MC

# WATER IN THE DESERT

*Recent Titles by Elizabeth Daish from
Severn House Large Print*

EMMA AND THE LEPRECHAUNS
THE BRONZE MADONNA
GREEN SPACES

# WATER IN THE DESERT

## Elizabeth Daish

**Severn House Large Print**
London & New York

This first large print edition published in Great Britain 2003 by
SEVERN HOUSE LARGE PRINT BOOKS LTD of
9-15 High Street, Sutton, Surrey, SM1 1DF.
First world regular print edition published 2002 by
Severn House Publishers, London and New York.
This first large print edition published in the USA 2003 by
SEVERN HOUSE PUBLISHERS INC., of
595 Madison Avenue, New York, NY 10022

British Library Cataloguing in Publication Data

Daish,   Elizabeth
   Water in the desert  -  Large print ed.
   1.   Women scientists  -  Middle East  -  Fiction
   2.   Love stories
   3.   Large type books
   I.   Title
   823.9'14 [F]

   ISBN 0-7278-7217-6

Printed and bound in Great Britain by
MPG Books Ltd, Bodmin, Cornwall.

# One

Away across the horizon, the first streaks of dawn showed Sarah that there was not much time left when she could be alone. She slipped the towelling robe from her shoulders and walked into the the glistening pool. The water caressed her thighs and then her whole body and she gave a shudder of pleasure. It was cool. Cool for the first time since she arrived yesterday in the small sheikdom that was almost next door to Oman in the Middle East.

Luxury, she thought. Everything done for the guests in the hotel almost before they knew what they wanted. The pool was warm but not enervating and the colours of the tiles made soothing reflections in the water.

She swam lazily and with a certain amount of care as the skin on her back was still taut. She listened for voices but there was silence and she enjoyed a good half an hour of blissful peace.

She shut her eyes and floated on her back, the rising sun warm on her closed eyelids and the soft mounds of her breasts peaking

5

from the water through the plain black high-necked leotard that she wore as a swimsuit. Her long hair, dark with the wetness, trailed behind like fine seaweed. She touched the side of the pool, ready to push away again but a shadow fell across the water, putting her body in shade, and she opened her eyes.

Above her, looming against the light, was a man. She couldn't see his face clearly as the sun was now bright and in her eyes, but she was aware of strength, a kind of animal force and the warmth of a hot male body.

Hastily she pushed away and swam to the far steps where her robe and bag were on a lounger. With one hand, she hauled herself to the rim of the pool, climbed out and reached for the robe, pulling the belt tight at her waist and feeling less vulnerable.

She glanced along the length of the pool. The man was bending down touching the water with one hand. He stood straight again and she saw just how tall he was, with powerful shoulders that were obviously used to lifting heavy weights, but the waist was slim, his stomach flat and his bare legs in the brief denim shorts well muscled, without being too exaggerated like a contender for Mr World.

'Carl?' He came rapidly towards her and she glanced back to where the voice came from. 'Come on, man, there's not time for a swim. Just take a quick shower and be in the conference room for a working breakfast.'

'Hell! I just got here! Can't I take five minutes?' He looked at Sarah and scowled as if it was her fault that he had to miss his swim. 'Some people seem to have all the time in the world.' He looked at his watch and then again at her, taking his time to really look at her this time, his dark blue eyes almost angry. 'Surely, even local girls have to be there on time, or don't they make you take notes or tapes any more?'

'I don't have to be at that meeting,' Sarah said, lightly.

'You speak very good English,' he said, with reluctant envy, eyeing her dark hair and concluding that she was one of the Muslim secretaries engaged for the conference.

'Thank you,' Sarah replied, trying to hide her amusement. 'Maybe that's because I am English.'

He viewed her with suspicion. 'No English or American girl that I know, with a good figure like that, would swim in that pool, wearing anything but a bikini, and she wouldn't run to hide under that terrible robe. I thought you must be Arabic.'

'There are still a few of us left who like to have a certain modesty,' she said, with a tinge of annoyance at the thought of a strange man watching her at the edge of the pool ... for how long? 'And this *is* a Muslim country,' she added.

He laughed and his laughter came in a gust of amusement that made his eyes sparkle and the laughter lines at the corners of his eyes crinkle in a way that showed that this was how he could be when amused. 'They've brainwashed you into thinking you have to keep your body covered at all times here? Tell me, is that awful swimsuit given out to the secretaries as a kind of uniform?'

'I'm not...' Sarah began but the voice called again more urgently and the man walked away with a swinging stride that made Sarah watch the muscles tighten on his wide firm back under the faded red shirt, his body moving as easily as an athlete's.

Carl? Sarah said to herself with a frown. She didn't recall a Carl among the delegates to the conference on oil refining. It was true that this was a big international affair with experts flying over from every corner of the world, but she had met a lot of oil men, she knew a lot of them very well, and somehow he didn't look the part, as a surprising number spent their lives dressed in city clothes, working in strip-lighted laboratories and seldom ventured out to the oilfields.

A smile made her usually pale face light up and her dark brown eyes glinted with laughter. No other delegate that she knew had such a body, such blue eyes and such badly cut longish hair, so it would be intriguing to know just who she had almost met at the poolside. He had a two-day growth of beard that wasn't tidy enough to be termed 'designer stubble'. His accent was American, with a hint of British influence. Perhaps he was an Englishman who worked in America or an American who had taken some of his education in England, she decided.

'And he thought I was a local girl, brought in to be a part-time secretary. If only life was that simple,' she said wistfully. She opened the large holdall that contained not only her sunglasses, make-up and towel, but the solid file of papers she had brought from the UK.

Her first thought was to study the papers by the pool, but she needed a shower now to rid her skin of the chlorinated water that was making the scars on her back itch. She slung her towel round her neck and put her espadrilles on, then walked into the cool of the enormous lobby on her way to the elevator. It was like entering a huge undersea world, with blue and green tiles painted with fishes and shells on the floor and diaphanous drapes at the open windows moving lazily under the gilt ceiling fans, giving an illusion of coolness and air movement.

The notice board stood where everyone must see it as they came and went through the lobby. She glanced at the words and saw

9

her name among the list of speakers: Dr S. Brackley.

Her gaze moved to the side where her attention was riveted to a name that had been added after the others had been placed on the board, the magnetic letters badly spaced but high on the list to indicate a name of some importance. Professor Carlson Ward, she read, and stared at the name in disbelief. Carl? Carlson? Surely the man by the poolside couldn't be *the* Professor Carlson Ward, the man who had been in the news last year after he had capped and tamed three oil wells in Kuwait that had been blown up by sabotage?

She remembered with horror the news pictures of the disaster, the wells spewing out fire and oil and molten rock, covering a wide area and putting countless lives in danger. She had seen pictures of the man in charge, but on reflection she knew she couldn't say that she had really seen him, as his face was black with oily smoke and his head was encased in a large helmet.

Fire! Sarah leaned against a mock marble pillar and took three deep breaths, her eyes clouding and the grip on her holdall slackening.

'Hey there! Get a grip, honey.' Strong hands pulled her towards a chair and pushed her into it. Her head was pushed down towards her knees and a note of irritation in the voice made her recover fast. 'You again? Are all the girls here scared of living and too darn dim-witted to stay out of the sun? It's strong in these parts, and you need a hat,' he said brusquely. 'You OK now? I have to fetch some papers or they'll be yelling for me in there.'

'I'm fine.' She spoke in a low voice and pulled her wrist away from his large enveloping hand. 'It's jet lag,' she lied. 'I arrived here late last night.'

'So they gave you the morning off?'

'No, I don't do anything until this evening,' she said.

He looked puzzled. 'It's the reception tonight, so there won't be any work done then,' he said almost accusingly. He handed her the holdall that had slid to the floor and the file fell out. Carlson Ward picked it up, glanced at the name on the cover and his face cleared. 'I get it. Dr Brackley hasn't arrived yet and you are waiting for him.' He grinned engagingly. 'I wish I had a tame handmaiden to hold my papers and make sure I don't leave them in my room, like now! I'm looking forward to meeting him. I've read his paper on the viscosity of crude oils – it's scholarly.'

Sarah blushed and he saw her rising colour. 'Thank you,' she said and took the folder from him.

'You look better. Keep out of the sun

11

today and get some food into you. You look as if you could break in half,' he added with a certain lack of feeling, as if he disapproved of slim girls with pale skin and dark eyes.

He walked away and Sarah followed slowly, standing by the elevator and watching the numbers glow as Carlson Ward rose to his floor. Third floor, she noted, and smiled. She walked into the other elevator with an Arab woman dressed smartly in a long-skirted black suit. The woman smiled and pressed number three, then looked enquiringly at Sarah.

'Three for me, too,' Sarah said. As they left the elevator, Sarah saw a now familiar back view disappear into the other lift to go down. Professor Carlson Ward was clutching a bundle of papers that were so badly put together that one had escaped from the elastic band and had drifted back on to the carpet of the corridor.

Sarah picked it up and saw that it had several columns of figures that were likely to be needed if he was to talk about the cost of a project.

She went to her room and rang through to reception. 'Professor Ward has dropped a paper that he will need in the conference room. Could you send someone to collect it? Yes, I have it here. Dr Brackley in room three hundred and eight.'

As she waited at her door for the boy

to come to collect the paper, she almost regretted sending for him. It would have been no real effort to have taken it to the conference room herself. She had attended enough of them to feel no embarrassment when confronted by a circle of strange faces, nearly all men as a rule, but she gave a secret smile. Let him think I'm what he believes, a secretary to Dr S. Brackley. I only hope I'm there when he learns the truth, she thought wickedly and felt more light-hearted than she had for some time.

She hastily wiped the paper on her towelling robe, realising that water had run on to it from her hair and made it damp. Thankfully she handed over the paper to the boy and went to her room to take a shower.

I really couldn't have delivered the paper, she decided. I would have dripped over everyone and they wouldn't have been amused at a woman bursting in on them at their solemn deliberations, damply dressed from the pool.

She stepped out of her leotard and covered her body with sweet-smelling shower gel, then revelled in the soft, warm water of the shower, the scars on her back and side relaxing and giving no discomfort except for one patch below her right shoulder blade where the skin graft had been extensive and was slightly sore.

She dried and smoothed her body with the

emollient cream that had been prescribed to stop the contraction of the burns. It was just possible to reach each part and she forced herself to look in the long triple mirror in the bathroom to examine the extent of the healing process.

She gritted her teeth as she looked at what she expected to see and tried not to think of what had caused it. Maybe it was the light or maybe she could believe her own eyes, but the scars were less livid and the edges of the grafts seemed to sit more neatly now over the ridges of mutilated flesh, with no harsh line of demarcation and only a slight difference in colour to the surrounding skin. She flexed her back and saw the other side of her body, taut and fresh and perfect. The line of her breasts and thighs was smooth and shapely and the dark pubic hair was beginning to dry and curl again.

What had that awful house surgeon said? 'There's nothing really wrong now. You can't hide for ever. Go away and lead a normal life again. You can go back to work or take a break doing something useful. You could even model tights or do nude videos so long as you do a full frontal and no side pictures. Take a lover! You are sensational ... in front and below the waist.'

She had wept after he had gone but now she knew that he wanted only to shock her into some kind of response, even if that

14

response was anger.

She smiled wryly. He had done a good job! The next day she appeared for work at the laboratory and refused any more time away from the rising pile of paperwork on her desk and the list of phone calls that must be dealt with soonest, and when she had been asked to go to this international consortium, she had shrugged and thought that at least she would be warm in the Middle East and be among strangers who would not fuss her and who knew nothing of her apart from what she chose to tell them.

'Hello,' she said softly when the phone rang. What was the Arabic for 'Hello'? she wondered but there was no need to try anything but English. She smiled to herself. Or maybe Welsh!

'Is that you, Sarah?' David Griffiths sounded relieved and delighted. 'I've been looking everywhere, and some guy from the States said that you hadn't arrived yet. He was at reception, see, when I asked. Said Dr Brackley's secretary was still waiting for him to arrive. Secretary is it? I said to myself. When did Sarah ever trail a lot of luggage about with her like that? Getting a bit posh are we, darling?'

'It's wonderful to hear your voice, Dave, and no, I'm not getting above myself, although I was offered a girl to cope with my notes.'

15

'And you refused, of course. You must be the only high-powered oil boffin who hasn't a bevy of helpers to make you look important.' He coughed in an embarrassed way. 'You show us all up, girl.'

'Don't tell me you've brought a minion or three with you?' she asked with delighted amusement. 'You swore you'd never get like *them!*'

'This trip shouldn't be all work and no play,' he said complacently. 'Miranda can send faxes and shuffle papers about but she's a bit more than that, I'm glad to say.'

'You mean she's 38-24-36?

'A bit more on top but I haven't measured. Let's say she wanted to come and seems to be looking forward to being shown around Arabia.'

'And you're looking forward to being shown around another contour map!'

'Let's not get coarse, darling. No one would ever think you had a string of degrees behind that ordinary sounding name. If you refuse to collapse into my arms, I have to find others who will,' he said as if he was in deep despair.

'The best of luck,' she replied lightly.

'Have you no mercy, girl? Can't you see I'm trying to make you jealous?'

'You must be hungry,' she said firmly. 'You always get sentimental when you need food, Dave. I think I'm going to look for a sandwich or something too, so if you aren't busy faxing, meet me in reception in ten minutes.'

Sarah had forgotten that David might be at the convention but it made sense. They would want to talk about oil production and oil platforms and oil wells, and David Griffiths was an expert on the erection of the enormous oil rigs that towered above the oil fields of the Middle East. He had degrees in metallurgy and an enormous fund of knowledge about the erosion of metals in salt or sandy conditions.

The flowing caftan-like dress that Sarah pulled on covered her from head to foot and the sleeves were loose, coming to her finger tips. The soft cotton fabric was cool and draped well, and the turquoise and peach abstract design suited her dark eyes and smooth complexion. She wore thonged sandals that showed off her elegant slim feet and she walked with confidence to the elevator, the dress billowing round her, first to touch and outline her thighs and then to flow away as if it wanted to retain her modesty.

She stepped into the elevator and turned to press the ground-floor button but a hand was already there and she faced the back view of a man with broad shoulders, dressed in a lightweight, pale grey suit and a pale blue shirt.

17

He turned and grinned. 'Going down?' he asked, then stared. Sarah felt that she was staring too.

'You've shaved,' was all that she could think of to say.

He roared with laughter. 'I do that sometimes,' he admitted. 'And you got dressed and combed your hair!'

The door opened and he stepped aside to allow her to pass before him. 'Dr Brackley not arrived, I take it? How nice for you to have such a lot of free time in this wonderful country.' His voice was mild but it held an undertone of rancour as if he resented the fact that she was looking graceful and attractive and she smelled of roses. His hand brushed her sleeve as if he wanted some physical contact, then drew away as if it was a forbidden desire. 'You look better,' he said.

'I'm fine,' she replied and smiled. She stepped past him to meet David Griffiths, who was waiting by the central column in the foyer, eyeing the physical attributes of a rather fat female marble statue.

Sarah was aware of the Professor's gaze on her back, or was it the scars that suddenly tingled with a new warmth? 'You'd never be asked to pose for that,' David said as a greeting. 'What happened? You've lost weight.'

'I work too hard,' Sarah said and laughed. It was wonderful. David had been away in

South America for six months and had obviously not heard about her. Nobody at the conference, at least nobody who she knew personally and who would want to talk about her private affairs, was here and would show any concern about her. After being cossetted for the past four months, she could be herself and not expect anyone to rush to help her, fuss over her food or make her relive that awful day and the pain that she suffered after it was over and she lay sedated in the intensive care unit of a famous London hospital.

'You look well,' she said approvingly and kissed his cheek, then drew away as she saw Carlson Ward walk by on the other side of the foyer.

'More?' David suggested with a wishful glint in his grey eyes, and put a hand on her arm.

'You can stop that right there,' she said sternly. 'We agreed to be only kissing cousins.'

'I seem to recall that it was your ultimatum! However, we do have serious work to do, Doctor, so let's get on with it.'

'I'm not working until this evening,' she insisted, mentally pushing away any sense of urgency.

'Silly lady. I mean food. I sussed out the eateries here and they have a nice small section that serves light meals and salads.

We shall be eating huge amounts tonight so I thought this might be good for now.'

'It's lovely,' she conceded as they were shown to gaily patterned cushions on low basket chairs in a room with one wall completely of glass, overlooking the distant desert beyond the well-tended flowerbeds of the hotel complex. 'Just cheese and pineapple salad for me,' she said.

'No wonder you're so thin,' he said as he studied the menu carefully.

'Slim would have been a more tactful word,' she replied with a trace of annoyance. 'I've always been slightly built and someone once said it was impossible to be too thin ... or too rich! I'm working on the last one.'

'That was Wallis Simpson, who married your king, but it didn't get her a crown.'

'Your king, too,' she said and mocked him with an exaggerated Welsh accent. 'Going all Welsh National are we? Or haven't you heard of any ruler since Owen of Wales back in the twelfth century?'

'Christ, no! Welsh I may be, but I do like to be able to read road signs in English. They have more and more of them in Welsh now. It wouldn't be so bad if I didn't have an accent but when I have to ask the way, I'm regarded as an idiot or a traitor.'

'Fresh orange juice for me,' Sarah said as the waiter bent over her. 'No alcohol, Dave,' she said softly and flashed a warning glance at him.

'We do have non-alcohol beer,' the waiter said, 'and wine will be served at the reception tonight.'

'I think I'll have orange juice,' Dave said in a resigned tone of voice. 'At least it will be genuine and not taste of old dustbins.'

'I've told you a *million* times not to exaggerate,' Sarah retorted, laughing. 'When did you ever taste a dustbin?'

'What have you been doing while I was away in South America?' he asked when they were served their food.

Sarah speared a piece of pineapple on a fork and dipped it in mayonnaise. 'Dead boring,' she said with a shrug, and added hastily, knowing David's interests, 'Tell me, are the girls in Peru very beautiful?

'Dark and some have lovely eyes, but you can never see their figures until you take off the wrapping. They wear voluminous clothes and Derby hats. You know, the old city gent bowlers that do nothing for a woman's image! They make wonderful coloured blankets and ponchos,' he went on. 'I brought one back for you, and I didn't forget the embroidered saddle cloth I promised to bring back for Mark.'

Her fork clattered to the floor and Sarah felt a cold sweat forming on her brow. She shivered in the cool air-conditioned room, and clenched her hands to regain her self-control.

David stared and looked anxious. 'What is it, Sal bach? Too cold in here? They make these rooms a contrast from the outside purposely and you need to bring a jacket to wear inside.'

He lifted a hand to summon the waiter, who came swiftly to take the order, his spotless white robe smelling of sandalwood. 'Coffee, and lots of it; not in tiny cups,' David ordered. 'The lady is feeling cold.'

'Thank you,' Sarah said shakily, as she sipped the steaming coffee. She regained her poise. 'I flew in last night and swam this morning in the sun, so it's a mixture of everything unfamiliar,' she said, as if that was sufficient explanation.

'What's the pool like? I think I'll go in before the reception tonight. You get a bit of a nap now and maybe you'll feel like joining me later for a swim.' He eyed her with concern as they walked to the elevator. 'No, on second thoughts, keep inside for the rest of the day.'

'I'm fine,' she protested.

'You don't seem to be your usual cheerful self. Something is wrong, isn't it? Is it the work? I know some mega American firm was after you and tried to head-hunt you from us but you turned them down. Is anyone putting undue pressure on you, Sarah? Just tell me and I'll sort them out,' he added cheerfully, flexing his biceps. Sarah half smiled. He loved his image as a tough Welsh halfback and macho athlete, and she knew that he really did care, as he was at least half in love with her.

'It's not the work,' she said gently. 'Don't ask me now, Dave. I may tell you later, but this isn't the time or the place, and I have to choose my moment to talk about it.'

Several people were returning to their rooms after lunch and Dave squeezed her hand and said he'd run up the stairs to his room on the fourth floor as he needed the exercise, leaving Sarah waiting by the closed doors of the elevators.

There were at least ten people waiting and suddenly she couldn't face the thought of a lot of bodies, sardine-like in the small enclosed space, so she started up the stairs, walking slowly and enjoying the views from the windows as she progressed upwards. On the next landing were two armchairs and a coffee table and on the next floor another set of similar furniture, too limited to take more than two persons at a time and so giving a kind of privacy. She made a mental note that these might be good places to return to after lectures as most people passed them in the lifts or walked by them on the way to their rooms and never paused to sit in the deep chairs to look out at the distant desert.

Somehow it was less lonely out there, away from her luxurious hotel room, and she resolved to bring a few notes to study there before she dressed for the reception that evening.

She sat among the pastel-coloured cushions in a chair on the third floor and knew that she could be alone there in comfort. She snuggled down and felt sleepy, even though she had planned a nap on her bed. She drowsed, half in and half out of sleep, and she was more relaxed than at any time for months.

A sharp sound made her start. She heard a telephone receiver slam down on to its rest. She peeped round the edge of her chair, thinking that if the telephone was the in-house instrument, she could order coffee to drink where she now sat. How lazy I feel, she thought, and stretched.

'Tell me, are there *any* office staff here who can take a message and send a fax without alerting the CIA, the White House and my old uncle from Oregon?'

The chair was one that enveloped the person sitting in it and was reluctant to let her go. It would take an unlady-like heave to escape and Sarah thought it better to stay where she was, although the man confronting her looked very cross.

'I believe there are a few,' Sarah began.

'Why not you? Each time I see you, you

are doing damn-all and obviously your employer hasn't arrived yet or you'd be busy.' Carlson Ward glowered at her. 'It's all your fault,' he added.

'My fault?' Sarah's eyebrows shot up.

'You did send that paper down to the conference hall, didn't you?' he said accusingly.

'If I'd known you were throwing away a valuable balance sheet, I'd have left it there,' she said coldly.

He made an effort to be reasonable. 'I was glad to have it back,' he admitted, 'but did you have to make it so wet that the columns of figures ran into each other and I found them incomprehensible?'

Sarah stifled a smile. 'Oh, dear, so you have to have another sheet faxed out here as soon as possible?'

'That's about it. Can you help me? *If* you can spare the time?' There was no mistaking the sarcasm in his voice and Sarah was annoyed.

'Sorry,' she said bluntly. 'I'm not here to be a dogsbody. Not yours or anyone here.' She dragged herself to her feet and smoothed down her crumpled gown.

For a full minute they stood in tense silence, her face expressionless, and his a mixture of disbelief and anger, tinged with a hint of reluctant amusement.

His face cleared. 'I get it! You came with that Welsh guy I saw you kissing in reception. I thought this was strictly business and no wives or camp followers allowed. I was told the only women here would be office staff, so how did he wangle a ... companion?' His eyes were insolent and seemed to rake her body, assessing her finer points.

'Neither a wife nor a camp follower, and I resent the implication, Professor. I don't have to explain my presence here to you or to anyone. David Griffiths is an old friend who I haven't seen for six months.' She walked past him and didn't look back. She fumbled for her room key and opened her door, then heard another key in another lock close by, and from the corner of her eye saw a door, on the opposite side of the corridor and two away from hers, shut as Carlson Ward disappeared into his room.

She rang down for tea and when David tapped on her door, she invited him to join her.

'Ready for tonight?' David asked.

'Why shouldn't I be?' she replied and poured out Earl Grey tea and added lemon slices.

'You haven't been here before, have you?'

'I gather that one conference is much like another in general format,' she said. 'I've attended several and I'm using the same material for this one that I used in my talk in the States. It was very well received and I have no fears on that subject.' She smiled more confidently than she felt, as David seemed uneasy for her.

'There's the reception tonight when we meet all the Sheikh's entourage,' David said.

'So what? I'll be neat and tidy and say all the right things,' she said in a teasing way. 'I can't imagine I'll be swept off my feet and taken into the desert to join a harem!' She laughed but David frowned. 'Why the glum expression?'

'They were expecting all men and you are a woman. This place is not as open and liberated as Oman.'

'I have better qualifications than most of the men here,' Sarah said firmly. 'Don't tell me I have either to be extra militant and very British or that I have to act the shy little woman ready to take orders from the Sheikh?' She went to her top drawer and pulled out an envelope. 'Here! He invited me personally and said some very nice things about my work, so he knows who is coming to the reception.'

David coughed and took the invitation. He grinned. 'He's in for a shock. You do know that the old Sheikh, for all his money, oil wells and influence, is a stickler for what is considered correct in his country?' He waved the invitation. 'Guard this with your life,' he said with a dramatic gesture. 'If he invited you, he will have to put up with the fact that you are a woman and his good manners will make him do that, but he won't like it! Have you read your invitation?'

'Yes, of course I read it! I can also write in joined up writing,' she said in an exasperated tone. 'Really, David, you are a nit at times.'

'Let me read it to you. "Sheikh Abdul Nizam desires the pleasure of the company of Doctor S. Brackley..." etc. etc.' He looked up but Sarah seemed puzzled. 'Not "Doctor Sarah Brackley," not "Doctor Samuel" or "Sean Brackley", just "Doctor S. Brackley",' David said patiently. 'Make sure you bring this with you and wear that dress or something like it.'

'Oh dear!' Sarah looked woebegone. 'It never occured to me that there'd be any trouble. Let me walk in with you David! Say you won't leave me!'

'She loves me after all! Now is my chance to blackmail you, my pretty.' He moved away as she gave him a threatening glance. 'Take my advice, chat up his son. He's stinking rich too and likes a pretty face. When he's in the UK or the States they say he is very westernised. He was educated at Eton and Oxford and lived for a year in the States.'

'Do you know him well enough to warn him about me?' she asked hopefully.

'No, but Professor Ward does. I can

explain it to him. I think he lives on this floor.'

'Leave it, David! The last person I want to be under any obligation to is Carlson Ward. I am definitely not flavour of the month with him and he certainly isn't with me.'

# Two

Sarah yawned. Her nap had been good and deep and she felt refreshed. 'Just as well,' she murmured. 'They stay up late here. The reception isn't until eight, with dinner after that.'

David rang through on the house phone to make sure she was awake. 'Wash behind the ears and put on a bit of war paint to impress the Prince,' he advised. 'I'll be in the foyer at ten to eight and we'll take it from there.'

'You're an angel,' she said. 'No, not that much of an angel!' she continued when she heard what he had to say. 'How's your little bimbo?'

'Actually she's not that. She is intelligent and we're going to get on fine.'

'Great. See you later,' Sarah said and smiled. If I said I'd have an affair with Dave, he'd run a mile, she decided. He's all talk and feels safe with me as he thinks I'm not free, but it's good to have a friend who I can turn to and trust without having to repel unwanted sexuality.

She bit her lip and brushed her hair hard

to keep her suddenly trembling hands busy. Dave and Mark, the two most important men in her life, had been friends in spite of both wanting her. If she was really honest, she would have to admit to herself that maybe now, David might not be as safe as he liked to think.

She had no idea when she'd have the courage to tell him that Mark was dead. They'd all been such good friends, right from university days, with her relationship with Mark blossoming into a low-key affair that did nothing to endanger the friendship of the three of them. It was a relationship that she often wondered might lead to a permanent liaison or marriage, and yet she held back from making any real promises.

'Do you love me?' Mark had asked many times, and she smiled and kissed him, making him shake his head in an exasperated way. 'You don't! I sometimes wonder if you are capable of really loving anyone!'

'I do love you, Mark, but it's a friendly sort of love and probably the better for that. No great passion, but a warm tender feeling that makes me happy to be with you.'

Angrily, she pushed the unwelcome thoughts from her mind. I mustn't look as if I've been crying, she thought, and washed her face in cold water before applying make-up carefully and sparingly and adding a rosy lipstick to her well-shaped lips.

The dress she chose was floor length and the slim-fitting line was obtained by thousands of tiny pleats from shoulder to hem like the lovely Fortuny dresses of the thirties. The dark grey silk shimmered like dull silver and the translucent sleeveless over-tunic, open at the front like a long, floor-length waistcoat made blush pink shadows like a sunrise on a grey sea.

She rubbed cream into her feet and made sure the dusky pink nail varnish was intact before pulling on black strappy sandals with heels high enough to give her confidence among the tall men with whom she would have to mix. Her tapestry purse held business cards and tissues, a small comb and her precious invitation.

David was waiting for her, looking unfamiliar in a smart, light-weight tuxedo. He whistled with appreciation when he saw her and kissed her cheek. 'Come on, let's brave it! The Sheikh is far more punctual than any other Arab I've met. The line of guests has started to be received.'

Groups of men drifted towards the ornate, wide-open double doors of the reception room and Sarah and David followed, hearing the voice of the man who called out the names as each one was introduced to the ruler of the Sheikhdom and his eldest son.

As they approached the door, two men

who wore the flowing robes of the Sheikh's entourage but looked as if they might be bodyguards, saw the only female among the guests and one came forward.

His English was excellent and without accent. 'May I have your name, madame?'

'Is something wrong?' David asked politely.

The man looked apologetic but firm. 'This reception is exclusively for delegates to the congress.' He ignored Sarah and addressed David as if he would understand. 'This is an all-male celebration and no office staff or wives have been invited. The Sheikh was explicit when the invitations were issued and there can be no exceptions.'

Sarah took her invitation from her purse and with icy calm showed it to the man. She hid her annoyance and made no comment. He looked startled and hurried back to the reception room where they saw him in earnest and agitated conversation with a tall elegant man in a soft white robe and silver-ringed burnous who went to a desk and consulted a list, then smiled.

Sarah watched as the tall man spoke to the bodyguard and made a placatory gesture that stopped the threatened out-pouring of indignant words.

The guard returned and almost smiled. 'My apologies, madame. Please follow me,' he said and Sarah glanced at David, apprehensively.

'I shall come too,' David said firmly and they entered a side room where the Sheikh had left his line of visitors to take his place on a velvet chair that was hardly less than a throne. 'Cheer up,' David murmured. 'You'll be fine. Just a slightly haughty expression, if you please, and don't be cross at what he is about to say. Just remember that you are one of the most important people here.'

'Dr Brackley?' It was the younger man, the son, who spoke in a cultured Old Etonian voice. Sarah inclined her head slightly.

'I apologise for the delay,' he said smoothly. 'There has been a slight misunderstanding. We assumed that Dr Brackley was a man, and here in this state, men are the ones who have education skills and come and go as they please.'

David seemed about to say something but Sarah touched his arm and he stood silently by her side.

'If I am not welcome here, then do me the courtesy to say so and arrange a return flight to the United Kingdom immediately,' she said coldly. 'I have many calls on my time and expertise and if you intend wasting my time, let me leave tonight.'

She regarded the Prince with steady brown eyes that matched his own in colour and depth but were now very unfriendly. 'I

make no apology for being a woman,' she
on. 'My work speaks for itself and I believe
that I am probably the best scientist here in
my own subject.'

For a moment, the Prince appeared to be
confused, as if he expected her to be apologetic and even servile. He cast an anxious
glance at the Sheikh, his father, then his face
composed into a bland expression that tried
to make light of the situation. 'When he was
informed that you were not a man, my
father was a trifle ... shocked, shall we say,
being unused to lady scientists, but now that
I have explained, he wishes to confer on you
the title of Honorary Man.'

'How absurd,' Sarah whispered, but a hint
of a smile made her lips twitch and she saw
answering humour in the eyes of the handsome man who was acting as go-between for
the Sheikh.

David nudged her slightly. 'It's been done
before,' he said quietly. 'A woman Prime
Minister and the Queen were both dubbed
in this way, so why not you?'

'Thank you,' Sarah said, looking directly
at the older man who she suspected had
understood every word exchanged.

He rose to his feet and began to speak,
first in Arabic, then slowly in English, saying
that while she was in his Sheikhdom and
whenever she visited him in the future, she
would have the status of a man in everything

she wanted to do. 'You may even drive a car,' he added, as if that was a great favour.

He walked out to the patiently waiting line of guests and the Prince suggested that Sarah and David might join them and be announced in the normal way, before he too went to the slightly raised dais to receive with his father. He paused at the doorway and looked back. 'What does the S stand for?' he asked.

'Sarah.'

'I like that.'

'Professor Carlson Ward,' Sarah heard and saw the Prince take the professor by the shoulders and kiss him as if they were old friends. As soon as they had finished lining up most of the guests stayed near the dais to hear the names of their fellows and Carlson Ward was among them.

'Dr David Griffiths,' the major domo announced. David made a slight bow to the Sheikh and walked on but the Prince delayed him and Sarah noticed that he spoke to him more than to the other guests who were new to the country.

'Dr Sarah Brackley.' The Sheikh inclined his head and made a graceful gesture of welcome as if it was no surprise to him that she was a woman, but a ripple of interest and amazement went through the assembly as Sarah inclined her head in acknowledgement.

She moved across to be received by the Prince and he said quietly, 'Well done. I like a woman with pride. Please call me Hussain when we meet again, as I promise we shall soon.'

Sarah smiled. It was good to feel she had a friend at court! Her smile faded. Carlson Ward was staring at her in angry disbelief. He walked towards her as if he knew her well and led her away from the main gathering. 'Why didn't you tell me?' he asked in a very aggrieved voice.

'Why should I? I don't know you, Professor, and we haven't exactly experienced ... an instant mutual rapport, have we?'

'I suppose an apology is due?' Suddenly he laughed. 'You must admit that you looked kinda homely by the pool, but now, this is something different.' He looked intrigued. 'I was anxious to meet Dr S. Brackley, but seeing you this morning, you couldn't expect me to think you capable of writing the paper you presented last year to the Royal Society. I can't believe that even now,' he said with growing wonder. 'You're much too beautiful and you still look as if a leaf could knock you down.'

'You are as bad as the Sheikh,' she replied scornfully. 'Worse in fact, as you come from a so-called democratic country where women can equal men. What have my looks to do with my work?'

He gave a lazy smile. 'Must open a few doors,' he suggested.

She made an effort to control her temper. 'It happens to us all, Professor. At the pool I saw a very grubby and, yes, smelly man with stubble that did nothing for his looks and I thought he must be a workman or a man from one of the oil drills, looking for his employer.'

'And now?' His eyes were calculating but he smiled.

'Now, I just find you patronising and rather offensive.'

She turned away. 'I still have the greatest respect and admiration for ... your work,' he said, as if her face and figure meant nothing, and followed her to the long table where soft drinks and fresh fruit juices were being served.

The guests had all been greeted and the Sheikh left his son to act as host. English seemed to be the common language but one man was available to speak in French where required. Prince Hussain was more relaxed now and laughed with several men he greeted as old friends who had visited the country on many occasions. Sarah accepted a frosted glass of freshly squeezed orange juice and saw that he was talking to David, listening to everything he said with interest. She knew instinctively that they were discussing her.

'The old man must nearly have had a stroke when he saw you,' Carlson Ward said. 'But he's a wily old bird and knows that they need you here, not just for the paper you'll read tomorrow but for your advice.'

He looked thoughtful. 'I keep in touch with Hussain. We were at Oxford together for a year doing a postgraduate course. He's a great guy but very ambitious.'

'He must be stinking rich,' Sarah said. 'What more does he want?'

'He told me that he might make Dr S. Brackley an offer he couldn't refuse. A laboratory with everything a scientist could dream of, and a house with all the trimmings that an oil-rich country can provide.' He regarded her with a frown. 'His idea was to make this a centre for oil-refinery expertise that would satisfy the old man's ego and make the country more than a mere dot on the map. He's more than a very wealthy Arab. He has several very enviable degrees in science and one like mine in metallurgy.'

'I'm afraid I haven't a wife and five children to qualify,' Sarah said dryly. 'Nor am I likely to want a dozen servants. This place would stifle me after a month.'

'Not here. You haven't visited the palace in the oasis a couple of miles away. It has everything,' he said simply.

'Including a harem?' Her tone was light

but she sensed that a house by the palace, under the eye of the autocratic old man, would be more than she could take.

'Yes, there is a harem,' he said.

'I shall be out of here as soon as the congress is over,' Sarah said firmly. 'Now they know I'm a woman they will see me off as soon as possible.'

He shook his head. 'They need you, Sarah. They really do value good work and when he's working, Hussain can out-do most of his men.'

She laughed. Hussain looked elegant and had all the hallmarks of expensive care. She wondered what his hair was like under that white covering, and realised just how attractive he was. 'I can't imagine him diving under an ocean oil rig to check for rust on the supports,' she said.

'You'd be surprised.'

'You mean, he does?'

'Of course.' Carlson regarded her with caution as if she might be insulted by what he was about to say. 'When working, he dresses in jeans and sweatshirts like the rest of us and is a very good diver. You will see him like that at times during this week, but don't be misled. He's a man of his own kind and under his westernised ways and his education, he likes women to be just that...'

'You'll be telling me he has a harem of his own,' she said, disbelievingly.

'He married a girl in Oxford against his father's wishes. She came here but she ran away. They were divorced last year. I met her a while ago and she said, "Thank God, there were no children or I'd have been a prisoner for life." I think she was very unhappy.' He shrugged. 'I love him as a brother but I'd not let a sister of mine within a mile of him.'

'Well, I'm safe. I'm a scientist and as you pointed out, not attractive when I'm soaking wet. Maybe I'll go for a swim with him if he falls for my limited charms.'

'Just tell him the truth, that you are living with a man in England and will probably be married soon.' He seemed vaguely unwilling to believe it. 'It's true, isn't it? I was talking to David Griffiths and he warned me off!'

'What?' Sarah couldn't conceal her irritation. 'How dare you discuss me behind my back.'

Carlson assumed a mock Welsh accent. ' "She's taken, boyo, and he's my best friend, so keep your dirty hands to yourself", or words to that effect. Very protective is David.'

Sarah laughed weakly. 'He never said "boyo". You Americans always catch on to clichéd remarks to put us into categories.'

'Maybe, but it's true, isn't it?'

She looked away, aware that he really wanted to know and this was not idle curiosity, but she put up a mental barrier to a danger that hadn't even shown itself. A sudden wish to confide in him made her catch her breath. I don't know you, she thought. We have nothing but our profession in common and I mustn't be drawn to a man I don't even like. 'David does know a lot about Mark and me,' she admitted. 'He was Mark's friend too.'

'Was? Are they no longer friends?'

'I'd rather not talk about it,' she said softly.

'Or have you broken with your lover?' The grip on her arm was hard and she felt as if he would never let go.

Sarah didn't move away but looked at his hand on her arm until he took it away. 'Thank you,' she said. 'I don't think that my love affairs are of any interest to you, Professor.'

'They could be,' he replied enigmatically and beckoned to Prince Hussain. 'Come and tell our learned colleague what your plans are for Dr S. Brackley.'

'All my plans?' he raised a dark eyebrow. 'Not all just yet, surely?'

Sarah ignored the bright dark glance and the sensation of being mentally stripped naked. 'Oh, do you arrange leisure activities, like visits to an oasis, belly dancers and camel rides and other touristy activities?' she enquired sweetly. 'I doubt if I have the time or inclination for those things. I *did* come here to work and exchange professional views,' she added.

'You are free to do as you wish,' Hussain said. 'Tomorrow, I shall arrange for a car and driver.'

'Do all the delegates have that privilege?' she asked.

'Not all, but you will need a driver when I am not free to act as your chauffeur myself.'

'Don't bother yourself, Hussain,' Carlson said casually. 'I agree that Sarah might be misundertood if she drives alone but I have a jeep here and she can ask me if she wants to be driven anywhere.'

'I hate to put either of you gentlemen to any trouble,' she said with a touch of irony. 'The Sheikh gave me permission to drive a car and if there is one for hire, then please may I have it?'

'I shall deliver a small but very good car for you tomorrow,' Hussain said quickly. 'You'll need air-conditioning and a little comfort when you use it, and tinted windows for privacy.'

'To hide the fact that a woman is driving alone?' she wanted to know.

He made a curiously Eastern gesture with both hands. 'It is better that you do not show your beauty to the common people. I do not want stones thrown at my car,' he added with humour. 'Only a few people here know that you are an Honorary Man.'

He laughed softly. 'If I find it hard to remember, then think how impossible your position would be with strangers.'

'He's right,' Carlson agreed reluctantly. 'After breakfast you give your first talk and then I'll take you out to the ruined fort. The view from there is terrific.'

'Sorry, old boy. I have other plans. My father has asked Sarah to lunch with him at the oasis and I shall be pleased to drive her there. We have a lot to show her and a pro-position to make.' He glanced at Carlson's set face. 'Of a purely business nature,' he added as if something amused him.

'I'm usually invited on my first day here,' Carlson said crossly.

'I hope you've invited David Griffiths,' Sarah said quickly, suddenly uneasy. 'His work overlaps mine and his views might be useful.'

'All right, Carl.' Hussain took a deep breath and raised his shoulders in a gesture of defeat. 'You can come to lunch and bring that Welsh dragon, who even now is eyeing us as if we might abduct his charge. I've had experience of British nannies but this is ridiculous!' He raised Sarah's hand to his lips and whispered, 'I shall manage to have you alone soon, Dr Brackley.'

His lips were cool and lingered on the palm of her hand, which he'd turned to receive his salutation. Sarah had the absurd vision of a woman making her palms fragrant and possibly henna-bright for such attentions. My hands probably smell of nail varnish, she thought and wanted to giggle, but she didn't rub away the kiss as soon as he left the reception room to lead them into dinner.

'Dr Brackley?' A small man with a gleaming bald patch stood before her. 'May I have the pleasure of taking you to dinner?' he asked. 'I'd like to discuss the latest find in Oman and how it differs from the wells here. I believe that you have done work on the samples in London and the results haven't been released.'

'My pleasure,' Sarah said and laughed as she saw the disgruntled looks of David and Carlson as she was firmly seated between her new aquaintance and a Frenchman whom she remembered from a previous conference in France and who had once taught her to play boules. No sexual undercurrents here, she decided with relief. These men don't care if I am man, woman or a thing from outer space, so long as I know my stuff!

'I have to talk to you,' David said later when they were having coffee in the tented garden lounge. 'Thank God the food was served at table and not Arab fashion on rugs. My legs weren't meant to be crossed for two hours at a time.'

'Maybe you'll have to do that tomorrow when we have lunch at the oasis,' she replied. 'You *are* going to be there, aren't you?'

'Yes, I've been invited and I'm glad, as I don't trust the smoothie Prince. You need to watch him, Sarah. He has his eye on you.'

'You sound like my granny. She thinks that any man under seventy is a threat to me, and she never quite got over Mark and me.'

'What's wrong?' David's voice was gentle. 'As soon as you or I mention Mark, you go cold and pale and look as if you've seen a ghost. Have you broken up?'

'I've tried to tell you, Dave, but I couldn't. Let's sit over there in the dim light by the palm tree and we can talk.'

'You had a row?' he began helpfully.

'No. You've been away for six months, so you haven't heard.'

'Heard what?'

Sarah took a deep shuddering breath. 'Four months ago I was in London with Mark and we went shopping.'

'Go on.' He took her hand in his and held it gently.

'We were in a big, new store – where they'd made a huge fuss about the wonderful staircases and windows round the atrium – when there was a bomb alert. They'd had a warning from a group of terrorists that a bomb was hidden in the store and was due to go off in fifteen minutes.'

He held out his arms and she rested her head on his shoulder, plucking at his shirt front with frantic fingers. 'And...' he prompted as if he already knew.

'There was less than five minutes. A lot of people wouldn't believe that it was more than a fire drill or a false alarm and Mark laughed. I remember that laugh. Suddenly there was an explosion and a wall of flame – Mark was flung over me, pushing me into a rail of coats. I rolled over, conscious that my jacket was on fire at the back and I dragged a coat from the rail to stifle the flames, then looked for Mark.'

He waited until her voice was under control and asked no questions, but rocked her gently as if she was a child.

At last she spoke again. 'Mark was dead. He lay there looking surprised and as if he was asleep, not even burned, but the blast killed him.'

David murmured in Welsh and kissed her hair. 'And what about you?' he asked after what seemed an age.

'I passed out and woke up lying on my stomach in hospital, where I stayed for three months or more. They were all wonderful to me.' She forced a smile. 'Even the horrible doctor who made me so mad that I woke up to the fact that life had to go on. I had four skin grafts and it's fine now except for one

47

area below my right shoulder blade that's tender if it's pressed.'

'This is your first time away from London?'

'Yes. It all seems like a distant nightmare now but when I saw you here, I nearly fainted.' She gave a weary smile. 'And I nearly passed out again when I heard that Carlson Ward had capped those oil wells last year. I almost saw the flames again and this time felt the heat and molten rock spewing from the well as if it was tied up with Mark and the bomb.'

'And I was about to warn you against randy men! As if you were ready for anything like that yet.'

'I'm numb and still cold and my scars remind me that I can never wear a bikini again or want a man to see my body,' she said quietly.

'Take your time, Sarah. There are a few of us who would never be put off by a few scars. This gives me scars too. Mental scars. Mark was my best friend.'

'I know,' she said simply. 'I hated telling you, but I knew it had to be me.'

'We shall miss him. He was a terrific guy.' David's eyes were moist.

She stood up. 'I'm exhausted and I have a lecture to give in the morning. Kiss me goodnight, Dave. I need that just now; a kiss from a real friend,' she added and held up her face to his.

'Never forget. I'm here for ever if you need me,' he said softly. 'Give it time and let me take a bit of the load.' His lips on hers were warm and comforting, and yet restrained as if he was controlling a much stronger emotion than sympathy and friendship.

'Is there another way to the foyer?' she asked. 'I couldn't face any more people to-night making me tell them what I'm going to say tomorrow at my lecture and I'm fresh out of small talk.'

David held her arm and they walked to an outside door. 'We can go this way, get a bit of air and slope off to our rooms without being noticed.'

'Goodnight, Dr Brackley.'

Sarah turned. Prince Hussain smiled and stood aside when the elevator came down to the ground floor. He watched her until the lift door closed and she had the feeling that he had seen her leave the assembly and had followed her.

# Three

Several four-wheel-drive trucks passed the car, leaving clouds of dust in their wake. Sarah sat back in the soft leather seat and gazed out of the tinted windows of the limousine that seemed not to notice the ruts in the road but went smoothly over all obstacles with barely a blip.

Carlson grinned. 'You must come here more often,' he said. 'It's not everyone who gets such treatment. I usually have to bum a lift in a jeep out to the oasis and arrive with my eyes full of dust.'

'That's why I'm here,' said the man sitting behind her in the back seat of the huge motor car. 'I'm Dr Clive Aran, Dr Brackley, a medic and not an oil scientist. The Sheikh has set up a clinic for eye disorders at the oasis and has asked me to oversee its equipment and to organise treatment for trachoma and other diseases caused by the sandy environment.'

'So all four of us are useful to him in different ways,' Carlson Ward said, with a slightly cynical smile. He shrugged. 'My part is simple this trip. After the conference, I stay for a while. I have to instruct his men on fire precautions and the need for constant drills about the use of rigidly serviced equipment. I also want to impress on them the need for having enormous supplies of cement and concrete and chemicals ready in case one of the onshore rigs blows its top.'

'It's interesting to find that most of the delegates are not concerned with the actual drilling,' David said. 'The Sheikh's men have got that licked now and are expert at getting the oil out once they've found it, after people like Dr Brackley tell them which sample cores from the drills show rich sources,' he added with an air of pride, as if he had real admiration for her work as well as his feelings for her as a friend.

'Is it true that you are coming to work here permanently, Dr Brackley?' Clive Aran asked.

'No,' Sarah said shortly, then smiled as her tone had been dismissive. 'Please call me Sarah, and I shall call you Clive. Everyone seems to be on first name terms here, even with Prince Hussain.'

'You sound as if a new lab, a lovely house and a huge salary aren't attractive,' Clive replied with a hint of incredulity. 'If I like the clinic I may well spend three months a year here and I would want to bring my wife with me.'

'Can you afford to be away from your practice for that long?' Carlson asked. 'I know your reputation as being one of the finest eye surgeons in Europe, possibly the world.'

'It's a tempting offer,' Clive said slowly.

'But surely you can write your own ticket anywhere,' Carlson said bluntly. 'You of all people have no need to put yourself out for any minor Eastern Sheikh.'

'With all the income from this oil-rich state, money is a commodity as free as water; free-er if anything, as this is still largely desert country, and as you say, I can write my own ticket anywhere. But here the rewards would be far above anything I can earn, even in private practice in Europe, and I could retire in five years and never have to think of money again.' He laughed, but the sound lacked humour. 'Wonderful in so many ways, but what would I do then? Sit on a beach or sail a boat and eat and drink far too much, while my children spent the money and got false ideas about themselves?'

'What about you, David?' Carlson asked. 'Does unlimited luxury not grab you?'

'Sure, why not?' he replied laconically. 'I like the heat and I can always cool off in the water when I'm inspecting the rig supports for rust.'

'Come off it! You sound like a raw redneck

diver doing routine work.' Carlson sounded annoyed. 'I heard that you have found a way of toughening metal to withstand the sea without adding to the weight or lessening the strength of the supports.'

Sarah eyed the two men with amused curiosity. On the surface, they seemed to like each other, but under it all was an animosity that hinted at rivalry, like two dogs circling each other with caution as if they couldn't decide whether to fight or wag their tails in friendship.

'Who told you?' David's face darkened, but Carlson gave a snort of triumph.

'You can't come here and not be spied on,' he said. 'Hussain knows and he told me he was inviting you here to do tests for metal stress. He has all the gear ready and, in any case, I saw your equipment being taken to the laboratory, so I suspected you had something new to test out here. You can't expect to hide big metal struts under a rug.'

'Is industrial espionage your hobby?' David asked with considerable force and rancour.

'Take no notice of David,' said Sarah hastily, knowing that his Welsh temper had a slow burn but got hotter as it began to be fed. She touched his hand warningly and he took her hand in a firm grasp that was not what she had intended, and she knew that Carlson Ward saw that they were holding hands.

'Sorry, bach,' David said in a silky voice that she immediately distrusted. 'Good thing you are here to keep an eye on me.' He smiled at no one in particular. 'Sarah always calms me down, like the angel she is.' He turned to Clive as if some explanation to a new aquaintance was necessary. 'Sarah and me go back a long way,' he said.

She dragged her hand away and edged sideways but there wasn't a lot of room to spare as Carlson was on her other side in the wide seat behind the driver, and if anything, close contact with him was far more fraught than with David's brotherly hand clasping hers. She looked back at Clive. 'You have the best seat,' she said. 'You also have the cool box all to yourself! I'd love a cold drink; orange or lime, if there is some.'

'Coming right up!' Clive sounded relieved as he sensed the atmosphere becoming un-easy. He whistled his admiration. 'Cut-glass tumblers, lots of ice and every fruit juice you could want, all carefully labelled. Soda water and tonic and spring water and even a few cans of non-alcoholic beer.' He pulled back a ring and the welcome fizz of a cold beer made them all opt for that.

The tension fell and conversation resumed on a lower key.

'The firm making this non-alcoholic stuff must have made a fortune in this part of the world,' Carlson said. 'I know a lot of Muslims who like less sweet drinks but are not allowed to drink alcohol. This is not bad at all, and has a pleasant bite that must be universally popular.'

'How far now?' Sarah wanted to know.

'Difficult to say, but I think it's over the next ridge,' Carlson said. 'We passed the disused oil rig they closed last year and the one on the horizon is the latest drill that doesn't look promising, but the Sheikh wants more onshore oil platforms as they are easier to maintain.'

'So there are areas where they find little oil?' Sarah asked. 'I suppose they can't win all the time and have the funds to pay for any that fail.' She almost stood in her seat. 'Is that the oasis?'

An island of green seemed to float in the sand and the bleak rocks of the gorge through which they were driving gave way to small tufts of coarse grass and stunted bushes as they drew near to the lush vegetation of the oasis. Like other islands that appear in the distance in the sea, this one grew larger as they approached.

Eventually the car came to an avenue of palm trees, heavy with dates. At the end of the avenue, a large white building emerged and another even bigger loomed up behind it. A few smaller buildings on the rim of the oasis were fenced in to keep out the sand when the wind threatened to let the desert take back what had been achieved and to return the land to dry desolation, and several elegant new houses were set in a leafy compound.

'It's unbelievable!' Sarah sighed with pleasure.

'You'd better believe it,' Carlson said. He added with an air of irritation, 'But don't let it get to you. The desert is a strange place; out of this world and not quite into the next, and it does odd things to people.'

'Feels good so far,' she replied airily. 'Oh look, we have a welcoming party.'

'Don't be influenced too much by the opulence here,' Carlson said in a low voice, and she was surprised by the urgency of his words and the sudden grim expression.

'Promise me you will never be alone with Hussain.'

'I thought he was your friend?'

'So he is. He's a great guy but he's from a different culture.'

'So what? I know people from nearly every ethnic group you can name and get on fine with them even when we disagree on some cultural matters.' She glanced sideways at him. 'Surely you aren't saying he's a threat? He's your friend.' She laughed and turned to meet the Prince, now striding towards them, hands outstretched in welcome.

Carlson said something that she didn't

catch, but it sounded like: 'But as yet we have never wanted the same woman.'

'Welcome!' Hussain bent over her hand and kissed it, then turned to the others. 'First we'll wash away the dust from your drive,' he said and led them through a deep archway leading into a vast hall in the first building. It was cool after the glare of the sun on sand and the lofty walls curved gently into a series of painted segments that resembled the ceiling folds of a huge tent. Soft draperies echoed this and the decor was as if an Arab tent had been transformed into stone and silk. Two men in spotless white garments brought trays of silver on which were flasks of iced water and fruit juices. There were bowls of fruit arranged on green leaves, and sticky Arab sweetmeats in pastel-shaded piles, surrounded by patterns in spun sugar.

Overhead fans spun noiselessly, sending out beams of soft light and stirred air and there were couches covered with rich fabrics and soft cushions along the walls.

Sarah gazed up at the ceiling, the gentle down draught of air from the revolving fans making her hair twist into soft, light swathes. She brushed the hair from her face and turned, aware that she was being watched, and saw that Hussain was staring at her.

'A bit too five star hotel, wouldn't you

say?' David said as if he disliked what he saw.

Sarah laughed and accepted a delicate glass of freshly squeezed orange juice from a silver tray. 'The service is better,' she said, smiling, then glanced up at the face belonging to the man offering the tray. His eyes were blank and unsmiling and looked beyond her. She lowered her gaze, realising again that she was in a part of the world that looked on women as inferior to men, and wondered if she really was resented, even by the servants.

They can't fault me on dress, she told herself. She had dressed in jeans and a sleeveless T-shirt after her morning shower but on seeing her reflection had changed her mind and put on a long wide denim skirt, her soft blue top covered with a semi-transparent over-shirt of deep sea green that buttoned at the wrists. Her hair was loose and shining and she wore no ornaments except for a small jewelled pendant in the shape of a turtle that had belonged to her grandmother.

The Sheikh made an appearance and welcomed the delegates, and it became obvious that he had asked them there as individuals, each one for a definite purpose.

Hussain translated, although once again Sarah was convinced that his father was quite capable of talking to them in English.

'Before lunch,' Hussain said smoothly, 'we would like you to see the departments that we hope will have the advantage of your expertise ... sooner or later,' he added as he saw Carlson frown and look at the others as if hoping they would ask the questions that hovered in the air. Did the Sheikh expect them to commit themselves at once to working in the laboratories and units obviously prepared for fresh and very well qualified staff?

'Clive? You will find a secretary and two paramedics already installed and Raffit will take you to the new department. I hope you approve of the operating theatre, which I think bears a strong resemblance to your own in Harley Street, London.'

'How do you know what my theatre is like?'

'I made it my business to see for myself and, with the consent of the theatre staff when you were away and the theatre was unused, I took pictures,' Hussain said, and his eyes sparkled as if he had pulled off a rather amusing practical joke. A tall man in a striped djellaba beckoned and Clive followed him.

'David?' Hussain handed him a key. 'This is for your changing room and lockers in the new unit where you will find all the protective clothing you require and scuba diving equipment should you wish to inspect our

59

offshore fields.'

'I can go with Sarah,' Carlson said swiftly. 'I know the set-up here from my last visit and don't have immediate plans to join you.' He laughed. 'Remember? I came here to visit you and to attend the conference, not to be brainwashed by all that lovely loot in there.' He turned to Sarah and grinned as if what he had to say was not to be taken too seriously, but she saw from his eyes that he really meant everything he said.

'Don't trust this guy, Sarah! He'll dangle all the gold in creation in front of your eyes to get what he wants, and believe me, there's gold in them thar sand dunes!'

'Not gold, just oil,' Hussain said gently, as if he missed the implication. 'Just oil, Sarah; oil that needs finding and an expert analyst to examine the cores from the drills; someone like you who can help, who has an instinct for her work and can translate it into practical forms. I need you, Sarah.'

'Why me?' she asked, and her mouth was dry as if she knew he was willing her to know that he was asking for more than professional skills.

'I read your treatise and the book you wrote last year and I knew that Dr S. Brackley must come here.'

'But now you know I'm a woman, that's impossible,' she said quickly. 'I too am here only for the conference and to deliver my lectures and I shall be glad to look at the new laboratory to advise if necessary while I'm here, but I am used to running my own department and I can't see me having much success working with your people if they thought that a woman was above them in status,' she announced forcefully.

The flicker of annoyance was gone in seconds and Hussain smiled. 'That is generous,' he said lightly. 'All I ask is that you see what I have to offer. Follow me and see the latest of our new toys.'

'I'm sure you are busy,' Carlson said, with a slightly aggressive grin. 'As I said, I know the way and I can take Sarah over there.'

'Everything is under control,' Hussain said. There was an edge to his voice. 'Obviously I want to see Sarah's reaction to the new lab, and lunch will not be for another hour.' He seized Sarah by the hand and almost ran her to the doorway away from Carlson, with a faint movement of ownership. 'I can't wait to see your face! It will be like watching a child unwrap a birthday present that he's wanted for months.'

Sarah laughed. He was almost childlike himself in his enthusiasm, and the firm clasp of his hand was more than the casual touch of new aquaintances. It held a *frisson* of awareness between two healthy young people and Sarah knew that when David had held her hand it was like the touch of a fond cousin and no more.

She felt light-hearted and freer than she'd been for months, and eagerly followed where he led her. Carlson came after them, hands deep in the pockets of his light linen trousers and his head lowered as if he was feeling morose and disapproving, an unwilling but necessary chaperone.

Hussain opened the tall wooden door and they went inside. Sarah gasped. It was cool and the air-conditioning made only the slightest purring sound. The benches and sinks and cupboards were of the finest quality, and the various pieces of high technology apparatus assembled made her aware of the care that had gone into choosing them.

One microscope alone must have cost more than the average luxurious American house with six bedrooms, swimming pool and acres of land, and she longed to work with it.

'See what I mean?' Carlson spoke softly when Hussain left them alone to bring in his staff.

'No, I don't see,' she replied stubbornly.

'Stop drooling over that piece of equipment. You can have it all. He prepared this set-up to impress you and believe me it doesn't come free. It has strings attached. You come with the deal and not just as a scientist.'

She regarded him coolly. 'Don't be ridiculous,' she said calmly. 'He was expecting Dr S. Brackley, a male scientist, not a woman, so I think that seduction was not on the cards.' Her lips twitched in a wry smile. 'I don't think he's gay so where would the seduction bit have come in?' She touched the glass knob on a cupboard door. 'It is all perfect and anyone would be mad not to want it ... passionately.'

'All of it? Be very careful, Sarah.' He gave a short laugh. 'He can charm even the most hardened oil man to do what he wants and with women, he's dynamite.'

'I'd noticed,' she said and walked away, oddly pleased at Carlson's reaction, but she wondered what he would say if she told him that she was immune to all masculine charm or ... bullying. Memories of the bombing, Mark's death and the ache of her scars were too raw to allow her much deep feeling apart from sadness. Pleasure in her work was real and must fill her mind to the exclusion of sexual feelings, but she glanced back at his serious face and knew that Carlson Ward was more caring than she had thought possible.

'Let me introduce your assistants, Sarah.' She raised her eyebrows at Hussain's assumption that she was already a part of his scheme for the laboratory. 'Jean St Gilles, who graduated from the Sorbonne in

63

Paris, Horst Müller from Berlin and Dwight Sioux from Harvard.'

The three men smiled warily as if unsure of her position and qualifications and Sarah saw that Horst held a slip of paper on which her name headed a short paragraph telling of her degrees and experience. 'It's a pleasant surprise to find that you are a lady,' Dwight said. He laughed. 'Too many goddam men here.' He stretched out his hand in greeting and she smiled back at him. 'I've wanted to meet you for months,' he went on. 'You really know your subject and it will be a privilege working with you.'

'Don't rush your fences, Dwight,' Carlson said with a barely hidden growl. 'Dr Brackley is here to read a paper and attend the conference, that's all.'

'Of course,' Hussain said smoothly, but his fingers tugged at his loose robe and his eyes were unsmiling. 'I voiced my hopes a little too emphatically – my dearest hopes – and once Dr Brackley honoured me with her presence in our country, it was so easy to imagine and hope that she would stay.'

'Sarah Brackley?' Dwight looked puzzled. 'I've known of Dr S. Brackley for a time but Sarah Brackley rings a bell of another kind. I know we haven't met before this conference or I'd have remembered, but your name wants to trigger off some other time or happening. It escapes me for the moment.' He laughed. 'Sign of old age creeping on but it will come to me. Something I saw in a newspaper or magazine.' He grinned. 'Don't tell me you're a fashion model as well as the famous Brackley?'

Sarah forced a smile. She had a fleeting and painful glimpse of the paper that Dwight had seen; a photograph of Mark's body after the bombing, with her huddled under a blanket, being wheeled away to the ambulance, her face turned from the camera but her name under the picture.

'You OK?' Carlson asked quietly, then laughed as if he had made a joke. 'Don't throw a wobbly here or you'll be whisked off to the harem and we may never see you again.'

'I'm fine.' She turned to Hussain. 'I was expecting men of your own country to be working here.'

He smiled complacently. 'There's no one to resent you here, Sarah. These men are all as impressed as I am by your record and I hope that you will all train my people to higher standards. We need to learn many things so that, as in the drilling fields, they may take a more important part in our work.'

'Cunning so-and-so,' Carlson said with reluctant admiration. 'Even at university you got what you wanted most of the time. Charm and money talks.' He gave a wry smile. 'You take the best from every country engaged in science and milk their knowledge until you have what you want.'

'Doesn't everyone?' Hussain asked with an innocent expression that fooled nobody. He looked at his gold wristwatch. 'If you can tear yourselves away, I suggest we join my father. Contrary to the general belief that Arabs are unpunctual, we like to have our guests ready for lunch at a given time and no later.'

Sarah had an idea that lunch would be served Arab style, from low tables while the guests sat cross-legged or reclined on cushions and she knew that if that was so, her long full skirt would be right for the occasion. She giggled to herself. Miniskirts just would not do here!

The luxury hotel in which the conference was staged was similar to other first class hotels all over the world and was geared to serve Western tastes with international cuisine and comfort, but the ambiance here was different. She glanced about her as they walked back to the main building. Men were at work watering plants and flowers, and sweeping pathways that the invading sand must have made an endless task, like painting the proverbial bridge.

She was taken to a cool flower-filled room where a female attendant poured water into a marble basin for her to wash her hands in cool water in which flower petals floated. The woman stood ready with a pale pink towel. I believe if I put my hands out she'd dry them for me, Sarah thought, and felt as if she had walked through the looking-glass into never-never land.

An ebony-backed hair brush was indicated and Sarah brushed her hair in long slow strokes, trying to ignore the fact that every movement she made was watched. At least I managed to go to the loo alone, she thought, and smiled. This was too much. She really wanted to be alone to adjust the fastening on her bra where it was digging into one of the recently healed scars at the base of her shoulder blade, but she felt she couldn't disappear again into the toilet or the woman might think she had something wrong with her, like cystitis! To take off her shirt and expose her back to a stranger was out of the question, so Sarah tried to exercise mind over matter and igore the vague discomfort.

To her disappointment, the dining table was laid in the Western manner, with fine silver and glass and ornate but typical dining-room furniture. While no spirits were served, the drinks were cold and delicious and the total lack of wine was hardly noticeable except when Dwight muttered that he could murder a large bourbon.

Sarah watched faces as the meal progressed. Carlson talked animatedly to the Frenchman and she found her gaze returning again and again to his craggy, handsome face and the dark, thick hair, which in spite of hard brushing was now reverting to disorder. His mouth was warm and humorous when he smiled but formed a hard line with faint deep etchings at the corners when he was silent and serious. She watched the Prince too, observing the almost sleepy eyes, the slightly hooked nose, and the well-formed but self-indulgent mouth, which held a promise of sensuality and even cruelty.

Hussain saw her watching him and smiled, raising his glass of lemonade in salute and making the simple gesture intimate even though they were on opposite sides of the table.

Sarah found herself blushing and was annoyed to see that her blush gave Hussain pleasure. She lowered her gaze and began to talk to Dwight who was on her right.

What had her counsellor said? After the bombing, Sarah had been driven nearly mad by sensible people saying sensible things to make her come to terms with the loss of Mark and the trauma of her own burns. She had resented the lectures but some things had penetrated her resistance to such unwanted help.

'Watch it!' the more abrasive of her therapists had said. 'Just when you think you have everything under control you could fall hard for someone just to fill the gap and to prove that you can still pull a great guy, scars or no scars.'

'Impossible!' she'd replied angrily. 'Leave me alone! The man I love is dead and I need time, just time alone and I'll sort myself out, thank you!'

'Just keep it casual when you meet him. Stand back and see him as he really is and if you want him then ... you might get lucky, but take care, Sarah. You will be raw in many ways for a long time and not only physically.'

'Don't worry,' Sarah had said bitterly. 'I'll only have to bare my body and any man will be appalled and say a polite nice to have met you but goodbye!'

'And if he doesn't?' the relentless voice went on. 'You'll wonder if he's some kind of a pervert who likes to see ugly scars and to know that you have suffered and could suffer again at his hands, to give him pleasure.'

'I don't meet people like that,' she retorted angrily and refused more counselling.

Hussain was talking to the Frenchman, and in profile he had a harder face, more like portraits she had seen of Arab tribesmen and Bedouins who lived harsh lives and took from the land what they needed.

69

Sarah shivered and knew that Carlson had been right. This man was dangerous to women.

# Four

From the windows of the laboratory, Sarah saw the gardeners raise their heads and listen, then put down their tools and file away to the mosque at the side of the oasis.

She went to the door and opened it and heard the strange, thin voice of the muezzin calling the faithful to prayer. Hussain strode across the wide path and disappeared through the ornate doorway and a minute later the Sheikh followed him. It was a transport back to the Middle Ages, with nothing changed by the intervening centuries and the desert sun hung low over the endless ever shifting, ever still sand. She felt isolated, as if everyone on the oasis had left her alone, but Dwight was busy in the computer room, and an Arab technician had been washing retorts and test tubes on the far side of the laboratory before hurrying away to the mosque.

The gleaming technology of the twentieth century under the purring air-conditioning seemed encapsulated in space, in a strange silent land, and the barrier between the two

71

cultures was palpable. Sarah was very much the foreigner.

The others had said they'd be back again soon after a break in their own quarters, so they at least weren't at prayer and she suspected that they would be drinking their ration of spirits, allowed to visiting foreign tourists if they signed a form to say that they needed it for health reasons!

The afternoon had been exciting, testing the new equipment and marvelling at the powers of the new microscope and Sarah knew that she could achieve wonderful things in such an environment.

A fresh batch of cores from exploratory drills lay in the huge tray and she couldn't resist the urge to do some real work.

'Going to take the bait?' Dwight asked. He brushed away the fog in his eyes and knew he'd been glued to a VDU for too long. 'He knows all our weaknesses. Mine is computers and the ability to put our findings on disc and analyse them. I might come back to stay for a while after I've been back to the States to settle a few things and make arrangements to take a sabbatical. For a year, maybe.'

'Your appointment isn't definite?' Sarah was surprised.

'I haven't signed but I think it's what I want to do for a time. Still, I have to go back first.'

72

'What about the others?'

'They've signed and I think that Hussain persuaded them because he promised that you'd be joining us.' Dwight laughed and eyed her with amused admiration. 'I reckon we didn't think Dr S. Brackley would look like you, honey, and neither did Hussain! You're safe enough with me, as my wife would kill me if I stepped out of line, but watch that guy! I have yet to know a man from this neck of the woods who can resist a pretty face and slim figure.' He chuckled. 'He's got a problem! Not every day he meets a good-looking female scientist with, I suspect, a mind of her own, and most of his Fatimas are ... fat.'

'Then he does have a problem,' Sarah asserted dryly. 'I'm not staying,' she added firmly. 'I give one more talk and advise about the new methods of assessing oil content and then I go home.'

He gave a lazy smile. 'You've already agreed to stay for extra days. Whadda you know? We may see you around for quite a time.'

'I'm staying because I am interested in the lab and the chance to do on-site work,' she said flatly as if he should know better than to link her with Hussain in any other way.

Dwight laughed. 'That's what they all say,' he replied with a maddening glance that assessed her vital statistics.

'I am Dr Sarah Brackley, head of my own university department and an authority on oil refining.' Who am I convincing, Dwight or me? Her chin was stubborn and her eyes angry. 'I am not a mindless bimbo with sex on her mind and I have never fantasised over handsome sheikhs who would carry me off on a white horse.' Her tension slackened and she laughed. 'You don't think he'll try, do you?'

Dwight looked serious. 'If I forget at times that you are what you are, the brightest scientist I've met in years, then how do you expect others to react to you, Sarah? Of course he'll try! He wants your expertise and a lot more if I'm not mistaken.'

'He wouldn't step out of line with his father watching,' Sarah asserted. 'He had a disastrous marriage to an English girl, without telling his family that he was getting married. Surely now the Sheikh has put pressure on to make it clear he never does that again. He wants him to have a nice Arab wife to give him lots of children.'

'That three monkeys act gives me the creeps,' Dwight said.

'What?'

'You know ... see no evil, hear no evil and say no evil, like those old models of the three brass monkeys they used to give away as prizes at State Fairs. I believe the guy understands and speaks English as well as I do.'

'I agree. We have a saying in Yorkshire that I think is more appropriate: see all, hear all and say nowt! I spoke to David in a very low voice at the reception and the Sheikh seemed to be straining to hear what was said.'

'Well, back to work. Got anything for me yet?' Sarah handed him a notebook. 'I'll set this up now but the potential yield doesn't look good from what you say.' He frowned. 'Is this for real? I could get more oil from my backyard.'

'It's a fresh drill and not deep, as you can see from the notes. It's a very easy test, Dwight, just to show what we can do.'

'If the oil is giving out then all this is useless,' he said, sweeping his arm in an arc to include all the expensive equipment.

'There's plenty left,' Sarah said. 'I've examined the results from the offshore platforms and the ones on the other side of the oasis. If the Sheikh wants oil from the land he'll have to drill much deeper and that means he'll need to have endless supplies of water to cool the drills.'

Dwight gave a low whistle. 'Which he ain't got. Right! So he pussy-foots about trying to scratch it from the surface.' He grinned. 'He's out of luck. There ain't any easy stuff.'

'So I can go home?'

'No, they'll need you even more as they get a bit desperate and hope for miracles.

75

It's like gold fever. I panned in the States for a while and nearly got the bug for gold. Some old guys have been at it for years, living in wooden huts and never leaving their claims. You think that the next time, in the next stream, there'll be one big goddam nugget to make your fortune.'

'But you never found one?'

'No. I ran out of funds and had a slight accident to my leg, so I went home to knuckle down to college and real work.'

'I've finished here,' Sarah said. 'I told Hussain I'd do one test and write up my findings. Pity about the potential output at that depth as the quality is fine.'

'Be with you in ten,' Dwight said. 'Have you seen the pool? All nicely hidden by trees but there and waiting for us. I need exercise and a swim will pull out the kinks.'

'I don't think I will,' she said.

'Scared that you'll be annoying someone? You have privilege here. Just say over and over, I'm an honorary man, I *am* an honorary man, and they'll never notice that you're wearing a bikini.'

'Bikinis are out!' Sarah said firmly. 'The old Sheikh would have a heart attack.'

'More like a testosterone crisis,' Dwight said calmly. 'So cover yourself with a T-shirt and long pants if you're that sensitive to local pred.' He grinned. 'I once judged a Miss Wet T-shirt competition and boy, was that something!'

'I have a good solid leotard,' Sarah retorted, laughing. 'That hides everything very successfully, and will not scare the camels.' She paused for thought. 'Sorry, that's not on. I forgot that we came here for lunch and go back this evening. All my gear is at the hotel, and I have notes to consult before my talk tomorrow.'

'Better swim there,' Dwight agreed. 'I'm having dinner with you tonight and attending your lecture tomorrow. This place is kinda claustrophobic. If I come here on contract, I shall stay at the hotel.' He grinned. 'No, dear, you can't take the nice microscope with you!'

'Sarah?' Carlson Ward walked into the lab. 'Taken root already?' he asked with grim humour. 'C'mon, the car's waiting and they've finished prayers, so we can say, "Thank you for having me," like good little slaves and get back to normality.'

'What's bugging you, Carl?' Dwight looked anxious. 'Something wrong?'

'Of course not,' he replied with an effort to speak naturally. 'I want to get back and send a few faxes, that's all.'

'I'm ready.' Sarah slid from the high stool and picked up her holdall, thrusting books and papers into it and closing the zip. 'Maybe we can swim before dinner,' she said to Dwight.

'In that glamorous get-up I saw you in?' Carlson raised his eyebrows. 'You could wear that here and not offend anyone, but I've seen better on a nun.'

'When were you in a nunnery?' Dwight bantered.

'I see videos, too,' Carlson said and relaxed.

'Oh, that kind of nun,' Dwight said and they left together, laughing.

The Sheikh was waiting by the car. He bowed slightly and said something in Arabic. Hussain told them that his father had enjoyed their visit and hoped that he would see them all soon on a permanent basis, working in the various departments that they had seen that day.

Sarah saw that two overnight bags were already stacked in the car by the cool box and Horst and the Frenchman, Jean, were sitting inside the vehicle. She hesitated, wondering where to sit, and Hussain touched her arm. She looked back and saw a scarlet Lambourghini under a tree. Hussain took her bag and led her towards it.

'Much too crowded in there now,' he said smoothly. 'I'm coming with you and bringing them back tomorrow after lunch.'

'In that?' she spoke as if he was offering her a lift in a jalopy that had seen better days. 'Four large adults and luggage?' She viewed the sleek lines meant for no more than two men or three midgets and laughed.

He seemed surprised that she was not impressed. 'They'll have a jeep,' he admitted. 'Don't you care for fast cars? This is customised to my tastes and goes like a bomb.'

'I'd rather it didn't,' she said faintly, then took a deep breath. 'The others have gone. Let's follow them at a reasonable pace,' she added as if she was afraid of speed and had not noticed his reference to a bomb.

I have to get over this, she told herself angrily. Every innocent remark still leaves me a quivering jelly.

Hussain gave her a curious glance and the car started smoothly, with all the latent power of an idling tiger. 'You are a strange lady,' he said.

'Me?'

'You have more brains than is decent for any woman and you rate my car as just a vehicle. Most women would be flattered to drive in her. Perhaps you've never seen anything like it,' he added hopefully.

'I know about cars,' she said. 'My father is a fanatic and drives the circuits for fun. He also collects vintage cars. He has an early Bentley, and a bull-nosed Morris.'

'Oh!' Hussain seemed chastened, then laughed softly. 'I can see that you are a challenge, Sarah. Luxury doesn't impress you and even that wonderful laboratory hasn't made you long to work here. What is your

Achilles heel, under all that beauty and intelligence?' He stopped the car and turned to face her. 'At times, you seem tense and I think that you work too hard. Stay at the oasis for a few weeks, doing nothing or working if that amuses you, but be spoiled and fed wonderful food. Let the women massage you and take away all care. Life is not all work, Sarah. We must get to know each other. There must be time for leisure and ... love.'

'I am perfectly happy with my life as it is,' Sarah said firmly, trying to ignore the response she felt as his soft voice took on an almost hypnotic quality and his warm hand brushed against her wrist.

'Do you miss the man you left in London?' he asked abruptly as she drew away. 'Is that why you don't soften a little towards me?'

'Of course I miss him, as any woman would miss her lover.' She spoke deliberately. 'You make it increasingly obvious that you want me for more than my work. Isn't it true that you must marry a virgin of your own race, at least to be your first wife if you are polygamous? I could never have an affair with you, Hussain. You are the most attractive man I've met for a long time, but any passion between us would be destructive and neither of us would be happy.'

'You know nothing. You speak as a woman

who has never been truly in love.' He reached for her hand and she let it lie passively in his grasp as if she had not noticed the contact, staring straight ahead at the endless sand dunes beyond the rocky defile through which they had driven.

'May we go on, now?' she asked politely, and hoped that he couldn't feel her racing pulse. She was alarmed at her own feelings. It would be so easy to let him make love to her. Passion might shatter the ice left after Mark's death but it would be a frantic greedy snatching at sex, not love, not for real and not for the future.

'I see it's too soon,' he said sadly. 'Forgive me for my eagerness, Sarah, but if you go away, I must make sure that you want to return.' He gave a self-conscious laugh that sounded beguilingly awkward and boyish. 'I know I'm a spoiled child who has never had his slightest wish refused him, but I know now what I really want. I want you, Sarah.'

'And if you can't have everything you desire, what then?' She eyed him calmly, restored to sanity by the synthetic plea that she'd heard from other men, and knew to be window dressing. 'Do you stamp your foot and throw a tantrum?'

His face hardened. 'No, I wait,' he said with cold emphasis, and pressed the starter.

A sigh came from the expensive engine, then another, as if apologising for letting the driver down, then nothing. Hussain tried again and again but the car refused to start. Sarah was amused more than scared, but the prospect of being alone with him in the desert for what might be hours, had a frightening edge.

'I know that running out of gas is the time-worn way of seducing a girl but this is ridiculous, and so corny that I'm surprised at you, Hussain. It can't be true,' she said lightly.

'It is not lack of fuel,' he said. 'It's a strict rule never to drive in the desert without a full tank and a flagon of water for survival if there is a breakdown.'

She squinted up at the sun and knew that if they stayed where they were, they would have a very uncomfortable three hours before the air cooled. 'Is there a rug in the trunk?' she asked.

'A rug?' He seemed puzzled. 'You can't be cold.'

'Put it over the engine to insulate it and when it cools, we can get on,' she said as if she was very impatient with expensive toys that didn't work well. He made no move and she smiled patiently. 'It's a case of fuel starvation. It's so hot out here that if you stop the engine of a finely tuned petrol-driven vehicle of this type, the fuel vaporises before it should and you must wait for it to cool down again.' She laughed with a hint of derision. 'Better use an old banger for this terrain or a diesel-driven Land Rover. This car is much too urban for the desert.'

'I know! Your father told you!'

'I do know about fuel oils,' she reminded him.

'As I am allergic to diving under cars in this heat, I have a couple of better ideas. One I have to discard as you are not willing and in any case, it's far too sandy for anything more than a chaste embrace, and the other is this.'

He reached into the glove compartment and produced a mobile phone.

'You are ringing the hotel, I hope?' Sarah asked firmly.

He cancelled the numbers for the oasis and sighed. 'I have work to do and a lecture to give tomorrow. I haven't time for this,' she said shortly.

'They'll be here in ten minutes,' he said in a resigned tone. 'We are only a couple of miles away from the hotel. But it would have been pleasant to have dinner together, alone at the palace.'

She smiled and relaxed, knowing that any danger was over. 'When I was a child, we used to play "I spy" when the car broke down, as it did with unfailing regularity if my father was trying out a new old car, but I wish you had chosen a more interesting outlook. All I can see is S for sand and R for red car.' She giggled. 'I thought that in the old desert movies the Sheikh carried the heroine away on a white horse. This is so different. A Lambourghini with a mobile phone does make a change.'

'You should look at me,' Hussain said. 'You would see many things that are more interesting than sand.'

'I *do* spy,' she said with a sense of relief. 'I spy a pick-up truck heading our way.' A horn blared as if to warn them of help coming and out of clouds of dust the grimy truck stopped by the car.

'What seems to be the trouble?' asked Carlson Ward with exaggerated courtesy. His eyes took in the scene and he seemed surprised to find the couple in the car un-ruffled and cool as if nothing had happened between them. 'I thought you'd been devoured by desert rats and I was ready to go pick up the pieces when you called, so I was on my way,' he said, and his smile nearly reached his eyes.

'Fuel exhaustion,' Hussain said abruptly and got out of the car to help load it on to the ramp. Sarah stood and watched, then climbed into the pick-up. The hawser tight-ened and the winch pulled the red bullet up into a very undignified position for such an aristocratic motor and the two men got into the cab.

'Hussain stopped to admire the view,'

Sarah said, solemnly.

'What view?' Carlson looked about him as if searching for something elusive and saw nothing but sand and scrub. 'Great,' he said with heavy sarcasm. 'Remind me to buy a picture postcard.'

He drove fast, as if the bucketing, jolting ride gave him pleasure and Sarah made no comment but clutched the safety strap with tense fingers.

Hussain asked her about the work she had done in the new laboratory as if he had nothing further than oil on his mind. 'My father worries about the lack of water,' he remarked.

'Plenty in the oasis, isn't there?' Carlson said.

'For our domestic needs, yes, but we need a good artesian well or two to use with the drilling rigs if onshore wells are to be a viable proposition.'

'Consult a soothsayer,' Carlson suggested. 'Isn't that what happens?'

Sarah was unsure if the remark was intended as an insult, hinting at the backwardness of thought of the Sheikh and his advisors, but Hussain took it seriously. 'It has been done,' he admitted, and shrugged. 'They said that water lies under the sand but failed to tell my father where to find it. There is a dried up wadi to the north but the original source of water remains a mystery. It may have changed its route underground.'

'Don't maps show anything? Old water courses and ancient wells?' asked Sarah.

'We've drilled in several such places but found nothing and surveys from light aircraft revealed nothing but the ruins of an old village long hidden, though the outline is just visible from the air.'

'They must have had water when people lived there,' Carlson said.

'Our engineers found nothing and you can be sure we tried to find the old wells, but if the inhabitants deserted the village it means that possibly the water supply failed.'

'You look pensive,' Carlson said as he glanced at Sarah's reflection in the rear-view mirror. 'Something on your mind?' His eyes held a challenge and the question: what gives with you and Hussain?

'Just thinking about Hussain's problem,' she replied demurely and thought that Carlson Ward could take it which way he pleased.

'I'll tell my servants to deal with the car,' Hussain said. 'Dwight said that you had a date to swim with him and I'd like to join you.'

'Maybe a shower and a rest before dinner might be better,' Sarah began.

'There's no need to be modest here. This is largely a tourist hotel, although it belongs

86

to my father and we reserve a suite for our own use. We get many guests who have no idea of the customs of my country and appear in next to nothing by the pool.' He shrugged. 'In that context, who notices anything immodest? I have seen it all in England and the States.'

'But you haven't seen Sarah swim! You really *must* join us,' Carlson said with an evil glint in his eyes. 'Hussain is dying to see how you look in the water, and so am I.'

She gave him a dirty look. 'See you by the pool,' she said, and the defiant lift to her chin showed that she would brazen out any rude remarks he might make.

Sarah applied emollient cream to her scars, using a long-handled applicator to reach every part of the thin new skin. She pulled on the leotard carefully and it sat snugly, with no tension on her back, then she shrugged into a bright caftan. The colours of the soft, heavy cotton were as deep and rich as the threads in an ancient tapestry and she tied her hair back with a crimson velvet band.

Sarah laughed softly. I look very good, she told herself. Even Carlson Ward will take a second glance ... until I take off the cover, then he'll watch Hussain's reaction.

The others were already in the water when she reached the poolside. Soft spotlights, directed over the pool, were dulled by the sun but ready to take over after the sudden dusk changed into the blackness of the desert night.

The air was warm and the water inviting. A few tourists were leaving to dress for dinner and the people left were mostly the delegates who would dine later in the private dining room set aside for them by the Sheikh. Sarah was aware of eyes watching her as she advanced to the row of white painted loungers with their bright cushions by the side of the water.

'Are you sure you should swim in this water?' David asked as he swam to the side to greet her.

'Shut up, Dave, and let me get on with what I want to do,' she said, but her smile took away the force of her words. 'And *please* don't ever mention what happened. Any reference to my physical deficiencies will meet with a frosty reception.'

'But they'll see,' he began.

'Wanna bet?' she slipped off her caftan with a flourish, as if revealing all. 'Ta-ra!' He slipped back under the water and came up spluttering with laughter. 'If anyone asks, say I have the local culture on my mind and wish not to offend.' She left the robe on a chair and slipped into the water.

'I see a disappointed man,' David said as they swam side by side. 'Hussain had his eyes out on stalks when you appeared and

88

now I can't quite make out how he feels.'

Sarah floated on her back and pushed ahead with her legs. 'If he's a son of his father, he should approve,' she said.

'Still wearing that old thing?' Carlson remarked and shook with laughter. 'C'mon, you've had your fun. Can't we see something more of you? You must have brought something other than that strait-jacket. Poor Hussain was drooling in anticipation and now he's a very sad man.' He eyed her with interest mixed with incredulous curiosity. 'Twice in one day? It must be a record, knowing his history. I gather you gave him the elbow in the car as you didn't have a hair out of place when I found you, but now, you're safe among friends and could give a little.'

'I like wearing this,' she said. 'I've another in my bag and that one's red if you prefer it. Same model and very comfortable.'

In the water, Hussain looked like any good-looking man with a sun tan. He wore a gold chain round his neck with an amulet of silver-gilt and amber on his almost hairless chest and his swimming shorts were well fitting and bright blue. 'Hello! This is a pleasant surprise,' he said. 'I almost gave up hope of seeing you here.' Sarah walked up the steps and sat on the side of the pool. He joined her and dabbled his feet in the water, ruffling the surface and destroying the image of the fishes portrayed in the tiles on the bottom of the pool.

'Don't do that,' Sarah told him. 'It's a very pretty picture.'

She stared down at the fishes and the giant octopus and the dolphins. 'Oh, there's a turtle. I'd forgotten that they breed here. I've never seen one in its natural habitat, not even in Turkey when we went up the Dalyan River.'

'We? Who went with you, Sarah?' he demanded as if he had a right to know.

'Mark, of course,' she said calmly. 'We sailed the Turkish coast and went to see the rock tombs, but the turtles didn't show up.' She didn't think it necessary to tell him that there were eight in the party, sailing in a large cabin cruiser that would normally take ten. With eight it gave them more room for gear but very little privacy.

'You aren't married to him?'

'No.'

'Why not?'

'It never seemed necessary,' Sarah replied. She wanted to say it was none of his business but thought it better to say nothing more.

He persisted. 'I don't understand. How can he let you remain unattached to him if he loves you? How can he bear to let you out of his sight if you don't belong to him entirely?'

'A few words spoken over us in church or before a registrar wouldn't ever make us closer, so why bother?' she said shortly.

'If you belonged to me, I'd want to shut you away where no other man could look on you,' Hussain said with such vehemence that Sarah was scared.

'Mark and I will never be married,' she said. 'But I shall love him for always.' She slid back into the water and swam over to Carlson Ward who suddenly seemed safe and friendly.

'Do they really shut women away, even today?' she asked him.

'I've never been in a harem, so how do I know?' He grinned. 'Go on as you are and they may try. You are not the kind of compliant woman they understand.' He regarded her with solemn eyes. 'Nor do I understand you completely.' he said.

'There's no need, Professor. You don't want to employ me, so I'm safe with you,' she said with a trace of mockery in her eyes.'

'Wanna bet?' He slid from the side of the pool and made waves as he swam a frantic length and left the pool.

# Five

Sarah was tempted to wear something plain and uninteresting when she changed for dinner, but she knew that if she had been at any other important dinner party, she'd dress up in her best and make herself attractive to bolster her courage among the delegates, who were mostly men and often brought glamorous wives with them.

Here, it would be even more important to make a gesture to consolidate her own status as there were no wives attending and the few local girls who acted as secretaries to the congress had gone to their own quarters. Being the only woman there might still be unnerving in a way that she had never felt when lecturing in America or the United Kingdom, and she knew that the Sheikh would be there, watching everything with those enigmatic eyes. She had no doubts about the delegates, some who had heard her talk at other conventions and the others, having attended her first lecture, knew who Dr S. Brackley was now and she felt their approval wherever she met them, in corridors or in the pool.

She blessed the local customs that discouraged low décolletage or strappy gowns and put on a long silk underslip of midnight blue that sighed as she walked, and a semi-translucent gown of blue chiffon with a dusting of tiny silver stars. The high collar of silver needed no ornament, but she hung the turtle pendant round her neck to glint dully among the soft fabric folds of the gown, nestling between her breasts. As always, she touched it before she left the room as if it was a talisman of great power to protect her from all danger.

She smiled almost guiltily. Nearly everyone had a good luck charm or some superstitious hang-up. She recalled a very serious professor who deplored such beliefs but who solemnly crushed his egg shells after eating boiled eggs, to prevent the witches using them for boats!

Some people wore a cross, others a keepsake from a lover, some a silver fish, and when she was in Greece the girls wore blue eyes in tiny balls of glass, round their necks on silver chains or pinned hidden to their bras, to ward off evil and the attentions of bad men.

Mark had bought her one and she had worn it for a while, then lost it and never missed it as it had no real significance for her, but the turtle was different and had belonged to her much loved grandmother and her mother before that. It was unobtrusive on its oxidised siver chain and fitted in with whatever she wore or lay hidden under sweaters or collars if she wanted to wear other ornaments. Tonight, she decided, I need all the support I can have. 'Thank you, Grandmother. Be with me tonight!'

David tapped on the door. 'I wish you wouldn't,' he said when he saw her.

'Wouldn't what?'

'Look like that. Even poor old Mark used to get jealous when you appeared looking a million dollars and he didn't get a look-in at parties.'

'Please, Dave ... no "poor old Mark". I loved him and it was Mark who took me home after the jollies I had to attend, but he's gone. I didn't go with any other man, and now I have to keep up my courage alone.'

'I'm here,' he said. 'Just say the word, Sarah – you know how I feel. I'll be with you if you want me.'

'How is your pretty helper?' Sarah laughed. 'I know you, Dave. We would never be able to stay together. Friends, yes please, and for ever, but nothing more, but you can help me tonight. I need a friend at my elbow to keep away the wolves ... and the ghosts.'

'Come on then. We have a special dispensation tonight. Wine will be served and even champagne to celebrate the success of the congress.' He coughed in an embarrassed way that Sarah knew to be spurious.

'Oh? What's cooking?' She smiled knowingly.

'Actually, I've been asked to say a few words,' he said.

'Don't have too much champagne or that Welsh spiel will go on for hours. Have you a lineage of Welsh chapel preachers in your family?' she teased him as they walked along to the dining room.

'Carlson's had a haircut,' she registered with surprise. His dark hair was still thick and curled about his ears but it had a tamed look about it, as far as his hair could ever be tamed.

'So have I, but you didn't notice that,' David said in an aggrieved voice. 'They really think of everything here.' He laughed. 'Everything from manicure, pedicure, to full body massage. I had the lot today but my masseur was a hefty lad who really knew where to hurt, and not the busty girl with the delicate touch that I had anticipated.'

'You didn't need a hair cut. You never look like a shaggy lion,' she replied. 'You usually look good.'

But not spectacular, she thought with a sudden catch of her breath. The white tuxedo fitted as if moulded to Carlson's body and the silken ribbons of several decorations were bright and yet subtle on his chest. His head turned as he saw other men looking towards the door and he advanced purposefully towards her, taking her hand and kissing it, with a rather wry smile as if to say, 'Look at us, all dressed up and not an oil rig in sight.'

'My, aren't you smart and gallant!' Sarah said to hide her sudden shyness.

'When in Rome ... or rather when I can get to you before your handsome prince puts tabs on you. I shall be urbane and very Eastern tonight to play him at his own game as he seems determined to steal my thunder.'

'He's not my handsome prince,' Sarah said laughing. 'As for getting into your act – Oh! I see what you mean.' She giggled. 'Shouldn't you wear a djellaba?'

Hussain was dressed in an elegant dark red dinner jacket that was more Saville Row than Oman and he too wore various orders on tiny ribbons but in addition had a sash of pale green from shoulder to waist across his jacket.

'Why the green sash?' Sarah asked.

'He's pulling out all the stops tonight,' Carlson said sourly. 'That is the green of Islam and he wears it as a hereditary descendant of Mohammed, which makes him a Sherif of the highest order.'

'Wow!'

'You don't sound impressed.'

'Believe me, I am, but in a way that will be a disappointment to Hussain. No wonder his father was mad when he married an English girl. It does make him much more remote than I thought, in spite of the European clothes tonight.' She looked up at Carlson. 'If he thinks I shall be impressed, I shall be, but it has the opposite effect as it makes me see that his heritage is special and he should keep within it.'

'That makes my day.' Carlson grinned. 'C'mon, let's go talk to His Highness and then pay homage to the Sheikh, who I see lurking over there talking to the Frenchman.'

'What freed his tongue? Or is he happier speaking in French?'

'He is a wily old bird and has plenty to say when he wants but he hates small talk. I've been here several times and I'm quite fond of him. He knows his country and is passionate about its future.'

'Sarah!' Hussain's exclamation of surprise was almost sincere as if he'd not noticed her arrival. He kissed her on both cheeks like a true European and Carlson, who seemed cheered by what Sarah had said, only grinned. 'Champagne?' Hussain offered as if he drank it every day.

'No, thank you.' Sarah reached out for a glass of orange juice and smiled. 'This is so

97

good. I shall miss it when I go home – I feel no need for stimulants here.'

'I wish I could send you a tanker-full,' Hussain said. 'I want you to enjoy our local products. Tomorrow I shall take you to a meal in a Bedouin camp, where we shall feast on Arab dishes and you shall know what we have to offer here.'

'Is it anywhere near the lost village?' she asked quickly.

'We can go that way,' he said, sounding puzzled. 'There's nothing to see there now but a few ruined walls.'

'Could we take maps of the place as it was and the photos taken from the plane?'

'Of course, but why waste time on morbid curiosity? I want you to enjoy your stay here. I want you to get to know me better.'

If I met you in London dressed like that, I'd be very attracted, Sarah thought. This was a different man, perhaps less dignified in appearance than when he was dressed in his own flowing robes, but, assessed as a cultivated international man of some importance, with no Arab dress to remind her of the difference in background, he was impressive and very sexy, and she felt her mouth dry as he took her hand to lead her into dinner.

Carlson Ward seemed relaxed now that she had tried to make it clear that she was not interested in Hussain except as a colleague and friend, and sat by the Sheikh, who nodded with approval at what his companion was saying. At one point, the two men glanced towards her and Sarah knew that she was under discussion. The Sheikh's eyes had lost the hooded expression that she had encountered on their first meeting, but he watched his son, and Hussain took care to act as if he was just being courteous to a guest, except when he whispered to her.

'I wish I could take you outside,' Hussain said softly. 'The stars in our sky would envy the stars on your gown. The night is warm and it would be quiet in the gazebo by the shore.'

'And miss my pudding?' Sarah raised her eyebrows and smiled. 'You don't have to try so hard, Hussain. I do like you very much but I'm here on business, with a few nice perks like this dinner and good conversation, so don't spoil it.'

'But you will come with me tomorrow?'

'If I can see where the village was,' she insisted. 'Who else is coming?'

He sighed. 'If I can't have you to myself, who do you suggest?'

'David, as he is a metallurgist and a geologist, who also takes good pictures, and Dwight to make notes on the maps to put on computer.'

'You're serious?'

'Absolutely, and when we have coffee, I'd

like to speak to your father, if that's possible and he won't clam up on me again.'

'I can promise you that,' Hussain said. 'I never expected that he could be so impressed by any woman.' He glanced at her cautiously. 'I really believe that he could forget my past mistakes and accept you as my wife.'

'He'll never have that traumatic decision to make,' Sarah said firmly. 'You forget Mark and the fact that I have a job in the UK that I love doing.'

'How can I think of that when I see your lovely profile and the softness and purity of your skin, even if I am not privileged to see it all? I shall dream of you tonight, not in that all-concealing leotard which I am pleased to see you wear when other men are with you, but soft and smooth under my loving hands,' he said.

'And if I wasn't soft and smooth all over?' Her mouth set in a line of pain.

'It is unthinkable. I know there can be no flaw.'

Carlson came over as soon as the guests rose from the table to take coffee in a lounge that was open to the distant shore and the desert night. 'His Highness wants to talk to you,' he said.

'Do me a favour, Carl.'

'Anything when you look at me like that,' he replied. 'Tonight you are all woman!' He laughed and made an exaggerated Eastern obeisance. 'How'm I doing?'

She looked away and tried to sound business-like. 'Find Dave and ask him to be ready to come on a kind of safari tomorrow, after my lecture. I'm going to see the lost village and I'll want two steel rods about a metre long, with a third of the length bent at right angles. He'll know what I mean, and ask Dwight to come too as I'll need him to take notes and plot things on a map to put on computer later.'

'For crying out! Don't you ever stop working? Can I come on this trip?'

'You accused me of doing nothing the first time we met,' she reminded him. 'If you want to come and eat couscous, clear it with Hussain. It's his party.'

'What a boo-boo that first meeting was!' He laughed and she warmed to his humour. 'Well, he's waiting for you with a tray of those horrible sticky sweets so that you'll be as fat as his women.' He touched her hand. 'Chin up, he likes you and you look great.'

'Thank you, Carl,' she said and walked across the room to the Sheikh, watched by the two men.

'Sit here, my dear.' The divan was piled with soft cushions of every pastel colour, making her gown look like a pool of deep blue water as she sank into them. She took a small sweet, and nibbled it reluctantly,

101

but with the strong black coffee, it was surprisingly good. 'Are you enjoying your visit?' the Sheikh asked her. His voice was without accent and he spoke with ease, about the laboratories, his difficulties over the onshore oilfields and a little about his family as if she had every right to know and to ask questions.

When he gently probed to find out more about her own background, Sarah shrugged. 'Very uninteresting, I'm afraid, Your Highness. You know my professional qualifications.'

'Your family?'

'My father inherited a little land and is a skilled motor engineer with a few cups for track racing and a garage full of ancient cars. My mother died a few years ago.'

'You are not married?'

'No.' She decided to be honest about her relationship. 'Mark and I never got around to that. We met at university and lived together.'

'Past tense?' The crisp question came as a shock. 'You no longer live with this man?'

'Mark will always be the only man in my life,' she said, shortly. 'Oh, look, Dwight seems to want to say something,' she added with relief.

'Excuse me, sir. It's been a long day and if Sarah wants me tomorrow, I think I'll hit the sack, if you'll excuse me.'

'Working tomorrow? I thought that my son was planning a picnic of sorts after your early lecture.'

'He is, but I asked to see the site of the lost village,' Sarah explained. 'I wanted Dwight and David along to make a kind of survey.'

'And you will be well chaperoned.' The brown eyes twinkled. 'Hussain will be disappointed.'

Sarah wondered how she could leave the Sheikh with dignity and go to bed. The soft cushions had enfolded her and she was reclining almost in a foetal position, curled round one huge pink cushion.

Dwight stared as if trying to recall something lost in the back of his mind. 'What did you say your boyfriend was called?'

With a kind of dread at the inevitable, Sarah said, 'Mark.'

'I've got it. It's been niggling me ever since we met. Sarah Brackley! It was you in that picture after the London bombing. I thought it was a terrible thing to do to show the photograph of the dead man, possibly before they told his family that he was dead. You were huddled up almost as you are now, and I couldn't see your face, but I remembered the name. It rang bells when I heard you were coming here.'

'Don't!' she whispered. 'Please don't tell anyone here. I want to forget it.'

'So Mark is dead?' The Sheikh sounded

103

almost pleased. 'But you are well? That is a blessing, to be unscathed after such a shock.'

'Please respect my privacy in this,' Sarah begged. 'It was a relief to come here where nobody knew about Mark and me.'

'Of course.' He put up a hand as if making a vow of silence and Dwight muttered something about keeping his big mouth shut.

'Tell me if you need anything for your survey but I can't believe that you'll find any indication of oil there,' the Sheikh said.

'Not oil, but there may be water,' Sarah said, her relief at the change of tone making her more expansive than she'd intended as she secretly thought her ideas would make everyone laugh with incredulity. 'It may be nothing but I'd like to try. I've asked David to make me some steel divining rods and we can quarter the site and try for water.'

'Have you ever done any dowsing?' Dwight asked. 'This I must see! It's a kind of magic that I know happens but I can't believe.'

'I've dowsed mostly with hazel twigs but steel works well too,' Sarah replied. 'My mother was good at it and I tried when I was a child and found I had the knack.'

The older man rose and bent over Sarah, his face tight with emotion. 'Find me water and you may have anything your heart desires,' he said, in a shaken voice. 'Find me water and you are my daughter, for whom nothing is impossible.'

She watched him leave, almost as shaken as he was, but by his fervent words, not the possibility of finding a well. His shoulders stooped as if under a burden and he left the room quickly without speaking to anyone.

Dwight helped her to her feet. 'You really creased the old boy,' he said. 'He nearly lost his cool completely.' He handed her the small jewelled purse that had dropped to the floor when he raised her to her feet. 'Sorry I shot my big mouth off in front of him,' he said in an embarrassed way.

'Just keep quiet about it to the others. It's all over,' Sarah insisted. 'I have to forget it.'

'There must be scars,' he said.

She nodded. More than you'll ever know, she thought and her back ached where the skin had stretched when she reclined in an awkward position.

'So this is to be a working expedition tomorrow,' Hussain said. He had followed his father from the room, alarmed at his sudden departure, and now was back with the guests. He gave a wry smile. 'I'm not doing too well,' he admitted. 'My idea of a romantic lunch, with Arab music and dancing and good food, seems to have gone by the board. As it will be very hot in the desert, my father insists that we take a picnic and have shelters erected by servants

105

to keep off the sun. It means that the Bedouin party must wait. The whole scene will be crawling with other people and I shall see very little of you,' he said resentfully.

'You could come back here for dinner tomorrow,' Sarah suggested, suddenly contrite and rather apprehensive at what she had started. 'It will probably be a bit of a damp squib and I shall emerge with egg on my face!'

'What a charming choice of words,' Hussain said, laughing. 'You underestimate the importance of this. Even if you do not find water now, you have opened up fresh possibilities and my father will pursue the search long after you leave here, after obtaining the best men with proven expertise in that skill. He seems to have great faith in your judgement.' Hussain looked triumphant. 'He already looks on you as a daughter.'

'An honorary title, just as I have the title of Honorary Man for this trip,' Sarah said flatly. 'Both meaning nothing in the outside world and neither of lasting value to me.'

David and Carl now joined them, talking together and not seeming to listen to their conversation, but Sarah was aware that they did just that.

'It may become more important,' Hussain said, in a meaningful tone. 'If you are to be fresh for tomorrow, you must have rest. May

I escort you to your room?'

'Carl and I can do that,' David said. 'We are on the same floor.'

'And you are coming tomorrow to look after Sarah?' His voice took on an insulting edge. 'In the past, our women were protected by palace eunuchs. I see I have no need to supply such a service.'

'Cool it, boyo,' David said, as Carlson took an angry step forward. He held his arm with the ease and strength of a Welsh halfback until Hussain was safely out of reach and walking towards the foyer and the elevator to take him to the penthouse suite. 'Remember? He's Mister Nice Guy when you're both sane.' David laughed. 'Sarah, my darling, you've a lot to answer for! You are ever so slightly muddying the water between two really nice men who love each other as two drunken football fans do on a Saturday night.'

His laughter eased the atmosphere and Carlson grinned. 'Point taken, but I do not like being called a eunuch!'

'I don't think he did,' Sarah said, her lips twitching with suppressed laughter at the sight of Carlson's enraged and offended face. 'He was explaining a bit of local folklore.'

'Like hell he was! He can talk! He was married long enough to get her pregnant but nothing happened. Maybe nature held back for her if she didn't want his child, but it could have been him lacking the where-withal!'

'Don't even think it and *never* say it!' David sounded alarmed. 'Never heard of the Pill, have you? Sensible girl if you ask me, as she could see that the marriage might not last.'

Sarah looked at the handsome passionate face and her carefully repressed sensual feelings struggled to make her acutely aware of him. '*Well*, are you escorting me to my nice safe room or aren't you?' she asked to hide her sudden emotion. 'I'd no idea what a *femme fatale* I had become. It must be the desert air.'

'Maybe.' Carlson regained his sang-froid and ushered her into the scented elevator with a flourish. 'Do me a favour, will you? Wear something really awful tomorrow, for all our sakes.'

'I didn't intend wearing this in the desert,' Sarah said dryly and left them at her door, the silk skirt sighing through the doorway and the tiny stars sparkling on the dark fabric.

Pensively, she stared at the closed door then locked it carefully. She stripped and showered, aware that her thighs were moist and her nipples raised. What had her coun-sellor said? 'You might fall for someone, just because you miss Mark and want to prove that you are still desirable, scarred or not.'

She smiled as she anointed her back with the soothing cream. After Mark's death there had been no need to use the Pill and certainly she had felt no need to bring a supply with her to the Sheikhdom of Abdulla Rifka.

That solves that little problem, if problem it is, she decided almost ruefully. I must not let either of these fascinating animals make love to me now. She didn't deny the temptation. They were both wonderful in different ways, and Carlson's reaction to Hussain that evening left her in no doubt as to his desire for her.

She slipped into bed naked and felt the caress of soft sheets unrestricted by a nightgown, leaving her scars free of tension, and she remembered the words of an aunt who disapproved of the Pill. 'We never did it, even during the war when the temptation was almost too much to bear,' she said. 'Fear was our best contraceptive and it might be better if some used that today instead of sleeping around and picking up all sorts of things besides babies.'

The turtle pendant was twisted on the chain and she took it off and put it on the dressing table. I don't need you any more tonight, she thought, but I might tomorrow.

With the light out and the drapes back from the windows, showing the stars, she settled down to sleep.

As if in a dream, she heard the stealthy twisting of the door handle, repeated three times, each time more firmly, then silence.

If I opened the door now, my whole life might have to change, she thought, and decided that she liked it as it was and this alternative was dangerous ... but wished she could see which of the two men had wanted her so much that he came in the night, hoping that she would take him to bed.

# Six

'You really started something.' David handed her the steel rods and watched while she balanced them in her hands. 'Bring a hat and a long-sleeved shirt. It's baking out there.'

'This is thin but opaque Sea Island cotton,' Sarah said. 'It's the coolest thing I have and has tabs on the sleeves that I can release to roll down the sleeves when we get there.'

She had hesitated between choosing this pale blue shirt and one of pale green with ochre stripes, but she recalled Hussain wearing the green of Islam and wanted no remarks hinting that she wore the colour with the same connotations. She put that shirt back in her case.

The thin denim jeans were old and soft and comfortable and she tied her hair back in a dark blue ribbon to keep her head and neck cool. This made her profile more severe than when her hair was free and she did it deliberately, wishing to appear really business-like and lacking in glamour. She picked up a battered straw hat that had been

111

in every hot country she had visited for years and did nothing for her. She recalled Mark eyeing it with disgust. 'Why not cut two holes in it for the ears and give it to some unfortunate donkey to wear, or to eat up if he could stand the prickly bits,' he'd said.

'I'm ready,' she said and followed David out to the waiting convoy of vehicles. 'Oh, *no*!' She stared in horror at the five jeeps laden with a mass of equipment that were already fast disappearing, to be on site before she arrived.

'See what I mean?' David laughed. 'This is all your fault, Sarah. The Sheikh insisted on carpets for the tent in which his favourite woman, sorry, Honorary Man, will condescend to eat lunch! Stop blushing. Just enjoy it. You might need a bit of courage if we find nothing today after he's gone to all this trouble, but until then you are the *man* of the moment and all eyes are on you! Go, work a miracle!'

'The last time I did a field trip, I sheltered under a leaky canopy of plastic,' Sarah said weakly. 'There were spiders and I saw huge beetles, and nobody did anything to help me cook my own lunch. It was on a small windy island in the North Sea when we came ashore from a rig. Ha blooming ha! They said it would be good experience to see the drill in action but all I got out of it was a heavy cold.'

'Well, don't let this attention go to your head.' Carlson took her small rucksack containing what she needed for the day. He weighed it in his hand. 'Why don't you carry this on your back when you get there? It's quite heavy and you'll find it much easier to cope with, leaving your hands free.'

'I'll be carrying it,' David said, casually. 'You forget that women have much narrower shoulders than us and Sarah will have better things to do than to make her back sore.'

She gave him a grateful look, which Carlson noticed. 'What happened to equality and womens' lib?' he asked in a bantering tone. 'I thought you were one tough cookie.' He began to walk away and called back, 'We're travelling in that Land Rover, the smart one specially laid on for Madame and her party.'

'Does that include you?' she asked.

'I'm gatecrashing.' Carlson swung the gear into the back of the vehicle and Sarah climbed up beside the driver, followed by the two men. 'I sent Dwight to the other one with Hussain, who has to ferry the Sheikh, like a good and obedient son.' He grinned. 'Bad luck, old bean,' he said in an exaggerated Oxford accent. 'He's in a black mood today. He hadn't bargained for Papa to be with us.'

Sarah wondered if Hussain's mood was a direct result of finding one locked bedroom door last night, and she felt immensely glad that she had not given in to the temptation to allow him into her room.

'You can relax now,' David said. 'You have only to clap your hands and the minions will come running. Did you know that the Sheikh sat in at your lecture, behind a few potted plants, so you probably didn't see him? But everyone was very pleased and you have acquired a few more devoted fans.' He grinned. 'They even liked what you said.'

'Do you really think you'll find water?' Carlson was almost derisive. 'They've tried everything and as they desperately need water, that does mean everything, so why do you think you can work a kind of magic? Are you or are you not an oil boffin, rather than a water wizard?' He smiled lazily. 'Not that you can't use magic. Some of us have fallen under a definite spell, and that includes the Sheikh. Better watch it! He has only one wife now and has more to offer than Prince Hussain, who gets a fantastic allowance but owns very little.'

'Don't be silly. What makes you think I would want either of them or they want me?' Sarah felt her colour rising and finger-ed the tiny turtle as she did when embar-rassed or uneasy. 'I go home in a day or so

114

and they will forget me. The desert will cover any memory they have of me just as it takes over everything, given half a chance.'

'Funny thing, sand,' David said. 'It never seems to move from those ridges and yet it shifts and covers everything. A bit spooky and I don't think I want to work here for ever. I miss the green of Wales.' He glanced at Carlson. 'It's all very well for men who know no better,' he said with a mischievous grin. 'From what I've seen of the States, it's one huge network of arid roads with a bit of scrub and trees if you're lucky.'

Sarah and Carlson groaned. 'What about New England in the Fall? What about the Smokey Mountains?' Carlson asked.

'And the Lakes and the deep South,' Sarah added. 'You've only seen the oil states and the bleak bits of Alaska.' She laughed. 'If all I'd seen of Wales was Cardiff on a wet Sunday night, I'd be as dismissive as you are about places you've never visited.'

David was enjoying himself. 'Cardiff and all that lovely cool rain? Don't remind me or I'll weep tears of homesickness and take the next plane back.'

'Good! I'll be glad to see the back of you,' Carlson said. 'Does he always try to wind people up?' he asked Sarah, as if referring to a naughty child.

'Always. Sometimes he drove Mark mad.' She bit her lip.

'OK, Sal bach.' David was suddenly serious and he patted her hand. 'How far now?' he asked with an abrupt change of subject.

'Not far.' Carlson was watching Sarah's fingers twisting the chain at her throat. 'That your own personal worry bead?' he asked gently. 'What gives with Mark? You've had a fight?'

Sarah took a deep breath. The desert stretched far away over the hills and a line of camels looked like paper cut-outs on the horizon as if the whole country was only a film set. What is real any more? she wondered. What will be real when I get back among people who know? She felt empty of hope and all emotion. Soon, everyone would know. Dwight was a great guy but she doubted if he could keep a secret.

'It's all over,' she whispered, and Carlson had to bend forward to hear her words. 'Mark is dead.'

He looked across at David who nodded and said quietly, 'Don't ask now, Carl. I'll fill you in later.'

Sarah sat tall and brushed a stray lock of hair from her eyes with a tired hand, then said with a valiant effort at normality, 'My worry bead, as you call it, is a family thing and I think it brings me luck. I wasn't wearing it the day that Mark was killed.'

'What is it? A terrapin?' he asked and touched it with one finger as she held it on

116

her palm.

'A turtle. It's very old and not valuable but it has a value for me.'

'Have you seen the real turtles here?'

'I don't think there will be time,' she said with regret. 'I hate to mention it to Hussain or the Sheikh or they'd want to lay on a safari! Today is bad enough. All I wanted to do was to come out here quietly, take a quick look and do a little dowsing for fun, but they've brought everything but the kitchen sink and a brass band!'

Carlson laughed. 'You'd better believe it! They've brought that and more!'

'Oh, not that nasal music again?' David looked disgusted.

'Can't expect a Welsh male voice choir singing "Bread of Heaven" here,' Carl said. 'Unless you can do it?'

'Not me,' David said firmly. 'I'm rugby and laver bread, not the singing bit.'

'Before you ask what it is, and not a lot of people know about this,' Sarah explained, solemnly, 'laver is a thick black-green sludge made from boiled seaweed and tastes foul but is the staple diet of the Welsh Celts who know no better.'

'I suspect that's the reason why Sarah refuses to marry me,' David asserted. 'And I don't think I want a wife who would refuse to cook it for me, rolled in oatmeal, and fried in bacon fat. Delicious.'

'I'm not marrying anyone,' she said firmly. 'That includes a man who would try to dominate me and who eats fatty lamb and couscous without a glass of house red to go with it, although I admit I do enjoy it for a change,' Sarah said.

'Why not settle for Maine lobsters and Texas beef?' Carlson sounded as if he was joking but his eyes held a question that Sarah couldn't face. Not yet, not Carl. She felt a moment of panic at her sudden long-ing for him to come closer, a strong man she could call her own. Mentally, she pushed him away to a neutral area of friendship where his mind couldn't dominate hers.

Dominate? Why did she think that every man she now met wanted that? It was a defensive thought foreign to her nature. Mark had been an equal, easy-going and calm; in fact, if she was honest, she had been the stronger personality, but here ... it must be the thousands of years of the tradition that women were inferior that had got to her, in spite of her ludicrous status of Honorary Man.

'Why not come turtle watching with me?' Carlson asked casually.

'Turtle watching? When? I've never seen them either,' David said, enthusiastically.

'Don't you ever leave little Sir Echo at home?' Carlson sounded bored.

'I'm looking after Sarah,' David said

118

firmly. 'Too many wolves in this desert.'

'I think that Sarah has built her own wall of protection,' Carlson said coldly. 'I can't see any danger for her unless she invites it. I was thinking of going tonight. You can tag along if you want, so long as you're quiet. I know that it's the time for turtles to come ashore and lay eggs and I want to see it again. It's a weird sort of ceremony. They come out of the sea and struggle ashore, then dig holes for the eggs and leave them to hatch. No mothering instinct there and sometimes they dig up other turtles' eggs to make room for their own. The whole beach becomes a maternity ward for baby turtles.'

'If they produce so many, why don't we hear of a glut of turtles and lots of lovely turtle soup? It's forbidden to hunt them, I believe, as they say they may be a threatened species. Isn't that so?' David wanted to know.

'Nature sure gets things wrong at times, that is if you're a turtle, but not if you're a hungry desert fox digging up eggs, with young to feed, or a predatory sea bird waiting to swoop down and pick up the tiny things as they emerge from their shells and try to make it to the safety of the sea. It must seem a long, long way to water when you hear the beat of wings overhead and no parents are there to fight for you.'

'Everybody say, *ahhh!* I'm on the side of

the turtles until I see a touching programme about the family life of desert foxes,' David said. He pointed ahead. 'That looks like a camp.' There were a few tents and a plume of smoke rising from a newly made fire.

'What luxury. Lunch and shelter without me having to lift a finger.' Sarah sighed. 'I could get used to all this.'

'Yes, you've got the easy bit,' Carlson agreed with an indulgent grin. 'Just hours in the hot sun, looking for dreams for the Sheikh, while we hold your bottle of mineral water in case you collapse with heat stroke.'

'Well, better get on with it,' she said crisply. 'There's Dwight with the maps and I can see a few old bits of wall which should pin-point the place where the old wells were.' She rammed her terrible hat down over her ears and grabbed her steel rods. David took her rucksack and went ahead to the table under an awning, where Dwight had the maps and the old geological survey.

Carlson took her by the shoulders in the shade of the Land Rover. He kissed her lips gently and said with a disbelieving smile, as if unwilling to have such feelings, 'You look terrible, Dr S. Brackley, and I love you.'

She slipped from his grasp, aware of pain in her heart and physical discomfort where his fingers had dug into the last soreness of her scars. 'No,' she said simply and fled to the shelter of the awning and the prosaic calm of the other American.

David was examining the last geological survey of the dry wadi and the diagrams of the old well that Dwight had laid out on a big trestle table. 'This is our best bet,' he decided. 'If the water went underground, it might still be on this line.' He looked again. 'Or, as they didn't discover any there when they drilled, it could have taken this route, diverted under a layer of rock that surfaces beyond that dune. That could mask a new progress of the stream to the west. Here,' he said pointing to the old dry wadi. 'We might find enough water that could revitalise a village, but what they really need is deep water that they can tap under pressure from the water table, to feed a pipeline to the new oil drill.'

'Let's try close to the old source first,' Sarah suggested. 'Even a little discovery would justify all this fuss and save my face! It's so embarrassing to think of all this effort just because I said I had dowsed a few times in the past.'

She rolled down her sleeves and took the rods, walking slowly in a line towards the shell of an old dwelling. The steel rods remained parallel to the ground and she felt no movement. She turned at right angles towards the place where David insisted the old well had been and walked slowly round the spot.

Nothing happened until she was walking back, taking a wide sweep to avoid a dense patch of scrubby bush and some loose and jagged rocks. The rods twitched slightly and came together slowly, but it was as if they were trying to run on spent batteries.

'They moved!' Hussain stood watching, his face stiff with anticipation.

'Not enough,' Sarah called. 'There's water to this side of the old well, but not enough to get excited about.'

'Let me try,' Hussain ordered peremptorily, and took the rods from her hands. He looked just like any other powerful charismatic man, dressed for work in faded jeans that clung to his body and a loose T-shirt of burned orange, but the arrogance of a long line of desert princes showed in the way he took over.

'Where was it?' he demanded impatiently. 'If you can do this, then so can I.'

'Try by that rock,' Sarah suggested. 'Then walk over to me, following my footsteps in the sand.'

'It doesn't move! This can't be the place.'

'The traces that Sarah left in the sand are still there except where you've trodden on them,' David said mildly. 'This could be a well for travellers to use and might be useful, but we should try further over there.' He laughed. 'It's galling to know there are things you can't do, isn't it?' He saw the

122

frustration in the Prince's eyes and added, 'I could write a book about my most profound failures but I think I'll keep a few illusions for a bit longer or I'll never pull a bird again.'

He called to the driver of a light buggy with an awning, who was waiting for instructions. 'One post here!' and the man hammered a tall, pointed stick into the ground to mark the place.

'Why doesn't it do it for me?' Hussain said in an aggrieved voice. 'Show me again.'

Sarah repeated the procedure with the same muted result. 'I think that women are better at this than men,' she lied, hoping that Hussain had never heard of several famous male dowsers who she had met.

'Women being closer to the earth, like,' David said soothingly as Hussain showed signs of losing his temper.

'So you do have some feminine qualities,' Hussain said acidly, and Sarah knew that he'd been humiliated when she kept her door locked during the night.

'My mother was really good at this. Much better than I'll ever be, but it does seem to be an inexplicable gift,' she said.

They piled into the buggy and went in the direction that David indicated. Three times, Sarah walked along lines suggested by the charts and the survey, and nothing happened. The heat was intense and the sun shone with relentless golden fire, leaving her limp until a beaten drum told them that lunch was served.

'I had no idea we'd come so far from the camp,' David said. 'I think we overshot the place where it could happen, as the maps don't show any usable faults in the rock here.'

Water to wash their hands was presented, together with spotless white towels and, Sarah suspected that it was in her honour, there was even a latrine tent set discreetly behind the main tented area.

Cushions surrounded the deep carpet and a huge dish of couscous and vegetables was set in the central space, with lamb and kid meat and bowls of dates and figs and oranges.

Sarah remembered to eat with the right hand only as she rolled balls of rice and vegetables in her fingers before transfering the food to her mouth, with enough aplomb to indicate that maybe she ate in this manner every day of her life. She ate well, which made the Sheikh look on her with approval, and after strong black coffee was served with the inevitable sweetmeats, she felt sleepy, but hoped the coffee would keep her alert as she wanted to get on with the project she'd set herself.

The Sheikh was too courteous to show his acute disappointment that a major find of water had not been achieved, but was unable to resist making no attempt to persuade her to rest or to stop her returning to the desert to try again, which proved just how much that he hoped for a better result before they returned to the hotel.

'Show me what you do,' he said when Sarah was putting her hat on again.

'We ought to try over there,' David said. 'Dwight and I have been studying the terrain on the charts and we think it's worth the effort.'

'I shall come with you,' the Sheikh said. 'Hussain shall stay here with Carlson and oversee the breaking of camp except for the small tent and facilities, and we can return to the hotel as soon as you have made one more effort. I must see what you do so that I can find a dowser among my own people.' He smiled. 'Hussain has discovered that it isn't as easy as he imagined, so I shall watch with care.'

Sarah felt that Hussain was in disgrace for being arrogant with an honoured guest and the Sheikh had shown him that he was still under his father's domination, but Abdul Nizam was the epitome of courteous regard for Sarah in spite of his own inner anxiety that must be as strong as his son's show of frustration.

Sheikh Abdul is treating my feelings as if they are cut-glass fragile and he's determind

125

that I shall not be upset, she thought un-
easily. It was one thing to call her his
daughter if she achieved what she had set
out to do, but was the reality the wish for a
more permanent relationship with her as
Hussain's wife?

The buggy stopped by a ridge and they
could see the depression left by the wadi
and a few stunted bushes that clung to life
but looked almost fossilised. The ground fell
away to the west and left a soft landscape
that led to the huge, shifting dunes.

Sarah climbed down from the buggy and
gripped the rods firmly. She was inwardly
excited as if some inner force gave her a
message that she couldn't ignore. The slope
of the ground was hard under the powdering of sand, enabling her to walk with ease.

Twice she walked lines of twenty metres or
so on the suggested route and then turned
away a little to the east, in spite of David
calling her to go the other way.

A tingling in her fingers made her want to
drop the steel, then the rods glinted in the
sunlight and began to converge, pulling her
hands inexorably until the rods pointed
down towards the ground and tried to leap
from her grip.

'Here!' she called but her voice was husky
and no sound came. The men ran towards
her and saw her pallor and her sudden
weakness as if she was drained of the power

126

that had helped her discovery.

'Show me,' ordered the Sheikh and she repeated the manoeuvre, going in ever decreasing circles to find the centre of the source of water.

The Arab servants pounded away at the stakes marking the area covered and the possible places to drill, and Sarah shook her head and said she could do no more. 'It may be a good supply but I can't promise that,' she said again and again. 'Just don't be too optimistic.'

'We'll take you back now, bach,' David said firmly and they began the bumpy ride back to the nearly dismantled camp.

'It might be a good idea if we took an aerial view tomorrow if we can have a light plane, sir,' Dwight suggested. 'From the air we can see the marker poles and plot them accurately and I can play around with the information on computer.' He sounded as if he had been invited to a marvellous party.

'I suppose that this is where I'm supposed to offer you half of my kingdom,' the Sheikh said to Sarah with a laugh that was spontaneous and joyful and showed how attractive and humorous he must have been in his youth. 'I have no intention of doing so but you may have a plane, men and equipment and much more.' He glanced at Sarah's set face and she dreaded what might come next but he was now calm and she took a deep breath, knowing that what was on his mind would be postponed, giving her space.

Carlson and Hussain ran to meet them, both annoyed that they weren't included as there had been no room for the pair of them in the small buggy now that the Sheikh was one of the party, and he had tactfully excluded both men to avoid tension, but the enthusiasm was infectious and they were soon busy discussing the next day's programme.

'Hussain will return to the oasis with me now as there will be matters to settle and supplies to order. He will fly the plane tomorrow for the inspection, while I rest. If this brings water, we shall be the envy of every small oil state in the Arab world,' he asserted triumphantly.

'Funny how money ceases to matter when you're rolling, stinking rich,' David said caustically as the Sheikh and Hussain drove away. 'It's power that matters afterwards and he's got it all. They'll bow and scrape to him at the meetings of heads of state that they hold to iron out Middle East problems and he'll appear modest and self-deprecating because of all that he has to back him up.'

'You sound bitter, David.'

'Not really.' He sounded more cheerful. 'It's not me I worry about. He's almost bought me and I think I like it, but it's you, girl. What they want, they have by one means or another, and make no mistake about it. It was a safe bet that he'd kick against Hussain marrying another Westerner but what would he get with you? A first-rate scientist, a beautiful daughter-in-law and a dowser as well. Once you are captive, he can drive you out into the desert to find water, more water, cracking the whip but making it a velvet-covered scourge, so you'll never notice a thing.'

'You are an idiot, Dave,' Sarah said, but her laughter was hollow and she knew that every word he spoke had some truth in it. 'I like them and they have been very pleasant company. You like them too, don't you?'

'Sure! They're charming,' was all he would say.

'I'm glad they left in such a hurry.' Carlson seemed pleased with himself. 'Hope you aren't disappointed, Sarah.'

'Why should I be disappointed?'

'Hussain seemed to think he had a hot date with you tonight.' Carlson regarded her with curiosity. 'I didn't think you were all that keen on the ancient culture around here.'

'I've liked what I've seen so far,' Sarah said, 'but unless Hussain thought he had a surprise treat for me, I know of no date tonight.'

'He hinted that he has priority with you

129

and that other men should keep their noses out of what does not concern them,' Carlson remarked calmly.

'And you let him tell you what to do?' David sounded belligerent. 'I'd have punched his stupid arrogant face in.'

'I'll bet you would!' Carlson smiled but Sarah felt that the slight smile hid a lot of anger. 'That's what he wanted: me to throw few punches and give him the excuse for sending me back to the States as soon as he could get me on a plane, but he and I go back a long way and I know how his mind works. I also like the guy and want no hassle there, so I said that I couldn't imagine us falling out over any woman.'

David glanced at Sarah to note her reaction. 'He hasn't seen you making a play for Sarah, has he? I didn't think you even liked each other that much.'

'Do you *mind*? I *am* here, you know, and I *do* have enough sense to make up my own mind who I like, who I tolerate and who I have dates with!' Sarah stormed away and sat with Dwight in the back of the jeep. The men followed, looking chastened, but she suspected that Carlson had enjoyed telling her in such a *nice* way that she rated low on his chart of what a desirable woman should be, and not worth fighting over.

'What about tonight?' asked David to ease the atmosphere.

'What about it?' Sarah said as if she had no knowledge of their former arrangement.

'Dave and I are going to see some turtles. Wanna come?' Carlson asked Dwight.

'Do I want to come? You bet!' Dwight glanced at Sarah and thought she looked tense. 'Why don't you come too, Sarah?' he asked generously, as if it was his party. 'All that hot sun must have given you a headache and the trauma of actually doing that dowsing must have taken it out of you. It'll be cool out there at night by the shore,' he added kindly.

'How sweet of you, Dwight,' Sarah said softly. 'I'll come with you, if that's all right?'

'Be my guest.' Dwight gave a wide grin. 'I hope you decide to stay, Sarah. We'll get along just fine.' He regarded her hat with interest. 'Might even buy you a new hat sometime. My wife wouldn't be seen dead in that.'

'I think it suits her,' Carlson said maliciously. 'It does good things to my blood pressure and keeps my mind on my job.' He looked at her with studied courtesy. 'Coming for a swim when we get back?'

'I might,' she said shortly and knew that he was teasing her about the leotard she wore in the water. 'I'll wear the red leotard for a change to give everyone a thrill.'

'The Sheikh and Hussain will be far away, so you don't have to be so bloody modest,'

131

Carlson said with a touch of irritation.

'Cool it, Carl,' David warned. 'When we get back, I want to talk to you.'

David took Sarah's bag and his own gear and walked into the hotel. 'See you in the pool,' he said to Carlson.

'What more is there for me to know?' Carlson asked as he walked back with Sarah. 'I know that Mark is dead, but don't tell me you made a deathbed vow of life-long chastity because he died?'

'No, there wasn't time for that.' She shook her head and dragged her hair to escape from the restricting ribbon band in an effort to hide her face.

'He wasn't ill? Was it an accident?'

'He was killed by a terrorist bomb in London.'

Carlson whistled softly and led her to a settee away from the reception area. 'And they had to tell you that he was dead?'

'I already knew.' Her voice was hard. 'I was there with him, taking an afternoon off to do some shopping in the West End and we were laughing about some of the colours. I reached over to feel the fabric of a jacket and I heard Mark say, "Leave it. You couldn't wear that." I was pretending to be cross but I was only teasing him as it was a terrible colour.'

'And then?' Carlson asked gently.

'The explosion happened and he was

thrown against me, half burying me under a rack of coats that had been tossed down by the blast. They muffled the impact but were on fire and so was I. I rolled on the floor to kill the flames and when I looked up, Mark was dead.'

She began to sob. 'There wasn't a scratch on him and he just looked surprised.'

'And you were treated for shock?'

'I was in hospital for three or four months with extensive burns,' she said deliberately, now dry-eyed. 'I often wished I was dead, too.'

'But your skin is perfect,' he said almost explosively, as if she was lying. 'There's no trace of a scar.'

'Perhaps now you'll stop making rude remarks about my really rather nice leotard,' she said coldly. 'See you in the pool, but you will never see more of me than you've already seen.'

# Seven

'Hold that.' David handed over an infra-red camera and picked up a rug and a raffia basket of bottles of mineral water. 'About Sarah,' he began in a low voice. 'Perhaps to avoid any further embarrassment, I should fill in a few details. Not that she told me very much,' he added ruefully. 'Very buttoned up is our Sarah, and I don't like to push it too much. When she looks at me in a certain way, I feel like one of her junior lab assistants who has just mucked up an experiment!'

'It's OK. She told me,' Carlson said. 'Wish I'd known earlier. It would have saved a bit of hassle.'

'She didn't tell me until I came here as I was out of the country for six months and missed the news. When she did tell me she begged me to keep quiet about it as she didn't want the people here to find out. It was a terrific shock to me as we were close friends and the three of us did a lot together.'

'It could have been different if I'd known,'

134

Carlson said accusingly.

'No.' David shook his head. 'Look at it this way. You can see how it was. At home, everyone knew and looked at her as if she was dying! She had no chance to forget, or if not that, to come to terms with it.' David looked pensive. 'People find it difficult to cope with such situations. They either ignore it but generate an aura of doom or they talk too brightly about it and say that you'll soon forget and isn't life great?'

'You're right,' admitted Carlson. 'It must have been a relief to get away from all that and the memories, and to be a part of the living scene, taking a fair share of responsibility for her own work and feelings without anyone making concessions just because she was hurt.'

'Thank God for work and over-work,' David said fervently.

'Who else knows?'

'I don't know, but Dwight recognised her name under a picture of Mark and the mayhem in the store. The Sheikh was there when he remembered where he'd seen her name, so he knows, and by now I expect he's told Hussain.'

'Is she badly scarred or just self-conscious about a few burns?'

'I haven't seen her back and she's not saying, but if she was under surgery for that long, it must have been bad,' David said.

'That isn't the worst of it, in my opinion. She's got a great big hang-up about herself now and works far too hard to try to sublimate it.' He tried to see Carlson's expression through the gloom of evening. 'She said she knew that no man would ever want to look at her body again.'

'She can't go on like that for ever!'

'It's well over six months now and she still hates her body,' David insisted. 'She may have to go back to hospital to have one last graft as one small area isn't solid, so please don't ever suggest that she wears her own rucksack! It really is sore at times.'

'I wish I'd known,' was all that Carlson could say. He recalled every snide remark he'd made and hated himself.

'Just one thing,' David said. 'Don't go soft on her. She'll know at once and shy away from any hint of that. Go on being offhand at times. It's good for her. I believe that one doctor was very caustic about her outlook and the fact that she was letting her career slide. She was goaded into getting back to near normal fairly quickly because her pride was hurt, and Sarah is a very proud lady.'

Carslon gave a short laugh. 'I'd noticed, but she should know by now that she has a lot going for her professionally, and she looks good enough to eat now that she's a bit browner and her face has lost that tense expression.'

'She doesn't need sympathy any more,' David continued. 'She must look ahead now and find someone who isn't repelled by a few scars, but who will have the tough job of convincing her that he's not a wimp who wants a woman who is less than perfect to boost his own ego, and who is not mad or perverted! Not me, I'm afraid,' David said with obvious regret. 'I was too close to them and she looks on me as a faithful pal. What man wants to be a good old pal?' he added with a note of disgust.

'Well, I'm none of those,' Carlson said with a wry smile. 'Rough and tactless, yes, but I'm sure you Welsh would say, in your own sickening sentimental way, that I have a heart of gold!'

David shook his head. 'Watch it, Carl. She's not into gold mining yet. You might find that you want to take her on before you assess the situation correctly. One-night stands are out unless you intend to shatter her completely.'

'Maybe I don't want her for that.'

'Anyone trying that would have to have the death wish of a male black widow spider! All that pent-up passion and a kind of hate released for nothing? I love the girl but I'd not dare to try to get her into bed, even though we are close and Mark is dead.'

'Maybe she'll marry Hussain?' There was anxiety under the simple question. 'He can give her anything.'

'God forbid! Not for all the black gold of Arabia. I'd kill him first!' David walked towards the jeep. 'Got everything?' he called. 'At least Sarah isn't wearing *the* hat tonight. We don't want the poor turtles to be frightened back to the sea with their eggs all addled.'

The desert was weird. Mountains of sand and rock loomed up on all sides as they drove along the valley leading to the shore-line, far from the hotel. The golden vista of the day was reduced to grey. The faint crescent moon hung suspended under the brighter stars in an almost black sky and the headlights of the jeep showed the scuttling figures of the creatures of the desert night as they escaped into the dunes. It was very quiet as they drove further away from the hotel and the faint sounds of Arab music from the village, and the air was cool even in the jeep.

Sarah zipped up the front of her anorak and wished she'd put on thick socks as the night air dropped by twenty degrees, not cold, but compared to the temperature of the day, it seemed really cool.

The air of unreality persisted as they parked the vehicle and carried their rugs and water and a huge flask of coffee to the spot where the dunes overlooked the beach. David seemed to have made up his mind that Carlson was no threat to Sarah and joined Dwight on the top of the ridge where they might get a good view of anything moving and be able to take pictures with the infra-red camera.

Lying flat on the rug, Sarah and Carlson were hidden from the beach but could see very little, so they moved the rug closer and then closer again until they were on the edge of the shore sand and could smell the seaweed and the fresh, sharp tang of salt water. Starlight glinted on the small waves breaking on the wet sand and the hiss of the undertow came with the night breeze.

'Even if we see nothing tonight, this a good place,' Carlson said quietly. 'No wonder the Bedouin never leaves the desert and the peace of the nights. Did you ever see such a sky?'

'It's wonderful,' sighed Sarah. 'There's not a sound except the sea and I really do feel close to nature, if that isn't a trite thing to say.' She stretched luxuriously.

'Have a nap if you're tired after your efforts today,' he suggested. 'I'll watch and wake you if they come within the next two hours.'

'That's kind,' Sarah said, touched by his consideration.

'Not at all. After that, it's your watch and if nothing happens then, we go home,' he said briskly.

She pushed a fist down in the rug to make the underlying sand into a hollow for her hip and lay down on her side, watching the sea until the water blurred and the light waned and she drowsed in a sea of her own, with fleeting visions of places and people and a feeling of contentment. She woke to find that one of her hands was being held gently and Carlson was watching her face.

'Good,' he said abruptly, and let her hand fall on to her chest. 'You were fine until you began crying, then I thought it was time for coffee.'

'Not now,' she whispered. 'Look!'

Out of the sea, like a fleet of clumsy, squat landing craft they came, losing their grace as soon as they were no longer floating on the water, labouring up the beach as if they were unwilling and almost unable to travel far on land. They were impelled by an instinct stronger than their own will and energy.

'Get down!' Carlson whispered. 'We're a bit too close. They might see us.'

He pulled her down beside him and put an arm round her shoulders as they lay prone on the rug, and they lay tense and waiting. A grunting, moaning sound and a flurry of scattered sand made them keep their heads down and the grunting became louder as huge flippers dug at the sand and sent it up in waves as the nearest turtle excavated a hole for her eggs.

Sarah wanted to laugh, and some of the the words of 'The Walrus and the Carpenter' ran through her mind; silly words ... 'The time has come,' the walrus said, 'to talk of many things ... of ships and sealing wax ... and if the sea is boiling hot and whether pigs have wings.'

This was as unbelievable as the poem. Perhaps here pigs did have wings, and the sea might be boiling hot. She'd got it wrong, she knew, but it was amazing that she remembered even some of the words. Mark would have laughed at her flight of fancy, but then he never could recall the words of any poem, however incomplete it was.

Carlson was laughing, too. 'Head well down! Here comes a real matriarch and I have a feeling we are very close to her patch.'

'I doubt if she'll know we are here. The breeze is coming our way so if they depend on their sense of smell, they'll not know about human bodies in the sand watching,' she whispered. 'And from the efforts they are making, they'll hear nothing. Whoops!'

A flipper-full of sand came over in an arc, covering the watchers with a light tilth and Sarah brushed it from her eyes.

'Do you want to ease back?' Carlson asked, softly.

Sarah shook her head. 'I wouldn't have

141

missed this for the world,' she whispered. 'Can we stay?'

'Yes.' His arm was firmly round her, but he took care to put no pressure on her back and with a conscious effort he refrained from caressing the softness of her body and the long line of her thighs. He brushed the sand from her hair and she couldn't decide if the light touch was from a hand or a gentle kiss. She discovered that she wanted it to be a kiss and turned her face towards him, but he was wiping sand from the neckline of his T-shirt and seemed not to notice.

Groaning and grunting came from all over the beach as dozens of turtles deposited the next generation, unaware that bright eyes were coming closer over the dunes as desert foxes waited for their feast of badly covered eggs after the turtles left.

A red glow, like a distant forest fire, came from the horizon. 'Dawn?' Sarah sat up cautiously and watched the last of the turtles amble and slither down to the sea, without a backward glance for their potential offspring.

Carlson filled a mug with coffee and handed it to her. He stared at the red glow. 'Dreaming, when Dawn's left hand was in the sky, I heard a voice within the tavern cry, "Awake my little ones and fill the cup, before life's liquor in the cup be dry,"' he quoted as if to himself.

'Omar Khayyam,' she said in wonder.

'Wise old sod,' Carlson said as if he disapproved.

'But you bothered to learn his words,' Sarah said.

'Doesn't everyone?' He looked into her eyes and she sensed his longing. ' "Unborn tomorrow and dead yesterday, why fret about them if today be sweet," ' he said with a wry smile.

She kissed him on the cheek and he felt her tears but clenched his hands to stop them taking her in his arms. 'Sand in my eyes,' she murmured and wiped her eyes dry.

'You hogged all the coffee,' David called. 'We got some good shots and now I want to crash out for few hours before we fly.'

'Forgot about that,' Carlson said. 'It could be a busy day. Let's go.'

The gardeners were watering the flowers and the pool was being swept clear of petals and leaves before the hotel woke up and the sun became too hot for the men to water the plants. The party returned and went quietly to their individual rooms. Sarah showered and washed away the sand that seemed to have got everywhere and imagined Carlson doing the same in his shower room.

She wondered if he was as hairy as his facial beard promised. In the pool his chest hair was flattened and hardly noticeable, but stupidly, she remembered the line of dark hair from his navel vanishing into his shorts, and she felt an unfamiliar thrill of excitement, quickly quelled by a jet of cold water that cooled her scars. Mark had little body hair and she thought that Hussain was like that, smooth as his voice when he wanted something, and as supple as a baby, but unlike Mark, hiding a streak of ruthlessness under the charm.

She towelled and applied the soothing cream that was still needed to keep the new skin soft, but she remembered Carlson's arm round her and the fact that it gave her no discomfort, only peace and a slumbrous feeling on the edge of wanting.

Sleep came quickly and she woke to her alarm, refreshed and cool. Dressed in jeans and a clean, thin shirt again, both laundered overnight and brought to her room while she was asleep, Sarah tied back her hair, thrust her feet into plain moccasins and braced herself for the day.

Mundane cereal and fruit seemed to be the acceptable food now and the hot rolls were delicious smothered with fresh butter and honey. 'I'd miss my kind of food if I had to do without it for long,' David said as he brought over scrambled eggs and bacon and ate as if he was starving.

'They seem very tolerant of Western needs,' Sarah said. 'I thought that bacon would be off the menu here.'

'So it is, officially, but when tourism rears its voracious head, bacon is served without a murmur of dissent in hotels of this rating. They have cooks who aren't Muslim, I believe.'

'Funny you should say that,' Sarah remarked, idly buttering another roll even now that her hunger had vanished. 'When Mark and I were in Turkey, we met a man who lived in considerable style and spent the winter hunting wild boar among other game. Mark asked what he did with the meat as we knew he was a devout Muslim. He said they only killed it but never touched even the freshly killed carcases. They sent word to a non-Muslim dealer to collect it and sell it to the tourist hotels, so it was used but he was not defiled by any contact.'

'You had a good holiday there?' David watched her face, alive with amusement and good memories.

'Wonderful,' she said. 'I want to go there again some day.' She giggled. 'Mark wanted to buy cheap trousers made from local cotton. He'd heard about the cotton, but to his horror he was measured for them and then fitted, standing in the window of the local tailor's shop. He hadn't the courage or the Turkish to say he didn't want them when he saw what they were like. They fitted well, but the material was as thick as the stuff

145

they use to make old-fashioned floor cloths and they were so hot he never wore them except once when he climbed up to destroy a wasp's nest back home. Nothing could sting through that lot.'

'I remember some good times too,' David said. 'With Mark alone and the three of us together. Those were the best times.' He attacked a large bread roll and covered the soft inside with butter and added the hotel red preserve that could be anything sweet. 'Not bad, but I pine for the marmalade my mother makes. Nice and bitter with lots of peel in it,' he said.

Sarah poured more coffee. 'We seem to be the only ones of our party at breakfast,' she noticed.

'They went swimming. Not in the pool but in the sea. Tempting but I'll get enough sea water next week when I examine one of the offshore drills where they're trying out my metal suggestion.' He regarded her with interest. 'Is it true that you are staying for another week?'

'Yes.' She moved restlessly. 'I have some leave due and there is a lot I could do here before I go to the States for the next lecture tour.' She sighed. 'They wanted me to agree to look in on a laboratory in Cairo on my way home, so the powers-that-be were anxious that I should have VIP treatment, hence the willingness to give me extra time here, but I doubt if I'll go there on this trip.'

'Partly political,' David said flatly. 'There's always a desk-bound member of parliament seeking some kind of concession from any part of the world where money drips freely.' He gave a cynical laugh. 'I bet they'll trade on your influence here and want the Sheikh to fund something or other, but you'll be the last to know.'

'I hate the thought of being used,' Sarah said reflectively.

'Grow up, darling. It happens to us all and the higher we go, the more pressure there is. I've been head-hunted often enough to know the score and what firms will offer if they really want something. Every time I have a very good offer, I look under the carpet to see the snags before I sign any-thing.' He looked at her with fresh interest. 'I hope you have a good lawyer? You'll need one if you stay here for too long. They'll make things too easy for you until you find that the desert sucks away resistance and you could end up with egg on your face.'

'Mike's fine, and I know what I want,' she said, but her mind seemed to be on other matters. 'Mark didn't like him but he's efficient and has never let me down yet.'

'Mike's the nice guy with the Robert Redford look? No wonder Mark was not taken with his influence on your affairs.'

Sarah shrugged impatiently. 'He was no

threat to Mark. He is very happily married and is a distant relative, which puts him in the big brother category as far as I'm concerned.'

'Did he upset Mark?'

'More than anyone told me, but any niggles came from Mark in the first place and he couldn't expect me to ditch Mike just because he didn't like him.'

'Mark did like to have his own way,' David said, mildly.

'I sound disloyal,' Sarah said. She began to fidget with the turtle pendant and her face was taut.

'Why didn't you two get married?' David shook his head as Sarah began to protest. 'It wasn't because he never asked you. He told me many times that he wanted you as his wife.' He grinned. 'He wanted to keep other men off the grass.'

'I know.' Her shoulders slumped at the memory. 'He did go on about it to me, but to save his pride he told other people we were happier without marriage. He nagged at me a lot until I threatened to end it. He accused me of having another lover, which didn't help. I blew my top and said I wanted to live with him but I must have space to do my work, and at last he saw sense and agreed.'

David saw Dwight approaching, and spoke quickly, then relaxed as Dwight was held up talking to a departing delegate leaving for home in Geneva. 'Every day in every way, you get better and better, isn't that what they say?' David remarked. His eyes were full of understanding. 'Let him go, Sarah. This is the first time we've talked, really talked about Mark since he died. Maybe it will put you back a bit when you stop mourning and look objectively at what you hoped he could be to you. It's healthy to begin to weigh his good side against the other that you always tried to ignore. He was my friend too, remember, but it doesn't mean we have to worship a plaster saint, shrugging away all his faults.'

'I loved him, Dave.'

'Sure you did. You said it. The accent's on past tense and you have a lot of life to live now.' He swung round. 'Hey there, Dwight! Any news of the plane?'

'Coffee?' asked Sarah in a subdued voice.

'Hussain is bringing it to the small runway in a few minutes from now, so I'm off for a leak and to get my camera. Meet you by the jeep. The runway is about five minutes away and Carlson is there by the jeep now.'

'The guy makes sense,' David said in an American accent. 'Guess I'll do the same. Can't bear sand in my fly zip. See you.'

'Idiot,' she said, but she was smiling.

'I love you, too,' he said and kissed her lightly, then ran to the elevator.

Sarah added sunscreen to her bag and a light headscarf although they would probably stay in the plane and return without undue exposure to the sun, but she wanted to leave her straw hat behind and decided that it must join a lot of her past, discarded for something new and unknown. She walked down to the jeep and Carlson waved a greeting.

'What? No hat?' he asked in mock dismay. 'You'll drive the Arabs wild.' He took in her freshly washed hair and clear skin. She had a bloom of health and something more. Even her limbs seemed more supple and she held her head high. 'You slept and you washed your hair,' he said, as if trying to find an explanation of the subtle change he saw.

'I ate breakfast too and remembered to bring some mineral water in case Hussain isn't that good a pilot and makes a false landing miles from anywhere!'

'You have to be joking! Just don't say that to him or he'll do stunts and we'll be hanging by our safety straps upside down.' He smiled. 'On second thoughts, he thinks you are too precious to risk anything and he wouldn't dare as the Sheikh would disinherit him if anything happened to you.'

'Nice to have friends,' she said, and heaved herself into the jeep. 'I bet the Sheikh would have helped me into this crate,' she remarked.

'Not the Honorary Man,' he mocked. 'Anything I can do, you can do better.' He sat beside her and inhaled the expensive and subtle scent she used. He sniffed audibly. 'Dangerous stuff that. What is it? Air freshener?'

She gave him a dirty look. 'Very costly and a present from an admirer,' she said, complacently.

'You weren't wearing it last night.'

'It would have been wasted there,' she said, and watched his face darken. 'Actually, it was delivered to me this morning as a thank you from the Sheikh.'

'Why didn't I think of that?'

'You have nothing to thank me for,' she said, calmly. 'I didn't find water for you.'

'You lay beside me all night,' he said and watched her blush. 'Not as a healthy man would wish, but don't deny that it had a certain magic.'

'I don't deny it,' she said. 'I fell in love with ... the turtles.'

Dwight drove the jeep and in the distance they saw a small executive jet plane, waiting on the runway. 'Nice one,' David said, admiringly. 'I never learned to fly, did you, Carl?'

'Yes, but mostly 'copters in my job except when I'm back home and we fly over the ranches.'

'That's your other life?' Sarah realised how little she knew about the man at her side, and the idea of him being a rancher appealed to her.

'So you swopped being a roustabout on a ranch to being one on a rig,' Dwight said and laughed. 'You know his old man owns half of Texas?'

'Less than that,' Carlson protested and seemed annoyed that Dwight should mention it, but the American persisted.

'Maybe as big as this Sheikhdom,' he marvelled.

'More steers than people,' Carlson said shortly.

'No oil? asked David.

'Who knows? In time,' Carlson said and looked at Sarah. 'What we need is water, so does anyone know a nice tame dowser that I can hire and take home with me?'

'I've always been scared of cows,' she said.

'I assume you can ride.'

She nodded. 'I can stay on a horse.'

'No problem,' Carlson said cheerfully. 'Steers take no notice of horses and riders. My father breeds a nice line in Palominos and makes sure there is one ready for any lady who calls.' He regarded her with exaggerated interest. 'On second thoughts, with your colouring, you'll need a chestnut or a bay and a bright saddle cloth.'

'And what do you ride?' asked David with

a grin. 'A stallion as black as the devil?'

'No, a very old friend. A piebald brought down from the mountains that my father tamed for me when I was twenty-one.'

'And he knows you when you return?' Sarah's lips were parted and her eyes wide and soft.

'He is restless long before I get there, and yes, he knows me,' Carlson said. He turned his face away as if afraid to show too much feeling.

'Get that!' Dwight gave a coarse whistle. 'Guess I'll have to buy a few bits of gear if I'm to stay here, and I'll warn my wife to dress pretty when she meets the Prince.'

'You know that this is for your benefit, Sarah?' Carlson's voice had an edge of scorn and latent anger. 'Be careful,' he added softly. 'He's dressed in all his war paint and lacks only the crown.'

'He's quite, quite beautiful,' Sarah said and her laughter was a mixture of comical disbelief and real pleasure.

They walked from the jeep and Hussain made no attempt to come to meet them, aware of the picture he made, leaning nonchalantly against the gleaming red aeroplane.

His dull black silk shirt was tucked into white designer jeans that fitted so closely that the line of his slim hips and the bulge of his sex seemed almost naked. Black desert boots and a bright red neckerchief completed a picture that shouted in a controlled but thrusting way, of wealth, youth and health and blatant sexuality.

Hussain waved a lazy hand, then swung up into the pilot seat, extending a hand to help her up. 'Sarah, come and sit by me,' he ordered.

She climbed into the seat behind him and gave him a dazzling smile. 'On the way back,' she said. 'If Dwight is to take photographs he must sit there and have the best view. What a pity this is a business trip,' she added, with regret that Carlson thought was mixed with relief. Suddenly, the waft of perfume as she entered the plane seemed too heavy, too musky, as if loaded with pheromones, much too erotic for a flight over a possible site for the discovery of water.

Hussain checked the dials in front of him and Sarah couldn't see his face. 'You're right,' he said in a level voice. 'My father needs good pictures and your results on computer, Dwight, so let's not waste time.'

Sarah relaxed, her shoulder touching Carlson's. He glanced at her with mocking eyes. 'Ever been fishing for the really big ones?' he asked.

'No. What's that to do with this trip? We are going inland and I hate fishing.'

'I think it is a male hobby, although some

women enjoy it,' he said. 'First you wait, as you don't want just any old inferior fish, then you see what you want where you want it, half hidden and unattainable. You cast your line and hope that the bait is acceptable, the line holds and the chase is on.'

'So you catch a fish,' she said.

'Not at once. If it is worth having, you are patient and let it run. The fish thinks it can get free at any time and it relaxes, as you did just now.'

'I'm not a fish!'

'The fish doesn't think of being caught,' he went on. 'But as it relaxes, then is the time to reel it in and land it quite gently. It may not know it is in the net until it finds there is no escape.'

'I suppose you were brought up on good old American fables,' Sarah said scathingly.

'No, that's one of my own,' he said complacently. 'Good, isn't it?'

'Include it in your next best-seller,' she teased him.

'I might just do that.' He bent forward to get a whiff of her scent and she was aware of his own brand of sensuality, less obvious then Hussain's, but potent and strangely frightening. 'Some fishermen use a scent attractive to the fish and it helps the catch to come faster,' he said.

'I don't think that the Sheikh had fishing on his mind when he gave me this,' she said calmly. 'Just a thank you, and very nice too.'

'A matter of taste. I find it too heavy in this heat, in fact be fair, don't you think it's one god-awful stink,' he added as if confiding something with which she must agree.

'I like it,' she said sharply, but her lips twitched.

'You don't,' he said. 'It isn't you.'

'The heat does make it a bit much,' she admitted. 'It was fine in the bathroom until my skin warmed up.'

Suddenly they were giggling.

'Poor Hussain,' Carlson whispered. 'He hasn't got it right yet, but he'll go on trying. I reckon he sent the perfume and hoped it would send you into a receptive coma,' he added. 'Maybe he likes his women to smell like a whore's boudoir.'

Sarah shrugged. 'Whatever turns him on, I suppose, but I prefer flower fragrances.' She turned her face towards him. 'And I'm not Hussain's woman!'

'Good. He wouldn't fit in with your plans at all.'

'Great view,' Dwight called back to them. 'We'll circle while I take pictures and then fly to the oasis to see the Sheikh for lunch.'

'I'm not dressed for that,' Sarah protested.

Hussain's voice came back to them, casual as only a rehearsed phrase could be. 'My father will understand, but if you are self-conscious, we can give you a *hijad*.'

156

'One of those all-concealing robes?' Sarah laughed. 'Modesty is one thing but I don't think I'd ever want to wear one,' she said firmly. 'Today, I am Dr Sarah Brackley, at work with no frills, and you must accept me as you find me.' She dismissed it as trivial but felt uneasy, as if something alien was being forced on her.

'Honorary Men do not wear such perfume,' Hussain said, calmly. 'My father will be enchanted.'

# Eight

From the air, the oasis looked like a model in a child's play village, complete with green plastic trees and a sparkling mirror used to portray water, but as the plane swooped low and made a turn to the landing strip, the full beauty of the area was evident. The two main largest buildings both had roof gardens and awnings that hinted at places for rest, cool from the heat of the desert sun, catching whatever breeze might come from the sea, and a welcome change from the efficent but dry air-conditioning used in some of the main salons, the laboratories and medical unit.

The slender minaret on the private mosque cast a shadow that pointed like an admonishing finger and when Sarah stepped down from the aircraft, she was aware of the silence. A face appeared at an upper window of the office block and a man paused from cleaning a dusty Land Rover to watch the party walk from the plane to the beach buggy waiting to take them to the shade of the buildings.

She shivered and David caught her mood. 'Spooky,' he said. 'Ever felt that there are hidden eyes watching everything you do? For God's sake, Sarah, don't pick your nose or scratch that insect bite you got last night. It all goes on your dossier.'

'Idiot,' she said with relief.

'At last I can really look at you.' Hussain took her hand in a firm clasp and kissed it. He made as if to kiss her cheek but she regarded him with a cool stare and he laughed and let her hand drop to her side. 'You should not smell so nice,' he said easily.

'I'd like to freshen up before I see the Sheikh,' she said.

'Of course, and Dwight must take the films to be developed.' He beckoned to a servant who waited impassively for his master's orders and Sarah was taken once again to the pretty rest room where the same woman who had waited on her smiled, opened doors and poured water as if Sarah was incapable of doing anything for herself. The warm water washed away most of the perfume on her wrists, and in the privacy of the lavatory, Sarah pulled off several sheets of tissue and used water from the tiny corner basin to rub off the perfume from behind her ears and in her cleavage under the shirt.

What a fool! she told herself. You must have known it was very, very good perfume, maturing on the skin and made to last!

Eventually, smelling faintly of rose-per-fumed soap, she emerged with freshly brushed hair and a face devoid of make-up. I should have worn my hat, she decided with a wry smile. Anything to make me unappetising, as I think I may well feature on Hussain's menu today.

He was waiting with fresh orange juice and ice and as he handed her the frosted glass, he stood close to her. 'Where are the others?' she asked.

He gave a mocking smile. 'You can't be afraid to be alone with me, Sarah?'

She looked up at him with carefully simulated surprise and innocence. 'No, why should you think that? I wondered what they were doing. Is Dwight ready with the prints as well as the polaroids? Obviously I'm excited to know what the engineers find and the pictures will be vital to their efforts.'

She strolled away to look out of the windows and to get as far as possible from the magnetism of the man who now stalked her as if she was a small and beautiful lamb ... or a sacrificial goat, she thought. I must be mad to stay another week.

The golden light through gauzy drapes lit her hair and face although she was unaware that she had moved into soft coloured sunlight.

'Don't move,' Hussain said as she heard

him approaching and she wanted to make space between them again. 'You have the most exquisite skin, Sarah. What man wouldn't want to touch and smooth it and move on from the peach bloom of your cheeks, unspoiled by the drying air and having no blemish, to your secret places where it must be even softer, even more inviting, and away from the sun, pale and pure and yielding?'

He made an impatient gesture, then took a deep breath of resignation as a servant walked towards them making the dignified obeisance of a man seeking an audience.

'Highness, I am sent to bring you and your guest to sit with the Sheikh and eat with him.'

'Very well.' Sarah noticed that Hussain obeyed at once as if switching off and shutting his mind to women, soft skin and possible seduction. She smiled and inwardly made up her mind to remember this when he was at his most attractive. She found that her pulse was unusually fast and suspected that her cheeks had more colour than was normal for her.

She followed him and watched the arrogant sway of taut hips and the set of his well-shaped head. Not an eagle, she decided, but certainly a bird of prey with gentle plumage that hid a threat of violence. The tension had been exciting and she wondered how any woman could resist him if he really wanted her, but found an odd kind of safety in the fact that she could never expose her ugly scars and was no longer using the Pill as there had been no need since Mark died.

Fear, the good contraceptive friend of the virtuous, she thought, and was smiling when she came to have her hand shaken by the Sheikh.

'You look happy, my dear,' he said and she thought that he glanced at his son to see if he had anything to do with her state of mind.

'I'm happy for you, sir,' she said. 'I am certain that your engineers will find what you need and Dwight has been very busy this morning. He will sort out the details on computer and that should be a thrilling time when we read his findings.'

'We begin drilling tomorrow,' the Sheikh said. 'I have a favour to ask. Would you be willing to dowse again closer to the new oil drill? There was a waterhole long ago, according to old maps, and if Allah wills, and you have the power, we may have water again there.'

'I have agreed to stay for a week, sir, and I had planned a fairly rigid schedule in the laboratory, but one day could be put aside for dowsing if that is what you want,' she stated in a business-like tone.

'I had hoped to persuade Sarah to stay for

162

longer,' Hussain said smoothly, and his sad, disappointed little boy expression was almost convincing.

'It is easy to forget that Dr Brackley is a scientist with many calls on her time,' the Sheikh ventured. 'One day would be generous and I shall put no further pressure on your time, but we all hope that you will return and take over the laboratory for at least a few weeks each year, even if you decide that you cannot live here permanently.'

Carlson was watching her face and his expression was a compound of curiosity and cynicism. He nodded when she said that she must have time to sort out her commitments when she returned to England, after her planned lecture tour of America.

She glanced at Carlson, recalling his homily of the fish that thinks because it is given a long loose line, it can get away.

'There is no need to feel rushed,' the Sheikh went on. 'We can pencil in a few dates that might suit you early next year, and I shall make all the travel arrangements for your comfort when the time comes.'

'I shall see you before that,' Hussain said, casually. 'I have business in London and I shall stay at Claridges so we shall be quite close.'

The scars on her back tingled, or was it prickles of apprehension? 'When do you expect to be in London?' she asked.

'Soon,' he said, and shrugged. 'My time is flexible and I may stay for a few weeks. Lawyers take their time and I have to sort out a few things.'

'Like alimony?' Carlson said softly to Sarah but Hussain glanced at him sharply as if he had heard.

'I haven't had lunch at Claridges since my father came up for the motor show last year,' Sarah said as if she had enjoyed the novel experience of eating in a small quaint roadside cafe. 'Better than most London restaurants, in my opinion. I shall look forward to being invited to lunch with you, Hussain. I'm sure we can fit lunch in with our busy schedules.'

Was there too much stress on the word lunch? But she knew that dinner dates might be dangerous. She realised that the Sheikh was watching her, slightly puzzled. 'I had hoped that you could make my son's visit to London less lonely,' he said.

'I'm sure that Hussain has a lot of friends in every city in the world,' she replied easily. 'I have work to do and in any case I leave for the States very soon, so I can't be available for very much of the time when he will be at Claridges.' She sighed. 'I look on being here as a real holiday and dread to think of all the paperwork piling up to greet me on my return.'

'Delegate it!' Hussain was angry. 'I have planned so much for us during my stay in England.'

'Dr Brackley is right,' Carlson said with studied formality. 'I too hope to see her again in London but I realise just how busy she will be during the couple of weeks she has before we travel to the States. I had planned the invitation before I met her, when I thought she was a man. That meant a slight adjustment to my plans but the basis of a professional visit remains firm.' He turned to Sarah, his eyes challenging her to tell him that he was a liar. 'You have your schedule?'

'I have no details with me but my office will brief me,' she said shortly.

'You are going to the States with Sarah?' Hussain forgot to appear urbane. 'What right have you to suppose she would want you there?'

'We shall not be together for long,' Carlson said. 'That is, unless Sarah has time free and can take time off for riding. My invitation to Dr S. Brackley didn't include a visit to my family ranch, but consisted of details about a congress in Boston and an inspection of a new oil find in Texas.'

'Where you live?' The sardonic anger spoke volumes.

'Texas is a big place,' Carlson said mildly. 'We may travel together for company, and I hope that Sarah can attend both places to our mutual advantage, but who knows what will crop up in our busy schedules before that?'

Sarah's mind raced. Carlson wasn't lying. She recalled such an invitation, signed by a personal assistant and the scrawled and unintelligible signature that could have been C. Ward. It had been relegated to a file that had to lie in abeyance during her illness and she had asked her PA to sort out such invitations while she was in Arabia, selecting those that could be reached without too much travelling over the same airspace in the States.

'I'm looking forward to meeting my friends at Harvard again,' she said. 'Will Professor Bentley be in Boston for the congress?' She knew that Carlson relaxed and she sensed Hussain's discomfiture.

Carlson smiled at the Sheikh. 'When are you taking up my invitation to visit the ranch, sir? My father is very anxious to show you his new stud farm, and in his last letter he mentiond that he had bought a colt thrown out of Argosta by Esmeralda.'

'Beauty and stamina.' Sheikh Abdul nodded and his eyes gleamed. 'What an acquisition! Is your father about to enter the world of horse racing now as well as breeding good stock for others?'

'He already belongs to a syndicate,' Carlson said. 'But he hopes to race his own stock soon.'

'Perhaps I should see what horses you have. We need more for our stables,' Hussain said as if horses were foremost in his mind.

'You know the way,' Carlson said. 'Any time. You know that my father would enjoy your company even if I am working, and you can have the whole of Texas to ride in, but seriously, we must get together again. I remember the last time when you came back home, with great pleasure.'

The tension between the two men slackened and the Sheikh eyed them with mocking humour as if he watched two stags wondering if tangled antlers might be unnecessary, and they could retreat with dignity.

'I may visit your father next month,' the Sheikh said. He regarded his son with an air of authority. 'We cannot be away at the same time, Hussain, so you must be here when I go away.' He raised a hand to prevent the angry response. 'However, this must not interfere with your visit to London and I think that Sarah could travel with you in our own aircraft.' He smiled and Sarah saw a hint of hidden cunning emerge. 'You will have time to conduct your business in London and still have time for pleasure with friends, before I leave.'

167

'You are very kind, sir, but I have made my own arrangements and my team will send someone to meet me and brief me on what has happened in my office while I was away. I prefer to use the flying time working and I can tie up a lot of loose ends in my next round of talks more easily with no phones and no people trying to talk to me.'

'You sound like—'

'A professional, I hope,' Sarah interrupted sharply. 'Remember that even here, I am an Honorary Man, who works on an equal level with men, and at home there is no distinction between me and a dozen busy scientists of either sex.'

She looked at the date on her watch. 'Which day would you like me to dowse?' she asked. 'I suggest tomorrow so that you can have my findings assessed before I leave in five days' time.'

The Sheikh nodded and she saw a new respect in his eyes. 'I wish all my busines contacts were as good as you. If only you were of my family and my faith...'

'Friends can be as valuable as relations,' she said gently. 'I know we have both gained from this visit.'

'Promise me that you will return?'

Sarah hesitated. She couldn't see the way ahead any more than she could see the future after Mark's death.

'Promise me,' the Sheikh insisted.

168

'I promise.' The words came out unwillingly but she knew that the desert had charmed her more than she cared to admit, and she wanted to come back, but later, when Hussain had married and forgotten her.

'You make me happy. I know that you would never break your word and I shall see you again as my personal guest in my home.' He glanced at the others, who were listening. 'Leave us,' he said imperiously. 'Yes, Hussain, I wish to speak to Sarah in private.'

Hussain looked back from the door as if he wanted to listen and didn't trust what his father would say, but he went with the others obediently and they took their places in the dining room while they waited for the last two to join them.

'You know that my son desires you, Sarah.' It was a statement, not a question, as if it was obvious to her as much as it was to Hussain's father.

'Yes,' Sarah replied steadily, as if the Sheikh had remarked that Hussain liked spinach or garlic, a strange desire but a personal one that didn't touch her.

'You do not return that feeling?'

Sarah thought for a moment before replying, then said as if she had never really analysed her own reaction, 'He is very attractive and I can imagine many women

169

falling in love with him, but as you know my background, I'm sure you can accept that I am immune at present to any thoughts of love.'

'Mark is dead,' he said almost harshly.

'Does love die, too?' she asked.

'If you were a real man and not an Honorary Man you would know that it is possible to desire more than one woman. Also, I have known women who loved widely, if perhaps unwisely.' He smiled as if reminiscing.

'I have slept with one man and that man was Mark. I did not sleep around and neither am I some kind of whore!' she said vehemently.

He waved a deprecating hand. 'You misunderstand me. To me you are a widow grieving for her husband but with a full life ahead where love, desire and a family are possible.'

'With a man who loves widely but maybe not so wisely?' she asked with an ironic smile. 'Mark and me were lovers for six years. We were faithful and we never looked further for sex. I am not a virgin, which I think is important to a man in your country. Unless, of course, you try to give me another spurious title and say I am an Honorary Virgin?'

She bit her lip. 'Forgive me. That was unpardonable but I resent you taking it for granted that I am ready, after only six months, to forget Mark and our life together. Hussain has been married and will be again, but not to me, sir.'

'Beware of men who stand in the background and seem to put no pressure on you. They are as dangerous to your virtue as men like Hussain who are perhaps too forward and compelling, but against whom you can erect barriers because you are warned of the dangers.'

Sarah laughed. 'I am quite safe, Your Highness. I can think of no man who feels like that about me who I can't brush aside easily if he became too persistent.'

'Dr David Griffiths is such a one,' the Sheikh said softly and his fingers tensed.

'David?' Sarah looked startled and amused. 'David is a dear friend and was a close friend of Mark's. We did a lot together but David and I were never as close as lovers,' she stated emphatically.

'You were seen to kiss,' he said. 'Not once, but twice, and he held you in his arms, in public, so what may have happened in private?'

'You spied on me?'

'I have eyes in every corner of my palace and in the hotel,' he said calmly. 'I need them at times for my personal safety.'

'I see.' She was silent for a moment to let her anger subside, then said slowly, 'David

171

is a dear friend. I have many friends who kiss on meeting and when there are moments when comfort is needed, as we did when I had to tell David that my lover, his best friend, had died tragically. At that time, I didn't want or need sex, just warm friendship and a shoulder to cry on, and so did David.'

She brushed the hair from her eyes and looked at him defiantly, her eyes hot with unshed tears. 'There are still men I can trust, who do not force themselves on me or try to get into my bedroom, as happened the other night.'

She walked towards the dining room. 'Am I right? Are we late for lunch, sir? I know that you hate unpunctuality in others.'

He followed slowly and she stood aside to allow him to enter the dining room before her. As he passed, he said, 'I see I have a lot to learn about you, Dr Brackley. I am beginning to think that you will be more than a match for my son, but a match I shall welcome, and I still believe that David Griffiths is a danger to my plans. Such men creep in before their danger is detected and, whatever you believe, he does want you.'

Conversation was general as the party was a small one and the table correspondingly intimate, allowing everyone to hear the others, but it did mean that private exchanges were impossible. Sarah's glance slid from one face to another and she listened more than talked. Hussain hardly looked at her and seemed engrossed in what Dwight was saying about the computerised findings that he had begun. Carlson talked to the Sheikh about horses and David ate solidly and smiled at her between mouthfuls.

Don't look at me like that, she wanted to say to him. I know it is just your usual friendly attitude, but the Sheikh doesn't understand platonic friendship between a man and a woman. She cut up the food served to her and after the meal couldn't remember what it had been. A sensation of foreboding made her restless and as soon as she could leave without seeming discourteous, she pleaded pressure of work in the laboratory and left the men to talk.

It's what the Sheikh expected, she decided with a wry smile. In his eyes I am still a woman who leaves the men to talk of higher matters that would be unintelligible to my poor female brain. In spite of what I do, his mind can't come to terms with me as a scientist.

Carlson had watched her leave and and soon after, when she was absorbed in an experiment, he came into the laboratory.

'What do you want?' she said crossly. 'Can't you see I'm busy?'

'I can wait,' he said mildly.

173

'Right. Just don't get in the way. Hold this.'

He did as she ordered and grinned. 'Are you always as bossy to your lab technicians?' he asked.

'They don't creep up on me to chat,' she said, shortly.

'Who's chatting? I came to make some firm arrangements without someone listening to every word we speak.'

She looked up sharply. 'Right. I'll be done in five minutes.'

At last she washed her hands and looked satisfied. She spoke into a hand-held recorder to note the result and the make of the equipment she'd used. 'I must twist someone's arm to get apparatus like this,' she said. 'It cuts the slog by half.'

Carlson laughed. 'If Hussain came with an armful of new retorts and pipettes he might make more progress than he did with the perfume,' he said.

'The Sheikh sent the perfume.'

'Correction. Hussain thought you might refuse it from him, thinking he had an ulterior motive, so he sent it from his father, hoping to lull you into a state of false security, dull your senses with it and make you fall at his feet.'

She gave him a withering glance. 'Do you mind! I'm not a complete idiot. Now what arrangements had you in mind? Coming dowsing tomorrow?'

'No. I have work to do here with some men learning about security and I have to contact suppliers of cement. The Sheikh doesn't realise the importance of having a lot of it near all the onshore platforms in case of accidents. He is a peculiar mixture of the result of modern Western education and Eastern faith in Allah, who holds our fate in His hands and nothing we can do will avert the outcome.'

'All the oil states must have learned from the tragedies of Kuwait?'

'They said so,' Carlson agreed. 'But admitting that they must take precautions doesn't actually tie in with modern development. We use snuffers in the States and they do now in Kuwait but here, probably because they have never had trouble with onshore rigs, the Sheikh sees no reason why they can't use the old methods and equipment, if and when an accident occurs, which means blasting off the top gases with nitro-glycerin instead of snuffing, before capping the well.'

'Sounds horrendous,' Sarah said with a return of the weak feeling that surfaced each time that fire or violence was mentioned.

'It can be,' he replied grimly. 'If they don't get a collar of cement round the rig, it can spew out oil and rocks and spread fire, so I have to convince the men here that their lives will be in danger if they don't learn to act quickly. I hope that some of them have no ambitions to go to paradise that quickly.'

'So you go teaching and I go dowsing. Surely that's the only arrangements we have to make.'

'About your lecture tour,' he began.

'I'll have to check with my office,' she said firmly. 'I left the itinerary to them, but I know it includes Boston, and maybe even Texas,' she added with a smile. 'If we are to fly together, give a buzz to my secretary and she'll co-ordinate the plane tickets.'

'I hope you aren't too democratic. I hate travelling in cramped conditions. Make it First, will you?'

She nodded. 'Of course, or I shall be fit for nothing when I arrive, and I'm being very self-indulgent on the way back.'

'Concorde?'

'West to East it cuts out jet lag,' she said simply.

'Your date of departure is settled? No hitches?'

'As far as anything is certain.' She hesitated. 'I do have an appointment with my plastic surgeon, but I think any further surgery can wait until after the tour.'

'That bad?' he asked gently.

'The worst is over,' she assured him, then turned away. 'At least the worst of the physical trauma is over, but I wonder if I shall ever feel perfectly normal again.'

'You can't live in an ice cube for ever,' he said bluntly. 'There's life out there and you can't tell me that you don't feel anything for any man, even now.' He came closer and she felt the force of his personality and his sensuality.

'After ... Mark, I was given counselling, which I resented, but they did warn me about letting myself drift into an affair that had no real long-term meaning for me, just to prove I wasn't a monster, and to ease my loneliness.'

'David said you have scars,' he ventured. 'I know you hate talking about it, but are they that bad that you really think any man in his right mind who really loved you would be put off by them?'

'Yes, I hate my body,' she said. 'I'm very lucky to be alive and to have a job I find all absorbing, so I can live with the other bit of my life missing.'

'Not you, Sarah,' he said and she couldn't meet his gaze. 'Maybe you're asleep and fooling yourself for a time, but it's waiting for some lucky guy to peel away the dust covers and find treasure.' He stared at her without expression. 'Does Hussain know that you were burned?' he asked abruptly.

She looked surprised. 'Now you mention it, I doubt if he does know. Dwight blurted out that Mark was dead, and that I was shocked and went to hospital, but he didn't know what really happened and no mention was made of burns to the Sheikh, who, if I remember rightly, said how lucky I was to walk away from it whole, or words to that effect.'

Carlson picked up an oily rag that had fallen to the floor and then washed his hands as if the topic of conversation had been exhausted.

'Why ask about Hussain? He's not likely to have a private view of my body,' she said with a trace of bitterness. 'Fortunately he thinks the leotard thing is modesty and he can go on thinking that for all I care.'

'Maybe I should put you wise to him,' Carlson said. 'He was besotted with his wife, at first,' he continued slowly as if choosing his words. He looked at Sarah as if he hated what he had to say. 'She had a pink and white complexion which was very pretty and delicate, like one of those porcelain shepherdesses that never look quite real to me, but she also loved the sun, and after they were married and he left her here alone while he went hawking for week, she got bored, lounged in the sun and went to sleep until she was burned.'

'So what?'

'Her skin began to peel and to have red patches.'

'Oh!' Sarah nodded. 'No need to warn me,

Carl. I go brown and never peel, but that is none of his business. I know that he has a kind of fetish about a woman's skin,' she said calmly. 'I can handle it.'

'I didn't want you to be—' He couldn't go on.

'If I fell for him, you wouldn't want me to suffer because he'd find out that my back is less than perfect, and he'd be repulsed by me?' she said.

'Something like that,' he admitted.

'But I did tell you that I thought he must marry a girl from his own culture,' she said firmly. 'He is very attractive and great fun but I couldn't take all this for ever, in spite of being invited to be the Sheikh's favourite daughter, Honorary-Man-Honorary-Virgin.'

'All that?' Carlson laughed and the tension between them broke. 'You're one hell of a lady,' he said.

# Nine

It seemed strange to be riding in an American stretch limousine across the arid plain, with an elegant but ageing Arab Sheikh and two of his engineers, neither of whom spoke much English. She looked into the distance at the line of a camel train on the horizon and wondered if the Bedouin were touched by the modern world.

Carlson was busy inspecting the latest drill and had taken a jeep load of technicians to see what was needed there. If they speak as little English as this lot, Sarah thought, he could be in for a difficult day as far as simple communication goes. Hussain and David were scuba diving for the sample experimental plates welded to the struts of the nearest offshore rig, to bring them back to the laboratory for testing, and Dwight was busy in the computer room with the Frenchman and the head technician.

She glanced back and saw the inevitable jeep following them, laden with comforts for the day: lightweight tents and rugs and a cook to prepare fresh food for his master and his guest. The motor car was cool but she knew that the sun, now an angry ball of fire, would be fierce when they reached their site of operations and it could mean a hot and tiring day.

We might even be as hot as Carlson Ward and his group, she thought. The new rig was quite close to the area that the Sheikh wanted investigated for water as he was eager to find water close enough to the new rig to be able to cool the overheated bits and make a deep drill for oil possible. Carlson wouldn't have the benefit of tents and servants and ice-cold water. Idly, she wondered if Carlson had been invited to eat with them, but decided that the Sheikh wanted her to concentrate on the work in hand and have no time for socialising.

She also had a suspicion that he wanted Carlson to stay away from her, and as for David, he had been very pleased to see him go to the offshore rig with Hussain and so out of contact with her.

Sheikh Abdul said little but she sensed his tension. At least this is a change from sexual tension, Sarah mused with a wry smile. Hussain was becoming a bore. Why does he pile on the charm as if smothering me with compliments and hand kissing would make me faint from overdone flattery? Carl was not a bore but more a threat to her sanity. She admitted that if she had to choose which man she would take for a lover, it would be him, but one twinge from her scars jerked her into the reality of remaining alone and made her forget such fantasies.

She bent all her thoughts and energies to the work in hand and when questioned, she answered the Sheikh enthusiastically about her work and ambitions and about the strange gift that her mother had possessed and now was hers.

The scar of the dry wadi stetched for a long way and Sarah studied the geological survey before venturing out into the heat. The old well had been situated a hundred yards from where the limo stopped and they drove slowly across the sandy rocks until she told the driver that this was where she wanted to be.

At once there was a flurry of activity as the main tent was put up and the Sheikh rested in the air-conditioned car until his cushions were piled on the carpet and the breeze came from the sea under the rolled-up walls of the tent. The harsh but musical voices, as servants were given orders and the driver of the car took charge of her equipment and put it in the jeep so that she would have transport when she moved away from the camp, became dear and familiar and she realised that she loved the sounds of the desert, the people and the wide spaces. I shall never get it out of my mind, she thought and had an uneasy feeling that everything was being done to convince her of that.

Even the acrid smell of camel dung on the hot sand would be evocative when she smelled it again, and London Zoo would have a certain nostalgia when she visited it on a hot day.

The distant Bedouin camp had a hazy smoke cloud above the black tents, and this fire was now echoed by the one that had been erected downwind of the Sheikh's tent, but this fire was not smoky and was the last word in modern gas-fired technology, with butane cylinders and grills and many burners.

Sarah crammed her hat down over her head, shading her eyes, and the Sheikh looked on with approval. 'The sun can be cruel to Western skins and women should never allow it to touch them,' the Sheikh said. 'You have exquisite skin and must never do anything to harm it,' he added with approval. 'The bloom on a peach is impossible to replace once it has been sullied.' Sarah wondered if he was remembering the girl who lost an adoring Arab prince because she went to sleep in the sun and ruined her complexion. She glanced at his arrogant face and wondered if he even cared what had become of her.

Sarah gave an involuntary shiver. People

183

were expendable here. Life was governed by fate, and death was settled at birth, and fate would find people even if they sought to escape.

'The moving finger writes, and having writ, moves on,' she recalled. Omar again? This place would have her reading the Koran soon.

Dust covered her safari boots and she felt the dryness of the air in her throat as she walked slowly along a line she had set herself. The steel rods remained static and she turned west and retraced her steps until she had covered a wide area and she was tired. She saw that the Sheikh now came towards her under a large ornate sunshade held by a tall youth.

'Rest for a while,' he suggested and she returned to the tent, gratefully sank on to the soft cushions and drank cool mineral water.

'I'll look at the charts before I go out there again.' They ate a lunch of couscous and lamb with a spicy sauce, fresh figs and dates, sweetmeats and coffee.

She pored over the charts that David had examined and noticed that he had pencilled in a few places and put question marks against them. Squinting up at the sun to get her bearings, she began again and followed a different line, but this time more in keeping with his pencil marks.

At first there was no movement but suddenly, as she walked across a patch of smooth sand, the steel rods trembled. She stopped and stepped back and the trembling stopped, then she walked slowly forward again, her excitement rising, calling to the man who had followed her patiently all day, carrying a long pointed stick and a mallet.

Another few paces and the rods became almost uncontrollable and then they swung down and crossed and fell from her grasp as if they were beyond her control. 'Here,' she said quietly. 'Put the marker here and tell His Highness that we have success.'

A servant shouted to the driver, who went back to the tent where the Sheikh was resting, and within minutes the Sheikh was being driven across the scrub towards her.

'Show me,' he said and watched impassively as Sarah demonstrated what she had done. He waved aside the man hovering with the sunshade and came closer. 'Why wasn't my son able to do that?'

'I've no idea,' she said lightly as she saw the autocratic face darken with annoyance. 'There are some things we can't explain scientifically. Some people can paint or make music. I can dowse.'

'I would like to try,' he said solemnly, and she handed him the rods and showed him how to hold them.

The ridges on the soles of her desert boots had made deep impressions in the sand and it was easy for the Sheikh to follow her path. He walked slowly, as she had done, his face set and his hands gripping the rods as if they might escape. Soon the sand was scattered under his feet and he came to the spot where there had been most of the activity in the rods, but nothing happened.

Sarah tried not to smile. He was so like Hussain in his disappointment and hurt pride. The aristocratic face now lost the benevolent expression to which Sarah had become accustomed and there was something frightening in his eyes.

'I did as you did,' he said stubbornly, and faced her, handing back the rods as if it was beneath his dignity to touch them. 'Is there some kind of magic that you use that makes the rods move?'

'I have no idea why I have the talent to dowse,' she said slowly. 'My mother was Irish and had a certain sensitivity to the supernatural but I have none of that.'

'She was a witch?'

Sarah laughed, trying to ease the growing tension. 'She didn't make magic or cast spells, if that's what you mean. No spells, no evil eye and no weird potions brewing in black pots, just a feeling of apprehension when she felt that some tragedy would occur in the family or in the small town where she lived as a child. She knew when she was about to die,' she added softly.

'Did you know that Mark would die?' he asked, and his eyes were as fierce as those of one of his falcons.

Sarah's eyebrows shot up. 'Of course not! How could I? It happened so suddenly and the terrorists had given no warning.' She began to tremble. The sun was hot and she felt the scars on her back contract. The Sheikh made an imperious gesture and the servant held the sunshade over her.

'But when you dowse, something leaves you. I saw it when first you found water and now you are pale and perspiring and some of your life force has left you,' he said. 'That is magic,' he added, as if his opinion was the only one worth considering. 'Why didn't my soothsayer know about this? Why has he no power to do this?' He smiled grimly. 'I think he sees only what I want him to see and to tell me.'

For a moment, Sarah saw a man who held the lives and welfare of his people in his hands. Had time paused here in the desert, and were there men even now, who had the power of life and death over their subjects? She pitied the soothsayer who she imagined might be in for a bad time. In another era, he would have been for the chop, she thought. It was ridiculous to think it possible now ... not now, not in this century, among all the modern technology of an oil-rich state. The Sheikh might be an autocrat and a paternalistic dictator but not a murderous tyrant.

Men hammered in many marker poles and broke camp while Sarah and the Sheikh drank mint tea and cooled off in the air-conditioned car before being driven back to the oasis.

'I think that another geological seismic survey is needed,' Sarah said. 'If you can calculate the depth of the different rocks, it is possible to tell where the water lies and may be you will find oil there at one level.'

'That shall be done,' he said.

'Make use of David and Carlson while they are here. You have two experts close by and they are the best, the very best,' she added with a note of affection in her voice. 'And of course, Hussain has a lot of knowledge of geology as well as having a degree in metallurgy,' she added, seeing that the Sheikh's face clouded whenever she mentioned David.

'I shall have the apparatus and the technicians ready on site at first light,' the Sheikh said. 'You are right. I shall not have the advantage of their expertise for much longer.' She glanced at him and wondered if the thought of losing David and Carlson gave him pleasure.

'You are going to Texas?' she asked.

'After Hussain returns from London,' he replied. 'I hope to meet you again in America and I also hope that you do not lose contact with my son. In fact, I insist on it.' He smiled. 'When you come back here next year, to live in a house that shall be prepared for you, we shall consider you to be a member of our family. If you marry my son, as he and I hope will happen, then my life will be full.'

'I have no plans to live here, sir. If I may, I shall return to work in the laboratory for a few weeks next year, but as for other plans, I'll have to take a rain check on that as I have many commitments,' she replied firmly.

'A rain check?' He smiled. 'I find the jargon of the West strange but succinct. You have no need of rain checks. You have found me a great gift of water under the earth, and whatever happens I shall be grateful to you for that for the rest of my life.'

Sarah inclined her head in response to the compliment but sat tall and almost warily. He was being very charming and she knew that father and son found that charm was a very powerful weapon.

'I have four more days before I return to London,' Sarah said. 'During that time I shall work in the laboratory here and not have time to go with David and Carlson to see the seismic tests or to see the site from the air. Dwight and I have a schedule that will make his findings on computer easy to track and will give him enough data to keep him busy for weeks.'

'Do you like that rather brash American?' The Sheikh laughed. 'At least you are safe with him. He is happily married, I believe.'

'I am safe with every man I have met here, and I have enjoyed meeting each one of them,' Sarah said with a certain amount of vehemence. 'In my work, I meet a lot of men and women and sex never makes an awkward situation for any of us.' She forced a smile. 'Thank you for making me so comfortable while I work at the oasis. It does save a lot of time driving from the hotel each day.'

'I was sorry that you preferred to sleep in the apartment where the other visitors are and did not take a suite in my palace,' he said. He shrugged. 'But if you were a man I would think you were right to be with your colleagues, close to your work,' he admitted.

'You made me an Honorary Man,' she pointed out. 'And I work as hard or harder than the average male scientist.'

'I shall rest now,' he said when they arrived at the palace. 'Hussain's jeep is over there, so they must be back here from the rig. I hope to be with you for dinner tonight, my daughter.' His face darkened as David walked from the jeep, carrying his holdall. 'I

190

believe that he is staying here, too,' he said with obvious distaste.

'Yes. I have a lot to discuss with him about the geological results and the findings about his metal struts. I hope to take a printout of exciting new data with me when I leave, to compare with other sites.' She smiled gently. 'David is a good and honest man who has been a good friend to me and Mark, and I love him as a brother.'

'Hussain says he is in love with you.'

'We are easy together, but that isn't desire,' she replied.

'There is no such thing as platonic love between a man and a woman,' the Sheikh said slowly.

'I disagree,' Sarah said, but her heart sank as David came over and hugged her.

'Not been overdoing it, have you, love?' he asked tenderly. 'It's as hot as hell out there today. I was glad to be under water.'

'I need a shower,' Sarah said. 'Meet me in the lab in half an hour and make sure Dwight is there too, and I'll fill you in with what I did today.'

She turned away as if dismissing an employee and knew that David eyed her with puzzlement. 'Yes, *ma'am!*' he said and slung his holdall over one shoulder and left her.

The Sheikh smiled, and while he was busy talking to Hussain, who had come to greet his father, Sarah escaped to her room and the bliss of cool shower water and a fragrant body rub. She applied the emollient cream to the scars and sighed. Each time it felt better and soon there would be no need for the cream except on that one annoying area that refused to heal properly.

'I'll get it done as soon as I go back,' she told herself; but when? She was leaving for the States soon and the plastic surgery might take a while to arrange. I could have it done in America, she thought, but I am used to my surgeon and they know all about me at the private hospital.

'You OK?' David's voice came through the door. She let him in and continued to dry her hair. 'Better temper now? I thought it was something I'd said, then I thought that maybe he'd given you a hard time today and you felt like hell,' he added cheerfully.

She bit her lip. 'Sorry, Dave. He's got a bee in his bonnet about you being a threat.'

'Me, a threat? Never! At least not off the rugby pitch. What have I done? I thought the old boy liked me. He's certainly ready to make use of me in any way he can, and that goes for you and Carl, too. Watch it, Sarah! He is after more than just his pound of flesh.'

'To put it bluntly, he wants me to marry Hussain and thinks that you are in love with me and could make me refuse him.'

'So I am. Hadn't you noticed?' David

laughed. 'Been in love with you for years, off and on between my other passions, but I know you would never marry me, so we are good friends.'

He made a movement towards her to hold her hand but she backed off. 'No, Dave! That's what makes him think we could be lovers, or at least moving towards it,' she said.

'I haven't made violent love to you in public yet,' he said mildly.

'To him, a kiss or even a bear hug such as you like to bestow on all things feminine means smouldering passion,' she said, but her smile was improving.

'The Welsh are a passionate race,' he said darkly and came towards her again.

'Cool it, Dave. I'm serious. I think that there could be trouble for you if you go on being dear old Dave who kisses his female friends and shows concern for me in particular.' A sudden thought struck her. 'You haven't had that nice Girl Friday they lent you to help your other girl with the statistics?' she asked anxiously. 'I think it might not be wise to take any local girl who is known to the Sheikh.'

'Funny you should say that.' He eyed her seriously. 'I think she's great but something makes me hold back.' He shrugged. 'You know me, I love forbidden fruit but these girls are at the top of the tree, out of reach and I am not climbing.'

'Scared?'

'Dead scared,' he quipped but she knew he was half serious. 'I think I know what you are getting at about the Sheikh. Men and women consider every touch to be sexual here, but you'd think that, having been to British universities, they'd both know that we mix on a friendly basis and don't think of the casual kiss as important.'

'The Sheikh said that there is no such thing as platonic friendship between men and women,' Sarah said slowly. 'He believes that, very firmly.'

'Hussain is very sexy, isn't he?' David watched her eyes.

'They all are,' she said a little shakily. 'The Sheikh must have been dynamite in his day and I think he has women stashed away in the harem, very discreetly, even today when officially he is monogamous.'

'Dry now?' David regarded her hair with interest. 'It suits you looking like a bird's nest, but better comb it, girl, and get along to the lab. You are a scientist, not a sex object for Arab princes.'

'See you in five minutes,' she said.

At the door, David paused. 'You wouldn't marry him, would you?' he asked, and she was astounded at the venom in his voice.

'No,' she replied simply.

'Keep that in mind. I may not be here to

look after you for ever,' he said.

For a moment they stared at each other as if he had said something terrible, then he closed the door and she heard him stride along the corridor outside.

She brushed her hair so hard that her scalp was sore. It mean't nothing, she told herself angrily. Too much Celt in both of us and a lot of morbid imagination. I can't lose Dave as well as Mark, and there's no reason why I should. He's young and healthy and safe here.

As she left the room and locked the door behind her, she saw the edge of a djellaba disappear at the end of the corridor. 'I have eyes everywhere,' the Sheikh had said, and she knew that he would be told that David had been in her room for fifteen minutes.

'Hi!' Dwight caught up with her and they walked across to the laboratory together. He was in a state of great excitement. 'This place is magic, Sarah. I can't wait to go back home to tell my wife about it all. She'll be thrilled. She does like her comforts and thought if she came here she'd have to live in a tent or some shack but she doesn't get this service in Los Angeles or Boston and I've taken pictures to prove it.'

'Ever felt you're being manipulated?' Carlson had joined them and was listening with a wry smile that seemed tired. 'Greetings, Dr Brackley,' he said solemnly. 'Ready for work?'

'What gives, Carl?' Dwight wrinkled his brow. 'Have I missed something. Are you two mad at each other?'

'No, but according to Dave, we have to keep our feelings for the lovely Doctor under wraps as we may have our balls chopped if we even look at her.'

'You're kidding,' Dwight said comfortably and chuckled. 'Boy, have I had a great time with that data you gave me. C'mon folks, let's get together with Dave and find out more.'

'Give the boy a lollipop,' Carlson said. 'At least it might shut his big mouth.'

'Dwight or Dave?' Sarah asked.

'Both. David had better watch it. He could just say too much to tease them and they haven't that kind of humour.'

'At least he can't get drunk and be too indiscreet,' Sarah said.

'He could get too relaxed. One of the boys sold him some *kif*.'

'Local hashish?' Sarah looked worried. 'I didn't think he smoked. He never did at university.'

They separated in the laboratory. Hussain worked with David, measuring the erosion of the original specimen of metal used out on the rig. It been there for a few months and now showed impressively little sign of sea water damage. There was no time for idle conversation. They worked at their separate projects in near silence, punctuated by comments that referred to the work in hand and to nothing outside the laboratory.

At last, a servant alerted them to the need to dress for dinner and they left reluctantly. Even Hussain seemed to have absorbed the relaxed manner in which the men worked with Sarah, as if sex was an unimportant myth, and when they gathered for dinner with the Sheikh, the atmosphere was good and full of shop talk.

Sarah looked from one animated face to another. If it could be like this all the time, I could work here, she thought, but the tensions would be there, released when the work was over and the subtle influence of desert and dark starlit sky and the scents of this strange world took over with insidious and relentless charm. Without the other scientists with her to keep the level of contact professional, would she have the strength to refuse Hussain?

David kept away from her and Carlson regarded her with a faintly cynical smile, but she found that he was there, all the time within reach, as if hovering to protect her, which she knew was ridiculous and unnecessary.

Coffee was served and Sarah felt as if she wanted to drop into a deep pit and go to sleep for a week. She begged to be excused, her excuse being a load of work to do on the following morning, but she waited while the Sheik made his round of goodnights after making sure that Hussain, Dwight and David would fly out to chart the new find of water at first light.

Hussain glanced towards the door to check that his father had left and touched Sarah on the sleeve. 'Before you go, I want you to try a special drink made from herbs and spices and very popular with the women here.'

'I don't think so,' Sarah began. 'I'd rather have some more orange juice.'

'If you dislike my drink, you may have orange juice,' he assured her.

David sat slumped in a comfortable chair. Sarah noticed with some disquiet that the cigarette he smoked was hand rolled and a bit shaggy at the end. His eyes were blank as if he saw inner dreams and his hand held the reefer limply. 'Dwight?' she said softly. 'Do me a favour and take that joint away from David. He's had enough for one night.'

They walked up to the reclining figure and while Sarah asked him about the work the next day, Dwight carefully eased the cigarette away and stubbed it out in a dish.

'Success!' Dwight looked around for approval and saw the Arab servant following Sarah, holding a silver tray on which sat a delicate Venetian glass holding a pink fluid. 'Cheers!' Dwight took the glass and downed the drink in one, then gasped. 'What God-awful sugary crap is that?' He put the glass down and Carlson picked it up before Hussain could stop him. He sniffed at the dregs of fluid and his face was devoid of expression.

'What's happening?' David asked, as if waking up.

'I'm afraid that Dwight drank the nice concoction that Hussain prepared for you, Sarah,' Carlson said in dangerously silky tones.

David shook his head to chase away the clouds. 'Trying to poison her?' he asked belligerently.

'Just an aphrodisiac,' Carlson said lightly, but the pulse in his temple beat faster.

'Why, you conniving sod,' David shouted and lunged out of his chair.

Hussain stood back but made no move to excuse his action or to repel the furious man, as if he expected the onslaught and welcomed it. Two men stood by the door, their hands concealed beneath the voluminous garments and Sarah was afraid. 'No, David,' she said but the words were a whisper.

Carlson caught David by the arm and swung him face to face. Calmly, but cautiously as if calming a raging bull, he punched David on the jaw and let him slump to the floor.

Hussain gave the two men a look filled with fury and strode away, followed by his two guards.

'Whaddya do that for?' David sat up and fingered his jaw. 'You could have killed me.'

'Correction.' Dwight looked horrifed. 'Did you see that guy's face? You probably saved Dave's life by hitting him.'

'Do all you Celts have iron jaws?' Carlson said, grinning, and sucked his sore knuckles.

'Thanks, pal,' David said weakly.

'Any time,' Carlson said laconically, then laughed. 'Get to bed sharpish, Dwight. Lock the door and think of the good old US of A and what your mother taught you.'

'You crazy?'

'No, but you might be soon, man. That stuff is powerful. You'll need a session of do-it-yourself in half an hour,' he added coarsely. 'That's if you can't order a houris on room service.'

'My wife would kill me,' Dwight said, and grinned. 'Maybe I'll ask for the recipe for when she's out here. It might brighten things up considerably.'

'Bed for you, Dave.' Carlson almost dragged the dopey man along the corridor to his room, pulled off his shoes and levered him on to the bed. 'Stop assing around, you son-of-a-bitch,' he said affectionately. 'I know these people and if they start gunning for you, it's serious.'

'Thanks, Mum,' David said sleepily, and began to snore.

# Ten

The geologists estimated that there was a large lake of water under the rock, on a bed of clay that kept it from filtering away, but it would need a deep drill to get at it, past a small area of oil-bearing rock which they felt in this situation was negligible.

The Sheikh was as excited as his dignity would allow him to show, and at first, his gratitude was claustrophobic, but after the first extravagant offers to Sarah to try to convince her that she could have anything she wanted in life if she stayed in the oasis, he was so taken with the new possibilities of unlimited water that Sarah felt she was of secondary importance and quietly got on with preparations to leave at the end of her stint. It was a relief to sense that he was fully occupied, and the limo and the man with the parasol accompanying the Sheikh were more often on site than in the luxury of the palace.

'Ready to go?' asked David when he saw that Sarah had packed.

'Yes, I can't wait to be back in reality,' she

said. 'This has been exciting but I could do with a nice cool shower on my face and a grumble about the weather,' she said, laughing.

'Good for the complexion,' David said. 'Dabbling in the dew makes a milkmaid fair, so my granny said, not that you need that as you have the skin of a ripe peach. No wonder Hussain wants to eat you.'

'In my case I'd need more than morning dew,' she replied. 'More surgery when I have the time.'

'Real trouble?'

'I hope not, but the heat doesn't help and I think the last patch might be infected.'

'Let the doc see it before you go.'

'No, I'll see my own man as soon as I get back. I faxed him to expect me and he'll brief me about future treatment, but the surgery will have to wait until after my tour in the States.'

'You could have it checked here. He's very good even if he is basically an eye specialist – they all do a general training before they specialise.'

She shook her head. 'And have everyone here knowing that I am so ugly?'

'Why not? It could put off one randy prince who will be there like a great big expensive spider when you get to London.'

'You don't like him.'

'Right first time.' He saw her anxious

expression. 'Don't worry, love, I'll be good. I've kept my mouth shut ever since that night and we work well together out there. He's a great diver and a good technician. That I will give him, but I wouldn't trust him further than I could throw a ball of sand.'

'I'll miss you, Dave.'

'Love you, too,' he said and his eyes were serious. 'Be very careful, Sal. I'd hate to see you at risk, without me or Mark around to look after you and keep the desert foxes away.'

'You'll be back in Britain, at least for a while,' she said.

'Yeah, sure.' He grinned. 'Let's get some lunch. Carl is around, so maybe we can eat together without brushing aside the djella-bas.'

'He's driving me to the airstrip,' Sarah smiled. 'I think he knew that I wanted no fuss and Hussain is under the impression that I'm staying on for another couple of days. Can't think how he got that idea, but it does mean no effusive farewells and the Sheikh said goodbye last night.'

Carlson Ward stormed in, looking furious. 'I can't make them understand that they need the right cement for the casings of the drills,' he said. 'Now that the Sheikh relies on his own men and not experienced out-side contractors, they've got sloppy and think that any old cement will do.'

'Stop glaring at Sarah. She has nothing to do with that. What's a bit of cement between friends,' David said, grinning.

'Out in the bay, they use special stuff that is compatible with sea water, but ashore, they'll need another kind that uses non-salty water to mix it. The hired help bought the right type originally, but now the locals seem to think that what's right for the off-shore rigs is right for anywhere.' He gave an exasperated sigh. 'I've given them the literature in English and Arabic and lectured them until I'm blue in the face but Allah will look after them and there will be no leakages when the casings are set round the drill holes.'

'If there is a leak, what happens?' asked Sarah.

'Hopefully not a lot, but it could mean real trouble.'

'How real?'

'If they hit gas, it could seep out in a cloud round the cracks and ignite. It might have to be cut off with nitroglycerin, and I hope to God they won't use dynamite or they'll have real trouble. If oil is found and a gusher results, and there is no way of controlling it to come through the right way, the whole thing could blow and we'd have to cap it and drill again alongside the concrete stopper.'

'Sounds easy, doesn't it?' David said dryly. 'I know that Texas breeds bigger and better everything, but even Red Adair didn't have an easy time capping all those wells in Kuwait.'

'We learned a lot then,' said Carlson. 'The last one I did wasn't too bad.'

Sarah was pale. 'You don't do that?' Her private nightmare of explosives made a shaky attempt to put her off her guard.

'Sure do, ma'am,' he said with a heavy accent. 'Why let the roustabouts have all the fun?' He eyed her with a curiously tender expression, soon quelled. 'Don't say that you care if I get blown up?'

'It sounds too dangerous for words,' she replied and he saw that she was in control again.

'When it has to be done, there's no alternative,' he explained. 'It does need experts who know what to do and what explosives to use or many people might be hurt, as well as it being a gross air pollution problem with damage to crops and cattle, as the oil gets everywhere for miles.'

'They've renewed the drill on the new rig now that the good water supply will be available soon,' David said. 'Everything is go, go, go! I saw the pylon go up yesterday and they have enough lengths of drill to get to the centre of the earth!'

'Well, you won't be here to suffer with us

if the thing blows,' Carlson said cheerfully. 'I'll get you to the airport before I drive out to check that they know what gives.' He laughed. 'I shall be glad to see the back of you, for all our sakes. Hussain will stop being like a hound dog after a bitch and David will be safe from those jealous feelings you cause.'

'Thank you! And you will just be glad to see the back of me?' she retorted.

'I can hardly wait, but that must be in the future,' he said softly. 'I shall meet you again at Heathrow in two weeks' time.'

'Well, look what the desert breeze brought in,' David said with an air of disgust. 'I thought he was far away. Just when we were having a cosy lunch before you leave, Sarah.'

'Down boy! Stiff upper lip,' she whispered.

'I thought you might be here,' Hussain said. 'Good news for me, bad for you, I think,' he added smoothly. 'Delays everywhere. and your plane will not take off today.'

'There was nothing on the fax about cancellations,' David said.

'The airstrip is to be closed for two days for repairs,' Hussain went on.

'As the local air strip is the property of the Sheikh, I don't understand,' Sarah said with a bleak glance at the Prince. 'Your father said goodbye to me last night and wished me a pleasant journey to connect with my flight to the UK. Nothing was said about repairs. What made this necessary? An emergency?'

'See you,' David said and left the table. 'I have some work that can't wait.'

'If I am not going today then I too have things to do,' Sarah announced.

'What difference does two days make to you?' Hussain smiled. 'It is a blessed bonus for me to keep you here for a while and now I can travel with you to London.'

'You've booked a seat for when?' she asked.

'I have to meet someone in Oman, so I shall leave you to travel there alone, but I shall be on the flight from Oman at one thirty the day after tomorrow,' he said with satisfaction. 'With you.'

Sarah stood away from the table. 'You'll have to excuse me. Two days makes a lot of difference to my schedule. I wasn't returning for a shopping trip! I have work to do, so I'll catch up with what I can here and have all my food sent to me in my room until I leave, if you could arrange it?' she said icily.

Hussain looked crestfallen. 'I thought it would be pleasant to travel together,' he said.

'Of course. I'm sure I would enjoy your company, but I can't see that I shall get any work done quietly on the plane as I had intended.' Her cold demeanour pierced his vanity at last.

'I apologise. I was mistaken, but I hate to see you leave.' His smile was lost-little-boy, and charming, but she turned away.

'May I have use of a small computer room with fax and photocopier?' she asked. 'I must be in touch with my office.'

'Anything,' he said and called his servant to arrange it. 'I hoped that we'd have dinner together tonight, alone,' he began, but saw her set lips and angry eyes and shrugged. 'As you wish. I am sorry to have angered you. That was the last thing I wanted.'

'I learned to cut my losses a long time ago,' she said, and sighed, then the humour of the situation made her mouth twitch into a smile.

'We are friends again?' And he really did want to know.

'Friends,' she agreed.

Carl fetched her bags from the lobby and took them to her room again, ignoring the hovering servants who looked as if they might get into deep trouble if they didn't do that chore. 'Well done,' he said quietly. 'I hope you get to last base, but he's a very determined man who has had his own way all his life and sees no reason for changing now. He also knows he's a nice bit of beef-cake and thinks that all women want him. I think you do, a little,' he added with a shrewd glance in her direction. 'Keep your head, Sarah, and ring me on this number if you need me in England, and this one in Texas. I'll come a-running, but trust a woman to louse up a perfectly good male friendship!'

'There's no need,' she began. 'I'll be gone and you can be buddies again.'

'I'll take you to the plane when they say it's there on the nicely repaired runway,' he said dryly. 'Until then, be careful and when you get to London be careful there too. I love them all but I know how their minds work and they can have tunnel vision when they want something very much and can see no reason for denying themselves. The Sheikh may look mild but he can be brutal.'

'You scare me,' she said and laughed, trying to believe that it wasn't true, then snapped her fingers. 'I've got it. I'll say I want to shop in Oman, but take the early plane home. I can leave a message for Hussain and ring him at Claridges to say sorry I missed you but I had urgent business.'

'If a man did that to him he'd string him up by his balls,' Carlson said mildly and left her to think about it.

She rang the airport in Oman and booked a flight on the early plane to Heathrow, and smiled. Hussain must not think he can get away with this, she thought.

Her office staff seemed stressed when they faxed back information that she needed but there was little she could do about it. The plans for America were complete and they'd have to manage without her again. They hardly missed me when I was ill, she told herself, but knew that this wasn't really true and her black mood lasted all day.

Stubbornly, she clung to her decision to eat alone and worked hard on some of the papers she had wanted to check on the plane, but knew that she really did need that flying time to get through the pack. Hussain sent messages begging her to join him for coffee, a meal, anything she fancied, but she replied coolly but politely in the negative and he gave up trying.

David rang her on the house phone: 'He's gone to the hotel,' he said. 'Can I come up?'

'No, Dave. It wouldn't be wise. If you are sure that we shall be undisturbed, I'll meet you in the forward lounge in ten minutes. I could do with a break. No, I don't want to eat. I had a tray sent up about an hour ago but I'd like to look out at the desert and have some fresh orange juice,' she said. She asked him to bring some more papers that she needed and hoped that this would be sufficient excuse for meeting David, and he would have no hassle when the ever-present eyes noted that they met and made a report to Hussain.

Why does he think David is a threat to him? She gave a wry smile. If he considered

Carlson in that light he might be nearer the mark, she admitted to herself. But Carlson had made no passes at her, and his cool attitude gave away nothing of the latent passion she suspected was there waiting for someone, under that strong, often impassive face, then realised that Hussain probably thought that Carlson had hit David to protect the Royal Person from harm! And that really does make them brothers, she decided.

'Did you have to lock your door?' asked David. He grinned. 'Didn't react as he wanted, did you? He's gone off to the hotel and, according to my Girl Friday, he will take solace there with one of the entertainers.'

Sarah raised her eyebrows and laughed. 'And I thought I was the love of his life!'

'So you are, but a man has to take what offers if he can't have you,' David said with a glance at her. 'Marry me, love, and make an honest man of me.'

'Once I've gone, you will forget I exist, until we meet again and pick up the threads of friendship,' she said firmly. 'It would be a disaster, and you know it, much as I love you, Dave.'

'Worth a try,' he said cheerfully. I do mean it, Sal. I do love you, but somehow you're right. We were such pals, and without Mark to make a threesome, it would be odd.'

'That was the odd situation,' she said slowly. 'Three of us, doing most things together at university, and then afterwards we drifted into a lovely relaxed friendship, even after Mark and I decided to live together.' She stared out at the dark sky and had never seen such stars, even when walking in the country with Mark. Everything was heightened here – scents, sounds and sights, together with the excitement of her work and the extravagance of the service showered on her. It was a drug, and she knew that she must get away to breathe less rarified air.

'He loved you, Sal. Did you really love him?'

'Of course I did,' she said vehemently.

'Yes, I believe you, and I know you suffered when he died, but was there real passion, Sal? That's what worries me.'

'I lived with him!'

'A lot of people who never know the gnawing pangs do that and they are lucky, as they don't suffer jealousy or the highs and lows of real passion. "Pleasure's not their's nor pain," the poet said.'

'Why does that worry you? You know I loved Mark.'

'I think you could be trapped and get involved too much,' he said. 'It might not be the safe, calm love you had for Mark, but a tearing of your heart, and might not even be

213

for someone you like. Passion, not love; sex and jealousy, and then what?' He stood up. 'If it's Hussain, then God help you or you'll be enslaved,' he said and walked away to the open window.

She followed. 'You don't feel like that about me, Dave. Who was she?'

'Remember Mark's sister – Michele?' He gave a short laugh. 'Younger than Mark and not even very pretty, but I fell like a ton of bricks and so, God help her, did she.' His voice was husky. 'We had one summer together and we were the only ones on earth, or so we thought, and it would last for ever.'

'She died of leukaemia!'

'Yes. I watched her dying and felt that my life was over, but Mark needed help too as he adored his sister.'

'It was then that I slept with Mark for the first time,' she remembered.

'In compassion, not passion,' David said, and laughed without humour. 'If you had only got over the steamy bits by now, we could have been happy together, Sarah. Do you know that? Now, I think you have that awful, wonderful time ahead and I tremble for you.'

'I have an ugly body and a lot of hang-ups,' she replied. 'I'm frozen solid and shall never suffer like that.'

'What happened to Science? Don't you know that ice melts under warm conditons?

Here, take my card.' He solemnly offered her a business card. 'When defrosted and having been through the mill and wrung out, contact that man and he will mop up the drips, if he's still around.'

'Going some place?' she asked lightly.

'Dunno. I've been to hell and didn't like it, so what's left? More juice? This air dries my throat like a lime kiln.'

'I leave the day after tomorrow,' she said. 'If Hussain has other ideas, I'll *walk!*'

'Surprise! Some goods appeared today by air, so the airstrip is OK and I hear that Hussain is leaving for Oman tomorrow.'

'Creep!' she said, without heat. 'You'll stay on when Carl leaves?'

'I said I would stay for a month but I have been having second thoughts. I dislike every move I make being watched and I long for a touch of greenery apart from the oasis. I'll stay for a couple more weeks and plead serious appointments in London. Now that you have worked your miracle they will have enough to do without me.'

'Must get some rest,' Sarah said. 'I'll let you have these papers back tomorrow. Now I'm really leaving, I can't wait to get back to see a few friends who don't look on me as a woman who has to be tolerated because she has a brain.'

'Carl is taking you away at dawn, I believe?'

'Yes, I just have to shop in Oman, don't I?' She smiled. 'I wish I could see Hussain's face when I am not on his plane to Heathrow.'

'I may not see you again,' he said. 'I have a full day on the offshore rig tomorrow and may stay the night there.'

'See you in London, sometime,' she said and slid into his arms for a satisfying goodbye hug.

'Goodbye, my darling,' he said and kissed her on the lips.

Sarah picked up the papers and walked to the door leading from the lounge. The round glass windows at eye level glinted and the door opened before she could put a hand on it. She was aware again that someone had been watching her and David and was ready to open the door as he knew that she was leaving.

Sarah locked her bedroom door but felt safe now that Hussain was away. She slept well and woke early, ready for more of the paperwork and the faxes she had to send. Carlson was not at breakfast and she missed David, too, but it was good to concentrate on work and to pay one last visit to her wonderful microscope and the other pieces of equipment for which she knew most of her colleagues would give their virtue or their souls, whichever was cleaner.

Dwight met her for lunch and looked

pensive. 'I think they are rushing things out on the land rig,' he said. 'Carl is out there now, trying to push some sense into the foreman. The cement is wrong and already they've had a slight leakage of gas as the casing began to crumble. They've rectified it but they are drilling again and using the same stuff. They should wait twenty-four hours. They have the other type arriving today.' He sounded impatient and worried.

'Can't Carl convince them?'

'The best that Carl could do was to send for tanks of sea water that is compatible with the cement, but when that runs out, as they use so much, they will use the fresh-water well already dug that produces a pissing amount, and then the water from the new water pipeline, which seems almost ready to gush. Then, who knows?'

'I hope he remembers that he's taking me to the airstrip tomorrow morning,' she said.

'If he doesn't surface, I'll take you,' he promised, and Sarah dismissed leaks and water and Carl from her mind until the next morning.

Sarah looked back into the room that had been so comfortable and checked that she'd packed her toothbrush and some tights she'd washed out overnight, instead of bothering the woman who cleaned her room and who seemed available day and night to serve her.

Breakfast was taken in the small dining room and, apart from Dwight and another house guest, she was alone. Air-conditioning hummed and fans rotated overhead, and in spite of the early coolness of dawn, no windows were open anywhere.

'Why this closed feeling?' she asked. 'The sun's not up yet and I love to smell the flowers and the sand.'

Dwight coughed. 'I've been on the blower to Carl,' he said. 'What did we do before mobile phones? There's been a hitch,' he announced as if it was unimportant.

'How bad?' Suddenly feeling claustrophobic, Sarah went to the window and opened it. She gasped. The air was filled with an oily smell and the breeze from the sea was too warm.

'What's wrong?' She raised an anxious face and saw that Dwight looked worried.

'They had a bad leak and had to blow away the gas, then found oil seeping through the casings,' he said grimly. 'If Carl hadn't been there they'd have had a major disaster but he's working on it.'

'Working on it? Then it isn't over?' She felt limp. He was working with explosives and there would be hot oil, mud and rocks spewing out of the drill.

'You have to leave,' Dwight told her. 'You have things to do and you seem a bit too concerned.' His friendly eyes regarded her shrewdly. 'I'll take you to the airstrip, but go, Sarah. If you stay you may stir up a hornet's nest for Carl as well as Dave.'

'It's senseless! There's nothing between me and Dave, and I've certainly nothing going with Carl,' she protested.

'Ayrabs are different,' he said succinctly. 'Both of them have a feeling that you might not come back once you are with your own people, and Hussain could louse up a good thing scientifically if they lose you to another man. It must be confusing for them as they are used to dominating their women. I'm all right as they can buy my services and I'm married. I'm a man who needs a job, but a female scientist who is immune to flattery and other inducements is more than their Eastern minds can take in.'

'You're right. At least I can phone Carl from the airstrip if you'll bring your mobile.'

'Right. Let's go,' he said and led her firmly out to the jeep that now had the windows fast shut and the air-conditioning working fast.

Her luggage was already in the back and she gave one last anxious glance towards the black cloud over the distant drill. Am I running away to escape the Sheikh and Hussain, or am I running from an involvement in what might be another traumatic disaster that I haven't the courage to face? she wondered.

'Carl will be all right?' she asked, but her hands were cold in the overheated jeep.

'Sure,' Dwight said. 'He'll survive.'

I survived, but I'm less than whole, she thought and her mouth was dry. Burns and disfigurement could catch up with Carl, too. She wanted to stop the jeep and run back to find him, but kept quiet and took deep breaths to calm herself as she'd been taught when she hyperventilated under counselling.

The Sheikh's private plane was ready for take-off and figures milled about the small tower and observation platform. Two men came to take her luggage and she went into the cool of the reception area. Dwight was talking to an official who looked grave.

'What's wrong?' she asked.

'They had to cap it,' Dwight said. 'Two men were injured but he doesn't know any more.' He pressed the buttons on his mobile phone and waited and Sarah thought that it would never be answered but at last under a lot of other noise, a voice came.

'Dwight here. You OK?' he asked as if wanting to know the time of day. 'Is Carl there?' He put a hand over the phone. 'That was the site manager,' he said in an aside.

He listened and spoke softly. 'If you locate him, tell him I called from the airstrip and Dr Brackley will be leaving soon,' he said.

'Was he there?'

'No.' Dwight frowned.

'Something's wrong!'

'It's OK, I'm sure,' he said. 'It's just that they can't find him right now, and think he took off somewhere away from the drill.'

'I can't leave,' she said shakily. 'I have to know that he is all right. He may be in shock!'

'You have to go,' Dwight said. 'Honey, you know you have to leave now! You have a busy schedule and you have no place here any more. To be blunt, you are putting men in danger if you show that you care about them. I saw the look in that guy's eyes when Dave wanted to punch him. I know a madman when I see one, and I think that Carl and Dave are in less danger from pissing oil drills than from that family with you around. I'll walk you to the plane.'

'I'll telephone from Oman,' she said. 'Here, take my phone number in London and promise me, Dwight, that you'll keep me informed.'

'Yes, ma'am.' He began to laugh. 'Didn't I say he was a survivor? Look what's coming!'

The dusty jeep slewed to a halt by the aircraft and a filthy pair of trainers slid down on to the tarmac, followed by even dirtier jeans and a body that looked as if it had been dipped in oil.

'Carl!' Sarah ran forward, her eyes shining. 'Oh, Carl, I was worried.'

'That's made my day,' said a tired voice. 'Anyone got a drink of water?'

Sarah quickly unscrewed the top from a bottle of mineral water she had carried from the jeep to finish on the plane, and watched fascinated as the liquid disappeared at the rate of knots.

'If I wasn't so tired I'd kiss you,' Carl said.

Dwight eyed the oily streaks on the man's face and the hair matted with oil and sand and grinned. 'She wouldn't thank you, Carl. You're a walking disaster area. She doesn't need to be mussed up now she's all prissied up and ready to fly.' He put a hand on Carl's arm. 'Don't even think it, bud, or someone will carry tales, and you are here for a few more days.'

He shouted to the men who had carried the luggage and asked if the goods that Professor Ward had ordered had arrived. One shrugged and turned away and the other returned to the reception area to enquire.

'Thanks, Dwight,' Carl said quietly. 'You are right, of course. Get the hell out of here, Sarah, and I'll be on that plane at Heathrow when you fly to Boston.'

'*Au revoir*, and thank you for coming here. I can be easy in my mind now,' she said.

'Thought that you might find another explosion a bit much to take on board even if it was just a colleague.' He grinned. 'I was lucky.'

As she climbed on to the plane, she saw the arm that he had held behind his back even when he drank the water. The sleeve of his shirt was a tight fit as if the bandage showing at the wrist went all the way up his arm, and she shuddered.

# Eleven

Wearing dark glasses and a headscarf, Sarah sat drinking coffee while she waited for her plane from Oman. She had made sure that her luggage was well labelled and it had gone through the plastic curtain to the luggage trailer without a hitch.

What did I expect? she asked herself, angrily. Men in white coats to cart me away? Hussain lurking round every mock marble pillar or a hit man out to get me?

The crowds were reassuringly normal, with a cosmopolitan variety of races and sexes and a good powdering of tourists on a package, who looked bent on rubbernecking at the local Arabs and grumbling at the lack of alcohol. 'I thought the agent was joking,' one man said. 'I can't take two weeks without a drink!'

'Do you good,' his wife said and laughed. 'They say the orange juice is lovely.'

Sarah heard her flight being called and picked up her briefcase and hand luggage. She settled in the wide first class seat and tried to ignore the hopeful glances of the man at her side. That's all I need, a pick-up, she thought, and concentrated on her papers, her eyes still hidden by the glasses. She refused food but drank mineral water, and managed to get through a great deal of the work she wanted to finish. At last, she sank back and closed her eyes. Her neighbour wouldn't trouble her as he was asleep and she felt released and safe once more.

The impact of freedom was amazing. I wasn't a prisoner, she thought, but I feel as if I have escaped from something really, really bad. They were good to me; too good to me, and I had everything a woman and a scientist could want, and I know that my work was appreciated, but now I feel that I've left a black hole that was sucking me down, and from which I had to climb to safety.

The taxi driver was not the chatty kind, to her relief, as she felt she needed time to reorientate herself to the sights and sounds of home. Red London buses, which she had never consciously looked at, seemed vibrant and the traffic fast and glossy against the grey walls and pretty window boxes of elegant Chelsea. Even the river had a welcoming sparkle.

Her small apartment in Chelsea was the obvious first stop as she had a lot of people to meet in London, including Hussain for lunch, she thought with a sinking feeling. I'll get down to Bristol for a break for a couple of days, she promised herself and smiled. It was good to worry about nothing but the fact that the Bristol house needed a new gardener and the Chelsea pad needed a fresh supply of food in the freezer.

She rang her secretary and caught up on the mail accumulated in the tiny lobby of the apartment. Junk mail was tossed away and personal letters eagerly opened, then the business letters which she spread out ready for Tandy, her Girl Friday, to tackle. Several invitations to give talks and to attend seminars made her purse her lips. If she accepted them all there would be no work done for months, but she knew that she could leave Tandy to deal with them and be tactful about it.

Sarah made sure she had plastic cards and cash and walked slowly to the supermarket, breathing in the cool air and loving the feel of the damp breeze in her hair. It was a change to have to think up food for herself and not to have it put before her on wonderful porcelain and silver. She filled the trolley and decided that she must have a taxi to take it home, so it was only when she arrived at her door that she recalled seeing the glimpse of a newsflash on a board by the sweet shop on the corner.

'Have you heard the news?' she asked the taxi driver. 'Was there something about an oil well?'

'Yeah. A kind of blow-out,' he said with no real interest.

Sarah unpacked the groceries and hurried down to the corner shop. She caught up a selection of newspapers and hurried back with them, feeling as if she would read of a major disaster, but there was only what she had heard first-hand in the sheikhdom, that there had been a minor blow-out and two men were slightly injured, one being an American scientist. Sarah silently blessed Carl for appearing at the airstrip and hoped that her residual panic would subside, but could not lose the sense of impending doom.

She went to answer the phone and after a lot of crackling and interference, she heard Carl's voice. 'Terrible line,' he shouted, 'but some of the lines are down and it's a bit fraught here. You OK?'

'Fine.' She spoke clearly and hoped he could hear her. 'What about you? I saw the dressing on your arm. How bad is it?'

Miraculously, the line cleared. 'A bit sore but then you know all about burns and it was treated quickly, so I hope I shall be able to escape plastic surgery.'

She caught her breath. 'That bad? At least I know a good surgeon,' she added, trying to appear calm.

'Cosy! Maybe we can lie on adjacent beds

while they scrape skin off our butts to make the patches.' He heard her gasp. 'Forget it! I'm joking. It's nothing, really. I just had to check that they hadn't abducted you at the airport.'

'It's silly but I didn't feel safe until I reached London. Nothing can happen now,' she said with a sigh of relief. 'Do I see you before you come to the States with me?'

'Depends where you are. I have to see a guy at Bristol University.'

'That's wonderful. I am going to my real home in Bristol next weekend unless the sky falls. My grandmother left me a house in Leigh Woods by the Gorge and there's masses of room, so you could stay there for a night or so instead of in a hotel. You can stay there even when I'm not there if our times don't coincide. I know we both have a lot to do before we leave again. I have a lady who's an absolute treasure. She comes in to get the place aired and leaves a few bits of food around, so I'll alert her to the fact that you might be there. She loves cooking for men, so be prepared for some solid food that will put inches on your waistline.'

She told him the address and telephone number of the Bristol house and when she put the phone down, she was absurdly happy.

Almost at once, the phone rang again and she spent the next fifteen minutes talking to

228

Tandy. 'Right!' Tandy said from time to time and seemed impressed by what Sarah had managed to do. 'Right!' she said again. 'That takes care of work. Now what have you been up to out there with all those wonderful guys?' she asked.

'Nothing,' Sarah said defensively. 'I worked damned hard.' She giggled. 'I fell in love with a microscope.'

'Did you wear that midnight blue number?' drawled Tandy, her curiosity showing.

'That and other things. I had to appear tidy as the standards there are very impressive, but I was made an *Honorary Man* as they hadn't met my kind of female brain before, so I felt I could wear my beautiful old straw hat on site!'

'Bloody Hell!' Tandy said inelegantly.' You mean no one, but no one tried to pull you? You walked into a sweet shop and never tried the candy?'

'The candy was there,' Sarah admitted, 'but too strong for my taste. I wish you'd been there to take off the heat.' She imagined Tandy's long legs and slim waist and her big blue eyes that looked so innocent. She also recalled her appetite for men and smiled when she thought of Hussain. They would be fine together, neither thinking further than the next lay.

'I think you're lying,' Tandy said with relish. 'I've been talking to a man with the most super deep brown voice, and he wanted your phone number.'

'And you gave it to him?' Sarah sounded resigned. 'OK, who was it?'

'Prince Hussain, who has just flown in and must have run to get to the phone as his plane is still hot on the tarmac, and so is he, I think. Not on tarmac, but he has the hots for you, ducky.'

'OK. He'll be in touch. If he calls the office, make an appointment for lunch, but not next weekend as I shall be away, so please don't give him the Bristol address. He's staying at Claridges and I said I'd have lunch before I go to the States.'

'I've time to set up those meetings before I go today, and I'll drop by with the contract this evening so that you can study it,' Tandy said and reverted to being a very efficient PA. 'Just as well I didn't go with you. Think what mayhem two intelligent and very beautiful women would have caused them!'

The phone had been put down for half a second and it rang again. 'Damn,' Sarah said softly and put the coffee percolator on before she answered it, half hoping that whoever it was would go away, but the monotonous tone got on her nerves and she answered it. 'Dr Brackley,' she said formally.

'Who is with you?' The unmistakable arrogant voice seemed to fill the room.

'Who is this?' she said as if she didn't

know, in as cool a tone as she could muster.

'Hussain, of course. Who did you expect? Or is someone there now? You took your time to answer and I've been trying to contact you for at least an hour.' He sounded thoroughly annoyed and upset, also unsure of himself now that she had made no welcoming sounds or any sign of contrition over the fact that she had foiled his plan to travel with her.

'Did you have a good flight?' she asked.

'I thought you had shopping to do in Oman,' he retorted.

'Wire bird cages and highly decorated ceramics?' She sounded amused. 'I took one look round the souk and caught the early plane. I did leave a message for you,' she added generously, 'and I did have work to do.'

'I wanted to be with you,' he said more calmly. 'I had a terrible suspicion that if you travelled alone, we might drift apart.' His voice held all the pathos of a practised Don Juan. 'You were leaving my country and I had to catch you before you were lost to me in your own surroundings with your own friends. Who is with you?' he repeated sharply, the jealousy almost palpable.

'Just the radio,' she replied, and took a deep breath. 'It's nice to hear from you and if you want to give me lunch tomorrow, that would be pleasant, but please listen, Hussain. I have never been anything but a friend to you and I have made it clear to you and to your father that I have no intention of marrying you. Why don't you understand that I am in earnest and leave me to enjoy your friendship and the contacts we have through my work?'

He made an inarticulate sound that was half sob, half rage and she continued. 'Your father wants me because I'm the brightest scientist he's met in years,' she said stubbornly. 'If I was a man, he'd try to buy my services. I know I have been of some help over the water divining, which is an extra bonus for him and I suppose that makes him even more keen to have me in his employ. If I married you, I would no longer be a private and independent individual, but be completely in his power. There is no way I could let that happen, much as I like you and your father. There are other scientists who can do anything for him that I can do and I think he would be more comfortable with a man.'

'Work!' The word came as an expletive. 'Why do you keep saying that? I love you, Sarah, and I want to marry you. Ask what you must. If you want me to live with you in England or the States, then I could do that, but I can't let you go.'

'Hush,' she said as if soothing a child. 'Leave it for now, Hussain. I'll meet you in

232

the bar at Claridges tomorrow at twelve thirty and we can talk again.'

'But, my darling,' he began.

'I'm tired and hungry and my PA – the girl you spoke to on the phone earlier – is coming with some papers. I really have a lot to do before I go to the States, so please let it rest. I'll see you tomorrow. Goodnight.'

Sarah popped a salmon en croute into the microwave and made a salad with mixed leaves and olives and cherry tomatoes. She opened a bottle of Chablis, thinking that Tandy would enjoy a glass when she came to the apartment, and she changed into a lightweight dressing gown of pale peach panne velvet. It was a relief to shed her shirt and bra and the soft fabric clung but made no real tension across her back.

It was wonderful to sip wine again and to smell the aroma of good uncomplicated cooking. No couscous tonight, she thought with a wry smile. Some day in the dim future she might want some with a desperate longing, as she had wanted Marmite and Mars bars when going round Greece with her university friends and when Mark refused to travel without Polo mints, but not now, not so soon.

She finished her supper and put the dishes in the washer before settling into a deep armchair with another glass of wine and a wicked box of chocolates that she convinced herself she had opened virtuously just for Tandy, who adored really dark chocolate and never put on an ounce of extra weight.

It felt later than it was and she wondered if Tandy would ring up and plead weariness, but knew that Tandy was a night owl and loved the evenings. She left the door on the latch so that she could let herself in if she decided to come.

Sarah yawned when she heard sounds from the tiny hall. 'Good. You made it. Have some wine, Tandy,' she called.

She turned to face the door. 'I never touch it,' Hussain said.

As calmly as she was able, Sarah held out the box of chocolates. He took one as if obeying in a trance, then put it on the table. His dark business suit and pale silk shirt were immaculate as if he had taken care with his appearance, his thick dark hair slicked back in limpid swathes, and in spite of herself, Sarah felt a reluctant thrill. She put her wine glass on the table. Enough of that if he was to be there with her for much longer.

'Can I get you some coffee? I have it ready as Tandy will be here soon,' she said firmly. He nodded and as she went into the kitchen she was aware that he watched her go, his gaze travelling over her whole body with a kind of hunger.

A tremor went up her arm when he took

the cup from her and his fingers contacted hers. Oh, God! This was terrible. She had seldom felt so vulnerable and her thin gown did nothing to hide the gentle swelling of her breasts and the long line of her thighs.

Hussain looked inscrutable. 'You are dressed to receive your PRO? Your female employee? I think you are expecting a lover. No woman dresses like that for business other than love.'

'I was waiting for Tandy and then I shall fall into bed and sleep for twelve hours,' she said with a laugh. 'I'm very tired.'

'Bed? Alone?' he asked with a cynical smile. 'What a waste. You should wear that colour more often, but only in private, with a lover, my darling.'

'I wear it because it is light and easy to pack if I take it when I go away,' she said, trying to sound practical. 'I have another in blue.'

'But that blends with your lovely skin,' he said and his voice was a caress. 'You have a nose that would drive one of the old Persian artists mad, hair that is silk and glowing darkness, and skin that looks so fragile and pure that it could bruise if touched roughly.' He came closer. 'Translucent like fine porcelain but with gentle colour,' he added, his eyes searching her face for a response to his hypnotic sensuality.

'My skin may look good on my face but it

235

isn't like that all over, Hussain. I know that you have a fetish about a woman's skin but please believe that I do not compare with most women.'

He dismissed her remarks as modesty and smiled, revelling in what he thought was feminine reticence. 'I've brought you a present,' he said as if she hadn't spoken. 'Have you any fruit juice?'

She nodded, relieved that his mood seemed to have changed and went to the kitchen to take the pack of so-called fresh orange juice from the fridge. She poured some into a Waterford glass and put sweet biscuits on the silver tray.

Sarah gulped. His mood hadn't changed. He had taken off his jacket and the blue silk tie and his shirt was open almost to his waist. He was consciously aware that he looked fantastic. Tandy, where are you? she prayed.

He sipped the juice and made a wry face. 'I will send you a juice extractor and a supply of good oranges,' he said.

'I have a juicer but no oranges,' she replied. 'I hardly ever use it,' she added.

'You will when I stay with you here,' he told her.

'You are staying in Claridges,' she said with a hint of panic.

'I have a suite there,' he admitted. He looked round the room and took in the good furniture, the tasteful drapes and the two original watercolours. 'I like this apartment. I see no need for us to change a thing.'

'I'm glad that you approve of *my* apartment and *my* choice of furnishings, but this *is* my choice and this is where I live when I am in London. Alone,' she added firmly. 'Mark didn't feel comfortable here so we usually met elsewhere, or in his flat.' She glanced at the ormolu clock on the bookshelf. 'It's late and I doubt if Tandy will come here tonight, so do you mind? I want to rest and my head is beginning to ache. Also, I have an appointment at nine tomorrow and I must keep it.'

He shook his head, indulgently. 'Isn't it time you forgot work and business appointments? Tonight we are here together and I want you to myself, with no thought for the outside world.'

What now? she thought with a feeling that the situation could go anywhere, with him being the perfect gentleman and leaving, which now seemed unlikely, or him trying to make love to her.

And would I really put up a fight? she wondered, aware of him as she had seldom been aware of any man, but she knew in her heart and mind that the sweet menace of animal attraction wasn't enough.

'See what I have here.' He snapped open a

tiny silver box and took out a ring. Sarah caught her breath. The turquoise and ruby centre was surounded by diamonds and their combined fire was gentle and fierce. Just like him, she thought.

Instinctively her hand went to the slender chain round her neck, on which was threaded the ring that Mark had given her long ago. It was a fun thing and meant nothing but friendship at the time that he had won it, shooting at plastic ducks in a fairground booth in Austria, and he had presented it to her out of all the girls in the party, with a flourish, saying, 'With this ring, I don't thee wed, but I know of no other girl I want to wear it.' The glass stone was wobbly in the setting but she had kept it, and when he died had begun to wear it on a separate chain to the turtle.

Hussain stared at her throat and saw the ring, exposed to him for the first time where her gown crossed low at the base of her neck. 'Mark gave you that?' His face was full of incredulity. 'That is rubbish! How can you bear to wear anything as cheap as that, Sarah?'

She pulled her gown higher to hide it and said nothing.

'Was it Mark? Or did David give you that, bought from a stall as a token to bind you, before he can give you the real thing?'

'There is nothing between David and me,'

she said.

'I am not a fool.' His eyes had the hardness of agate and an emotion that was deeper than mere dislike simmered under the deadly control. 'He is nothing! He can never satisfy you as I can.'

'I am not in love with Dave and he is not really in love with me,' Sarah tried to explain, but Hussain's growing fury made her recoil, physically.

'The night before you came away, you were seen embracing and he kissed you on the lips,' Hussain accused. 'My father is convinced that he is a threat and I agree with him.'

'David said that you and he worked well together,' she remonstrated mildly.

'That is work. Women we do not share,' he stated as if that was acceptable.

Her temper flared. 'David is a good man and true friend and I do love him, but only as a dear friend and the friend of Mark,' she retorted, her eyes bright with tears and anger.

'Has he asked you to marry him?'

'Only in a rather half-hearted way,' she said and tried to smile and lighten the atmosphere.

'He smiles and makes you feel safe?'

She nodded.

'He is dangerous,' he continued. 'He would slip into your bed like a snake and like a snake tighten the coils so that you cannot escape.'

'A devious mind is something that Dave does not possess,' she told him firmly. 'He is an honest man and if I wanted to marry anyone I could do a lot worse. I would have a loyal and loving partner and a lot in common with him.' Her chin rose defiantly. 'He would also be tolerant of my defects and not expect perfection in my body or in anything I did.'

Hussain gave a short laugh. 'He would take everything for granted and not revel in your beauty as I will. He would never pause to wonder at the texture of your skin and think it heaven-sent by Allah and to be treasured above all things. He could not give you wonderful clothes and the privacy of the oasis.'

'And the harem?' she asked quietly.

'When you bear my sons,' he said and the expression in his eyes grew soft.

'I wouldn't marry you if you were the last man on earth,' she said, quietly. 'I could never survive if I was spied on and made to bend to any man's will.'

His face contorted with fury and hurt pride. 'You will marry me, even if I have to make sure that you bear my child,' he said with icy calm. 'I want you, Sarah. I love you and desire you, and now I have to make sure that I have you before you go back to your own friends. I do not think that David would want you if you had my child in your womb, and my father has told me to take you under any circumstances.'

He moved swiftly and tore the chain from her throat. The cheap ring fell to the floor and was crushed under his foot. She saw the maddened gleam in his eyes and backed away but the only escape was through the doorway into the bedroom, so she stopped moving, sure that if she collapsed on the bed, his superior strength would lead to rape.

Wildly, she looked about her to find a weapon if a weapon was needed, but the heavy glass ashtray was on the shelf as few of her friends smoked and the vase was slender and more fragile than his head, she surmised with a hint of hysterical amusement under her panic.

With both hands, he tore the robe from her shoulders, bringing it down, imprisoning her arms and exposing her breasts. He gasped as if overcome by what he saw and slackened his hold to caress her, but she jerked away and turned her back to hide her nakedness.

She cowered away but he made no further attempt to touch her. His breath hissed in a long exhalation of horror and she glanced back to look at his face. He seemed to have shrunk. His hands trembled but not with desire, and he stepped back and stared again but now Sarah was covered and he was filled with disbelief and hope, mingled with his revulsion, as if it was a nightmare or a trick to confuse him.

To make sure that he had no doubts, she slipped the robe off her back again, deliberately, and he saw the scars once more. Hussain closed his eyes and shuddered and Sarah knew that his dream of her perfect body, perhaps floating idly in the petal-covered, scented pool in the harem to await his pleasure, had died.

He found the outer door and fled, leaving his jacket and the ring, and his tie hung over the arm of a chair, a silk reminder of his visit.

Sarah sank into a chair and wondered why she felt no emotion other than relief.

A minute later, Tandy tapped on the door and came in, carrying a bulging briefcase. 'What did you do to him?' She took in the fact that Sarah was dressed in a very flimsy gown, now tightly belted. 'I take it that the dishy Arab in the lobby was your prince?' She looked at Sarah with mocking accusation. 'You didn't scare him off with chains and bondage, did you?'

'Idiot,' Sarah said with a tight smile.

'Something happened.' Tandy regarded her with some anxiety. 'Did he rape you?'

Sarah shook her head.

'He looked as if he'd been offered choco-lates and found a can of worms.' She whistled softly. 'Get that ring! It must be worth a king's ransom. Was that the bait?' she asked, shrewdly.

'Something like that.' Sarah recovered her mental faculties. 'Tandy,' she said. 'I know it's later than you like to leave the office and you might have a date, but could you do me a big favour?'

Tandy sensed the tension and saw Sarah's hands restlessly pulling her gown ever closer. 'Sure,' she said simply.

'Take this jacket and tie and the ring to Claridges. Go by taxi so that you can be put down at the door and have no hassle with doormen. Hand it all into reception after showing them the ring and asking for a receipt for it before they put it in their safe, then ask them to send a message to Hussain that they have it secure. Get a receipt,' she said again.

'Pity.' Tandy tried it on her engagement finger. 'Sure you don't want it?' She eyed Sarah with affection mixed with a kind of protective care. 'One good deed deserves another. My electric heating has packed up,' she lied. 'Can I shake down here tonight? I can't even have a bath, leave alone cook.'

'I thought you had a gas stove?' Sarah smiled more naturally. 'But thanks, I'd like to have company. Go now; we'll finish the

Chablis and I'll make you an omelette and lend you everything you need,' she added.

'He was coming in the door as I left, looking like the devil was after him,' Tandy said cheerfully, later. 'He didn't notice me so he must have been upset. Usually the Eastern types go for me in a big way. I'm glad you are in contact with the oil states now. I might have a bit of fun.'

'As soon as they mention oasis or harem, run like hell,' Sarah suggested. 'I thought all that was back in the *Arabian Nights* and silent films, but it's all there alive and well when the chips are down.'

She swished butter round her omelette pan and poured in the beaten eggs. 'One Madame Poulard coming up, as seen in Mont-Saint-Michel.'

'I bet he didn't know you can cook,' Tandy teased her.

'He saw enough,' Sarah said quietly. It was ridiculous to think of any man wanting her once they knew.

'Let's get this straight.' Tandy filled her glass again. 'Great food, great wine,' she said, appreciatively. 'Now tell me what's really bugging you. Shock about tonight or something more?'

'I'm back to square one,' Sarah said, slowly. 'I began to think I could feel something for a man again and that maybe he would take me as I am, scars and all, but after Hussain tonight, I know I am worse than a sexual leper. I'd be more acceptable if I had Aids!' she added with more passion.

'The faithful David?' Tandy asked with raised eyebrows that showed her disapproval.

Sarah moved restlessly. 'No, although he did ask me to marry him. He was one of our crowd and I love him as a kissing cousin.' She laughed. 'The Sheikh got it all wrong. Because David kissed me and gave me the odd hug when the Sheikh's spies were watching, he thinks he lusts after me and I encourage him, but David could never be the one who might be a threat to his plans for me and Hussain.' She sighed. 'I did too well out there, discovering water for them, and he wanted two for the price of one, a skilled scientist and a wife for Hussain, firmly set in the oasis and well under his control. What that man doesn't know about the iron hand in the velvet glove is not worth recording!'

'So who is he?'

'What?' Sarah looked startled.

'Come off it. In the office, I take orders from you and touch the old forelock in public, but now, I'm Tandy. Remember the woman who saw those burns when you were almost in coma? I saw them again later and marvelled at the result of the treatment, but I also know what hang-ups you have about them in private. So who is next, who might be put off by a bit of discoloured skin?'

'Is that what it is? A bit of discoloured skin?' Her voice was shaking with anger and despair and every fibre of her body came back to life. 'Look!' She pulled the gown away from her back and exposed the scars.

'Great,' Mandy said with enthusiasm. She ran a finger along a ridge of flesh that stood proud to the surrounding muscle. 'Amazing what they did to get this in line again. When I saw it, it was a bit of a mess.' She looked dreamy. 'Remember Dr Simeon? I had quite a thing going with him over your back.'

'He's married,' Sarah said viciously and dragged her gown into line again.

'I know and I never tangle with married men but I do flirt with them and they love to feel an illicit tingle in their pants.'

'You are impossible!' Sarah relaxed. 'How about another bottle? Say a half bottle this time as we are working women?'

'Same type and cold? I'll get it.'

The phone rang and Sarah started up but Tandy took the receiver from her hand and as she listened she smiled. 'No, sir, you can't speak to her,' she said in a heavy North Country voice. 'A bit of a misunderstanding was there? Me? Oh, I'm just a nurse who is keeping her quiet tonight. She has been muttering of attempted rape and we are waiting to see if she wants to make a statement tomorrow, but I doubt if she will do that. No harm done as far as I could make out when I examined her. Just a bit upset, but she's sleeping like a baby now. Jet lag has a lot to answer for; it makes people excitable in my opinion, and it would be a pity if the media got hold of a story told when the lady is hysterical.' She listened again and tried to sound serious. 'I see, sir, your date for lunch is cancelled because you have to return to the oil fields early tomorrow. Yes, I'll tell her as soon as she wakes up.'

'You sounded like a PC Plod from an Agatha Christie book,' Sarah said, half laughing.

'He's scared shitless,' Tandy said with relish. 'Bed for you, my girl,' she said, reverting to the terrible accent.

'Yes, nurse,' Sarah said meekly. 'I have a present for you. Just promise me never to wear it when I can smell it.'

'Super!' Tandy said as she took the huge bottle of perfume. She was about to unscrew the top and smell it but saw Sarah's expression and just put it into her bag. 'I know who will chase round the bed if I wear this,' she said with satisfaction.

# Twelve

Sarah hoped that as soon as she went back to Bristol, she would relax. The past few days in London had been full of work, people and phone calls and by the time she was ready to leave for the weekend, she was limp and felt that she was not concentrating well.

'For Chrissake, *go!*' Tandy said when Sarah expressed doubts about sparing the time to go away. 'You aren't thinking straight and you're getting up my nose!' She laughed. 'I'd come with you but I have this really lovely man just waiting to be hooked.'

'You aren't invited! Get back to your desk, woman, and stop bullying me.'

'I've booked you on the shuttle and a car to pick you up from the airport,' Tandy said. 'Lucky you. When I go home I have to take the train, as we have no local planes.'

Sarah checked her flight bag and briefcase and knew that she could travel light as there were clothes enough in the Bristol house if the weather changed. 'Carl might join me but he's busy just now.' Sarah sighed. 'I know the feeling. It's amazing what I have to take to the States. He complained on the phone that he has been lumbered with parcels for friends as well as his notes and a few pieces of equipment.'

'He sounded nice when he rang,' Tandy said and eyed her with interest. 'Not much of an accent, but surely Texas? I love Americans.'

'No, he isn't a possible lover, Tandy, so take that expression off. He's a very tough person and very attractive, but I know I can't have him.'

Tandy's eyebrows shot up. 'Are you telling me that you want him?'

'Of course not,' she replied too quickly. 'He's a new friend and he's very bright and sometimes can be fun, that's all.'

'Rich and unattached?'

'Both, but not for you, either, Tandy. He hated that perfume and he can be very abrasive.'

'You haven't seen him since you came back?'

'No.' Sarah didn't add that she had avoided him except for phone calls and was half dreading meeting him again. 'He's a great buddy of the Sheikh and Hussain. In many ways I envy that, as I liked them and had a great admiration for the Sheikh until they began to put pressure on me to marry Hussain, so it could be awkward when we

249

meet and mention them, if Hussain has talked to him about that evening.'

'All boys together?' Sarah nodded. 'Maybe not. I think that Hussain will say nothing as he must have had a jolt to that arrogant pride,' Tandy went on.

'Shock, more likely,' Sarah said grimly, remembering the look of horror when he saw her scars.

'I could kill him! I thought that you were getting a bit more confident in your social life and now he's put you back to when it all started.'

Sarah looked dreamy. 'I do have some regrets. I love the people and the country but I shall never go back to the wonderful laboratory, and I shall never possess that marvellous microscope.'

'Bloody Hell! Get on that plane before I blow my top.' Tandy picked up the bags and took them to her car and Sarah locked the door to her apartment with a feeling that she wanted to stay, safe in a cocoon of work and solitude. Hussain had gone. Tandy had checked with Claridges and the airport to make sure of that, and even David wasn't there to make lukewarm emotional demands on her.

The small plane made a good landing at Lulsgate airport and the car was waiting. Sarah smiled. It would be there on time as Tandy had organised it. She blinked and looked again. The man holding the card with Dr Brackley written on it was not the chauffeur of a hired car.

'Taxi, lady?' Carlson said in a Bronx accent.

'What are you doing here?' she asked.

'Your PRO told me when you might arrive. I checked the flight, so here I am.' He eyed her curiously. 'Does she look on you all the time as her favourite duckling? I'd hate to get on the wrong side of her. I almost hired an ambulance after she told me that you were sick, but you seem OK to me.'

'Tandy exaggerates,' she said, 'but she's a wonderful PRO. I work too hard, or so she believes, and I need a break.'

'Fine.' He led her to a low-slung red Porsche and tossed her luggage into the trunk.

'When did you arrive in Bristol?'

'Two days ago, just after I last phoned you. My contact at the university was free yesterday and it seemed a pity not to get away as I was drawn to your description of Mrs Morgan and her food.' He sighed. 'I haven't had real home cooking like that in years. She was very pleased to hear from me and has fed me so well that I shall have an overhang as deep as that Avon Gorge of yours.'

'It doesn't show,' she said, and knew that she had been staring when he manhandled

251

the luggage.

'Great. In that case I shall ask her to marry me and follow me everywhere with a field oven.'

'You won't get her out of this country unless she goes back to Wales,' Sarah said comfortably. It was wonderful to see him again and she sat back to enjoy the ride.

The deep gorge was greening up in a rehearsal for Spring, and for once the tide was up and the mud banks hidden under the silver river as it wound under the suspension bridge from the city centre to the sea at Avonmouth.

The sweep up to the Downs and on to Leigh Woods made her eager to be at home again. He glanced at her rapt face. 'You have lived here all your life?' he asked.

'No, but my grandmother lived here ever since she married and it's her house I have now. I came here when I could while she was alive and it was a haven when things got tough. I wept for her passing,' she added in a soft voice.

'Good tears,' he said and accelerated as if he wanted no reminder of tears.

Mrs Morgan greeted them with a smiling face. 'You must be exhausted,' she said. 'I've put a couple of hot bottles in your bed if you want a nap.'

'I've come from London, not New York,' Sarah said. 'What's cooking?' She didn't feel hungry but knew that food had priority in Mrs Morgan's scheme and the mention of it would take her mind off tired executives.

'A nice cup of tea or coffee and some fresh Welsh cakes now, and some nice braised beef for tonight,' she said. 'Mr Ward likes my dumplings,' she added with pride.

Carl grinned and eyed her ample bosom. 'Very nice,' he agreed and Sarah laughed.

'I'd like to walk in the woods,' she said. 'We'll have tea when we come back.' She listened. 'What's that?'

Mrs Morgan looked guilty. 'She isn't any trouble, Sarah, and she doesn't often bark like that. I felt that living in now as you want me to do, I like a bit of company, and in these times you never know who's about,' she added darkly. 'I keep her in my flat and you need never even know she's here.'

'Spoil-sport. Afraid I'll take her away from you?' Sarah teased her. 'Where is she? And *what* is she?' she added when a ball of mixed colours flung herself on the housekeeper as she opened the door.

'Walkies,' suggested Carl and the multi-variety of mongrel bitch transferred her allegiance to him. Mrs Morgan handed him the expanding lead and he clipped it to her collar, trying to avoid the busy tongue that licked his hand.

'Where did you get her?'

'I went to the dogs' home and she looked

at me,' Mrs Morgan said. 'She was all matted up and dirty and looked horrible but her eyes were so bright and appealing that I couldn't leave her there. I've had her for two weeks now and she's putting on weight.'

Carl grinned. 'She would. Did they tell you she might well be pregnant?'

'But she's only a puppy herself,' Mrs Morgan said.

Carefully, Carl pressed her abdomen and looked at the maturing nipples. 'I'd say there are at least five in there,' he said. 'My mother used to breed dogs and I helped.' He looked up. 'Take her to a good vet. She's too young to have this litter if the father was a big dog or she was raped by a pack. She was torn and there's still some infection there. It may seem harsh but her best hope of being a healthy companion is to have her sterilised at once.'

'Ring Mr Bennet in Clifton,' Sarah said. 'He was at university with me and is good. If you agree, I'll take her in tomorrow and leave her until she's over it.'

'You're right. I was silly to take her without a vet's say-so, but I wanted to have her,' Mrs Morgan said.

'A good walk will do no harm,' Carl said. 'Come on, you ugly bundle of rags! What have you called her?'

'Myfanwy,' her mistress said with dignity. 'Fanny for short.'

'That's all I need,' Carl said. 'I can't call her with a name like that.'

The edge of the Gorge came into view and the delicate structure of Brunel's bridge hung against a pale blue sky. Sarah breathed deeply and enjoyed watching Carl, racing along with the pup dragging at the lead.

'Careful,' she called. 'Your arm is still bandaged. How is it?'

'Better but sore, but the dressings are not too painful now.' He slowed to a walk and the pup panted happily by his side. 'I know now how painful a burn can be. I have had only minor scalds in the past, but this was really bad at first.' He looked down at her, his face serious. 'I know you must have suffered,' he said. 'Much more than this minor thing and I think much deeper.'

'In so many ways,' she admitted, softly.

He coughed, in an embarrassed way. 'You have one lippy PA. She hinted that I am to mind my manners and look after you when you come to the States.'

'Tandy does sound off at times, but it's only concern for me. What did she say to you?' Her mouth was dry and yet she couldn't believe that Tandy had said anything of the attempted rape.

'She says that you are really, really off men.' Sarah smiled at his very good version of Tandy at her yuppiest. 'She said that Mark's death was still with you and could I keep the wolves away?'

'She's impossible but I couldn't do without her.'

'I assume that she includes me among the wolves,' he said dryly. 'I never force myself in where I'm not wanted,' he added and he looked straight ahead so that she could not read his eyes.

'I can cope with a few fumbling attempts at seduction,' Sarah said. 'If I survived Hussain, I can survive anything.'

'You really have survived him? I did wonder at times. No regrets that you have refused a fortune and all the fleshpots that Arabia can provide? He is a very fine man when women are not in the picture, and you have confused them both a lot,' he added. 'According to their rule book such women don't exist, and they are at a loss how to treat you, so try to make allowances for centuries of male domination.'

'I can't wait for braised beef and dumplings,' Sarah said. 'But tomorrow I shall take the pup in to the vet and eat out at lunch time. I shall not tell Mrs Morgan but I ache for fish and chips that I can eat out of the paper, sitting by the Downs, watching the Bridge.'

'I started up the engine of that uninteresting car you have in the barn and it's fine,' he said. 'I suggest we use that as I can't have mine stinking of fish and chips and hairy dogs,' he said calmly. 'I might want to take out someone important in it.'

'Who said you could come too?' she asked.

'I did.' He grinned. 'I'm scared of your dragon back there in London, so I have to look after you. Here, take the lead now as my arm aches and I can't use the other one just now.'

'Have you seen your friend in Bristol?' she asked as they climbed up to the observatory on the far side of the Bridge.

'All done. I can relax for another day or so; one more day here and then back to London until we go away.' They walked in comfortable silence and then he asked, 'Why did you get Mrs Morgan to work for you? She is obviously devoted and I heard a lot about you before you arrived here.'

'That sounds ominous,' Sarah said lightly.

'Not at all. I gather that she was in a bad way when you found out that she'd worked for Mark's college as housekeeper but had a wife-beating husband, so you brought her to Leigh Woods.'

'He attacked her more brutally than usual and she killed him in self-defence, but although she was aquitted, her job was gone and she had no pension. Believe me, I am not acting out of charity. She is very good and, as you know, cooks like a dream, so why not give her a job? Where would I find anyone as good?'

'Why is it always hard to justify our good deeds?' he said.

'I want an ice cream,' Sarah said, to hide her embarrassment. 'I haven't walked over here for ages, although I promised it to myself often enough.'

'Not since Mark?'

'Now that we have a dog, I can come here again like any good dog walker and not feel odd, alone,' she said.

'Did you come here with Mark?' he persisted.

She shrugged. 'With Mark and Dave and others,' she said. 'Dave liked Bristol better than Mark did and he came here alone at times and with Mark's sister while she was mobile.' She glanced at him. 'Michelle was the love of his life, not me, Carl. That's why it's unfair that Hussain could ever think that Dave was going to marry me'

He frowned. 'I tried to reach Dave a few times but was told he wasn't available as he was out on the rig. I hope he isn't diving too much. They have a limit on hours under water and he does need monitoring. I know him, the senseless Welsh bum.'

'I'll write from Boston,' Sarah promised, licking the melting ice cream from the cone. She gave the rest to the dog and they headed for home, with a very sleepy pup and a sense of belonging to her favourite city.

From the Leigh Woods side of the Bridge, they looked back at the tower. 'It has an observatory in the top, called a camera obscura,' she explained. 'It's Victorian and offers a 360-degree panorama of the surrounding countryside, reflected on to a concave canvas circle and any place can be picked out by rotating an arm on a periscope – gets any part of the Downs that one wants to see. It was shut today, but one day I'll go up there again and see it. As the notice says, among other things, it gives gratification and amusement to all who see it.'

'Isn't science wonderful,' he mocked her.

'Bet you couldn't have invented that,' she retorted, and they argued happily over a few minor inventions that they claimed were sheer genius.

'You're lying!' she said happily. 'That hasn't been invented yet.'

'Nor has your gadget for putting clothes away by remote control,' he retorted.

'Which reminds me that I haven't unpacked and Mrs Morgan will be simmering along with her beef if we're late.'

'She calls you Sarah and you call her Mrs Morgan? Seems the wrong way round.' His expression was quizzical. 'I know it is a Georgian House and in those days they called servants by their last names, but they didn't call their employers by first names, so if you are clinging to the past, you've got your history wrong.'

'Bella Morgan was so shattered by the court case and all the snide remarks in the press, that I answered questions about her, but refused to answer until they called her by her right name. Calling her Mrs Morgan gave her a bit of dignity. Morgan is her maiden name, to which she has reverted, and it stuck.'

The pup, released from the lead, ran into the house. Carl stopped in the doorway and bent to kiss Sarah on the cheek. 'You're one hell of a nice lady,' he said.

'I'll unpack,' she said and almost ran from the hallway.

He's going tomorrow, she reflected with relief as she put away her clothes and changed into a velvet leisure suit of deep emerald green. No way must I take him seriously. He's just a very nice guy and a good colleague but that's all. Hang on to that, Sarah! You can't take another episode like the one with Hussain. Her reflection as she brushed her hair was disconsolate. Maybe he wouldn't even try.

'That's nice,' Mrs Morgan said. 'When she puts away her business suit and wears things like that I know she isn't going to do her homework.'

Carl grinned. 'She doesn't know what hard work lies ahead. I saw a very good chess set in the study and I shall beat her this evening.' He handed her a glass of good amontillado sherry. 'First, I shall get her drunk so that I have the advantage and then I shall cheat.'

'Join the club! I learned to cheat before I was five,' she retorted.

'A child prodigy,' he said and sighed. 'I shall accidentally tip the board over if I'm losing.'

'What wine did you want, Sarah?' The housekeeper's tone was warm but always deferential and Carl was touched.

'I sneaked into the cellar and saw what is there,' he said. 'Was your grandfather a tee-totaller or an alcoholic? There's enough there to last a lifetime.'

'You choose,' Sarah said.

'Something robust to go with the beef, and a liqueur to sip over the chess board,' he suggested.

'You should come here more often,' Mrs Morgan said, beaming at him.

Sarah picked up her sherry glass and followed him down to the cellar. In the dim light she looked about her. 'I must have these catalogued and maybe sell some,' she said. 'I know very little about fine wines and I'd hate to let them exceed their sell-by date.'

Carl shuddered. 'Don't you know that wine and all good women mature most beautifully with age? They never reach a time when they are no longer good to see, and good to enjoy.' Carl selected a bottle of Châteauneuf-du-Pape and wiped the neck clear of cobwebs. 'Don't do anything in haste,' he begged. 'Promise me you'll leave it until my father visits you, as he would think this Aladdin's cave.'

'Is he coming to England?'

Carl's eyes were dark in the candlelight. 'I don't think I'll have to twist his arm, when he knows what I've found,' he said. He blew out the candle. 'He'll want to see the wines, too.'

'My grandfather was connected with a famous Bristol wine shipper and had shares in the company,' she explained, ignoring his last remark.

'Let's see if he bought a bargain,' Carl said and took the bottle into the kitchen to open it.

Mrs Morgan served the food as soon as Carl said the wine was right. She refused to taste the wine and disappeared back into the kitchen when they had been served, and after apple pie with feather light pastry and thick cream, they both refused cheese.

Coffee arrived as if by magic and again Mrs Morgan went away to her own rooms. 'Her service is as good as any at the oasis,' Carl remarked. 'If you are alone, does she remain a bit aloof like that?'

'Always. When she came here, she made that a condition; real friendship and service but no undue familiarity. She has a lot of inner healing to do and a certain formality helps to give her parameters inside which she can function.'

'And you understand that.'

'Yes,' she said. 'The arrangement suits us very well.'

'And you see no rifts in the personal wall round you? All battened in and safe?'

'Not always,' she said carefully. 'There's a stupid advertisment on the television, showing a girl hemmed in by dark woods, and when she uses the preparation advertised, she comes out into the sunlight through a convenient gap.' She looked down at the grotesquely beautiful knight in her chess set. 'I see glimpses of light but the trees grow up too fast and I'm lost again.'

'I had noticed,' he said dryly. 'Check!'

'It can't be! I'm sure I didn't...'

He laughed and the deep sound was good. 'So I cheated!'

'You pig,' she said mildly and giggled.

'Come on, let's take the pooch for her last pee,' he said. 'Mrs Morgan can let her out in the garden at night when we aren't here but tonight we can take her into the woods.'

'Beware the badgers,' Sarah said. 'No wolves, but we might see a fox and I think there are badgers.'

'Great.' He fetched her waxed jacket from the hall cupboard and she laughed. 'In houses like this there are always jackets in the hall cupboard,' he said. 'I borrowed the larger one. Was it Mark's?'

'No, it was left by someone who never came to claim it and I forget who that was. It should fit you as you are bigger than Mark.'

'I'm glad,' he said and called Myfanwy.

The woods were dark and Sarah was glad to have a man with her. As if reading her thoughts, Carl said with mocking satisfaction. 'Being an Honorary Man is no good here. No one can see the difference and you have to admit to being a woman.'

'You sound like them,' she retorted, but made no effort to draw away from the arm that he placed casually across her shoulders.

They stood by a gap in the trees that showed the river below, now with the tide out, a thin line between dark grey banks of mud. 'People jump off the bridge, sometimes,' Sarah said.

'How nice for them,' he said. 'Suicide isn't a good idea.'

'They don't always die. It depends if they fall on the banks or into the mud. In Victoria's time, a girl of eighteen jumped off after a bad love affair and her crinoline skirt acted as a parachute. She landed safely in the mud and was rescued.'

'You're kidding?'

'No, it's true. A surgeon friend of my grandfather operated on her for gallstones when she was eighty-five and she did very well after the op.'

'What happened about the guy concerned?'

'I have no idea. I suppose she forgot him.'

*'Tout passe,'* he said. 'Who knows, you may forget Mark one day; I may forget a lot of people and things, but never the night we watched the turtles.'

'That was magic,' she agreed and walked away. 'Come on, Mrs Morgan will be worried. Not about us but in case we've let Myfanwy run over the edge of the Gorge and she isn't wearing a crinoline!'

Breakfast was late as Sarah's alarm failed to work and Carl agreed with Mrs Morgan that she needed the extra rest. As the appointment with the vet was at eleven they had to hurry, and by the time they had reassured Mrs Morgan that a visit to the vet was best for all concerned as she was beginning to have second thoughts, the pup was put in the back seat of Sarah's car, on a rug that protected the seat in the event of an attack of car sickness or worse, en route.

'Well, that's one job I didn't enjoy,' Sarah said as she took a last look at the front door of the vet's surgery. 'If Mrs Morgan had seen the expression in that dog's eyes when

265

we handed her over, she'd have snatched her up and taken her home again.'

'She can't know what they will do to her. She was scared because the smell of disinfectant is similar to that stuff they use in dog pounds.' Carl grinned. 'Forget her and concentrate on *me*. I go away early tomorrow, so show me something of Bristol and then we can have that gourmet dish of fish and chips unless you've changed your mind.'

'What do you want to see? The museum? The Zoo?'

'I can see them anytime,' he said.

'Right! One tour coming up.' And when they returned to the car in the late afternoon, Sarah was happy. They had walked the back streets and the dock area and Carl had been impressed by her knowledge of local events, past and present.

'Slaves and wine,' he said. 'When I come here again, I shall go into both of these subjects and I know my father will be fascinated. He read *The Sun Is My Undoing* years ago and didn't believe it, but it's all here.' He looked at her as if to impress on her the force of his words. 'It was not so different from the lack of social conscience that prevails in some countries today, but we know better now.'

'Do we? Does the Sheikh believe that he is wrong to have the oasis run as it was two

266

hundred years ago, with unpaid labour, fed and clothed by him, in reality slaves, under harsh justice, with women under the thrall of men? It's archaic and wrong,' Sarah protested.

'If you had lived then, with a good family background and ample means, you would have had slaves and gone to church and felt very moral and generous.'

'And where were you when the slaves were given emancipation in America?' she asked caustically.

'My family had slaves, and saw the good and bad side of that when they freed them. We employ a number of people who are descended from former slaves and are now on the payroll like any other person, but some families threw them out when free, and as they had no patriarchal family to see to their needs, they starved. Not all slave owners were bad, Sarah. Hussain and his father care for their people and would be shocked if anyone classed them as slaves.'

'But women are criminally underestimated,' she said.

'Women like you are redressing the balance, if painfully,' he said. 'I don't know what happened between you and Hussain but I gather he has gone away and you will not meet him except at professional gatherings.' She nodded. 'Try to forgive him, Sarah. The Sheikh is genuinely fond of you and admires your brain.'

'Hussain has a fetish about skin,' Sarah said slowly. 'He came one night to my apartment and brought a ring, which I refused. He then became angry and said he would make me pregnant so that David would no longer want me. He thought that he could then take me and impose what future he liked on me.'

'He raped you?' His fury startled her.

'No, he didn't get that far,' she said, with the calm of despair. 'Worse, he shrank way from me and fled and I shall remember the look of revulsion in his eyes as long as I live. Now do you want to know why I can never let a man touch me?'

'You know that I love you, Sarah?'

'Yes,' she whispered.

'I thought that you were thinking along those lines, too,' he said gently.

'How can I? I would die if you saw my body and looked at me with loathing.'

He drove into the barn and shut off the engine, opened the door and stood by the old farm cart that had been left by a farmer long gone. 'You forget I've seen the worst of you?'

'When?' Acid bile rose in her throat.

'I saw you in that terrible hat with sweat running down your nose,' he said. 'You nearly asphyxiated me with that whore's perfume and scared me as I thought you were after my body, and I didn't really like the shirt that should have been given to a garage sale five years ago.'

'You say the nicest things,' she said and laughed. 'So now you know, I feel better and you can go gracefully, as the police say when giving evidence in court about a brothel: "I made my excuses and left." '

'Good night, Sarah,' he said solemnly at the foot of stairs. His kiss was firm but without fervour and she climbed the stairs slowly, her feelings mixed and very sad.

# Thirteen

Misty rain blurred the view over the Charles River as it ran between Boston and Cambridge and Sarah Brackley was glad to turn back to the lecture room in one of Boston's biggest conference centres. The vista of interested faces of men and women gave her a sense of security and she knew that her talk would be noted and quoted long after it was given.

She even took comfort from her slick appearance in the smart but understated grey business suit and pale yellow shirt. This is my world, she thought, and in it I can be professional with all kinds of races and sexes with no hang-ups about status and sexual overtones. The water jug on the desk shone with aggressive cleanliness, the ice in the water glistening and sharp, an uncompromising aid to any temporary loss of voice or inspiration.

Maybe there is some sexual discrimination here, she thought with a smile. The previous lecturer had a reputation for having vodka and tonic in his glass when he paused for a slurp, but she had been offered no such stimulant.

Her back felt easy and she had taken the last of the antibiotics prescribed for the slight infection of the last graft. The news had been good and it was almost certain that no further treatment would be needed, unless she injured the fragile skin before it was set in place firmly.

Applause, which invariably surprised her, came over spontaneously and warmly and she sipped the iced water and sat down after the lecture, suddenly shy as if she had given a party piece that she had not thought was good enough and now had this great acclaim.

'Lunch,' suggested the organiser, a determined woman with a large bust, who had chosen badly when it came to clothes as the tight skirt wriggled up over her ample seat when she sat down and she had a nervous habit of pulling it down even when she was standing. 'There are a lot of folk anxious to meet you but I said to wait until you have a breathing space this afternoon,' she said with unctuous kindliness. 'So follow me, Dr Brackley, and we'll meet only a very few for now,' she added as if many people had made a great sacrifice to pass up the opportunity to meet her now but would do so later.

Cameras whirred and reporters hovered as Sarah was shepherded to the smaller dining room exclusive for VIPs. She helped herself to a paper towel in the wash room and smiled. No silent Arab woman to hand her scented soap and soft towels and no bowl of warm water ready for her. A lingering regret made her wistful. It had been wonderful in so many ways.

The few people there, instead of the many who wanted to meet her, were enough, she thought wryly. At least forty guests for luncheon and a set top table that looked as if someone was expected to say a few words at the invitation of the host.

She was vaguely puzzled. As a scientist, within her own profession, her talks were popular and her reputation fine, but surely there were far more people interested in her today who had never heard of the viscosity of oils and the analysis of oil-bearing cores, as if she might be famous for something of which she was unaware. The luncheon room looked very formal and grand and she sensed an air of curiosity and expectancy as she walked in.

Her heart sank as she recognised the fact that she would be flanked by civic dignitaries who would know nothing of her subject and hadn't the slightest idea of what she had said that morning, but had been brought in by the sponsors to give weight to the seminar as far as the civilian public was concerned.

'No speech,' Sarah said clearly as the organiser led her to her seat.

'Just a few words about the opportunities for young people in the oil world,' she begged, giving a vicious tug to her skirt.

'You say it,' Sarah said firmly. 'I know nothing about selection for jobs.' She eyed the woman with a cold stare. 'If you ask me in public, you'll have egg on your face as I shall sit there looking very puzzled,' she said. 'Don't be greedy. I've done my stint and you are overstepping your brief. I don't recall my PRO saying that I have to meet people this afternoon, either.'

'I've arranged it,' the woman bleated. 'I thought you'd enjoy a trip up the river with a few invited guests and the press are alerted. It's a great fund-raising opportunity and everyone is fascinated by your work in Arabia. They are just panting to hear the low-down on life on that wonderful oasis.'

'The river, in this weather? You have to be joking, and I tested for oils and water, gave lectures and got very warm in all that hot sun and sand,' Sarah said in a flat voice. 'Nothing more happened.'

Sarah sat down and addressed the florid man on her right. 'Tell me, Senator; you have a big estate. How do you heat your house economically?'

For the next two courses, she ate and nodded and let his words flow over her head as he warmed to what she had long ago decided was a subject dear to all men who had to pay household bills.

The elaborate iced pudding was offered but she refused it, her mouth still full of the taste of bland chicken. She sipped more wine instead and had two cups of strong black coffee. Mrs Morgan would have dismissed the pudding as rubbish, and she wondered if Carlson Ward had been brought up to like such confections.

'Sorry. What was that?' she asked as the man on her other side tried to gain her attention.

'I said that you must have had a wonderful time in the oil fields, Dr Brackley. My wife was telling me that out there you have become some sort of guru.'

'Guru?' Sarah looked blank. 'I'm sure that your wife was mistaken.'

'Now don't be coy, Dr Brackley. She read about you in a magazine and said that you discovered water for a very important sheikh.'

'It does happen sometimes when we look for oil,' she said in a downbeat way to discourage him.'

'You made a lot of waves out there, I believe, with your discoveries, and she wants to know if I can persuade you to talk to her ladies' group and give a demonstration of water divining.'

Sarah gulped. 'That was a one-off accident,' she insisted. 'There are many people who do that for a living and have much more expertise. I am an oil scientist and have no real interest in dowsing for water.'

'It would take only a day and you can stay with us. We have a very fine pool and sauna and a lot of friends who would like to meet you,' he said eagerly. 'My wife is in a very militant women's movement and we welcome ladies who have proved that they have a leading place in the professions normally run by men.' He bent over, his voice low and confidential, and Sarah was aware that he actually nudged her. 'I think that what they really want to know under all that militant female nonsense is what the men were like and have you photographs of those sheikhs.'

'I'm really sorry, but I have to move on to Texas and I have no time for any other appointments,' she said with a sweet smile.

Inwardly she seethed. I am not an exhibit in a fairground booth, and I am not a militant feminist, so what would they expect from me? So many people pulling in different directions and I have no place with any of them.

She went to her room and read again the letter she had received from the Sheikh. It was obvious that he thought she had quarrelled with Hussain but he had no idea why they had parted in such a hurry. He referred to her as 'daughter' and begged her to return after her American tour.

'Even if you cannot marry my son, I want you here, selfishly for two reasons: your work, which will bring much prestige to me and my state, and for your own sake, as a flower in my palace, but free to come and go as you please.' It read deceptively as if he felt humbled and the tone of the letter was placating, but she visualised his proud eyes and the set of his chin when he wanted something.

He went on to say that he hoped to meet her in Texas when he visited Carlson Ward's family.

Sarah felt a tug towards the peace of the oasis. America felt brash and at times, humourless, and the intrinsic good manners of the Arabs had made a great impression on her. One man must never make her bitter towards them.

She sat on the bed and picked out her diary and address book. First, she tried to ring the Sheikh's palace and then the hotel where she had stayed, hoping for news of David, but the lines were busy. David had sent a card saying he was busy on the offshore rig, as a few snags had appeared in the anti-corrosives he was using, but he hoped to be through quite soon and able to leave the rigs for Wales and laver bread.

I could easily marry David and accept that we would never set our souls alight, she thought. He could be the only man I know who's able to dismiss my ugliness as unimportant, and be a real friend who puts no great significance on such a deformity.

She bit her lip. Did she really want a minder, as if she was a handicapped younger cousin, needing care and love because she was disabled?

What of the love she knew she now felt for Carl? That was impossible, and he must never know her feelings. If she gave way to him and he turned from her, she thought she would have to die. She remembered the woman who had jumped from the suspension bridge and knew she would never have that courage, but she could not go on living if Carl saw her body and found her repulsive.

The phone trilled. What had happened to privacy? She cupped the receiver and put on her Spanish maid voice.

'Nice try but not the real thing. Not for me, at any rate.'

'Carl!' Relief and pleasure sent a current along the line. 'I thought you had gone home.'

'I was delayed. I have another day in Boston. Want to walk the Freedom Trail?'

'It's raining!'

'So, you'll get wet, but you're wrong. It

stopped an hour ago and we can get the walk in before dinner.'

'Well,' she drawled. 'If it's a choice between a river trip packed with local dignitaries paying huge sums to fund some obscure charity, hoping I have salacious tales to tell them about Arab sheikhs, a talk about dowsing to a group of militant feminists, and the walk, I guess I'd choose the walk.'

'Christ! Is that what they lined up for you? Pick you up in ten.'

She laughed into the silent phone, then kicked off her high heels and put on flatties. Her light raincoat was soft and deep red and she took a silk scarf instead of an umbrella. She squinted up at the sky through the net drapes and saw blue patches. 'Enough to make a sparrow a pair of trousers,' her mother once said, and it was a good sign.

The squirrels running about in Boston Square were shaking off the drops falling from the trees and the tourist trams had started up again after the rain, with people huddled against the almighty draughts that scythed in through the half-open roofs.

Carl produced a leaflet. 'We start here,' he said, and intoned a piece about one of the buildings. 'Come on, we've lots to see.'

Together, they walked along the red painted line that marked the trail and went in and out of the main buildings illustrated on the map, including the old state legislative buildings.

Many tourists on the same trail were impressed by the antiquity but they were Americans from other states on holiday, and Sarah forced herself to make no snide remarks about the lack of really old history, but she did murmur to Carl, 'What about Salisbury Cathedal and Westminster and every small monastery in Britain, all hundreds of years older than any of this?'

'Not to mention Luxor and Delhi,' he replied solemnly. 'Stop being a superior little shit and enjoy what we can show you. We are a young country but we do have some things that make the Brits blink! A lot of you were eager to come here when they ran out of goodwill back home.'

'I love you, too!' she said resentfully.

'Say that again!'

'What?'

'Say you love me.'

'No.'

'You said it in front of witnesses.' He pointed to two bedraggled pigeons perched on the back of a wooden bench.

'Idiot,' she said and walked faster. 'What do we see now?' She laughed. 'I don't believe it!'

'Yes, one of our greatest triumphs against the English,' Carl assured her. 'The Boston Tea Party. Want to have your picture taken?'

'Where?'

Carl had a mischievous glint in his eyes that Sarah distrusted, as he pushed her towards a booth and she found herself being led towards a replica of an old three-master moored permanently by the jetty. She stared then recoiled and rushed back to Carl shaking with laughter. 'You beast,' she said weakly. 'They can't really do that seriously?'

She watched as a man threw a box that looked like a tea chest into the water of Boston Harbour. The camera clicked, then he stepped down as if he'd achieved a life-long ambition and another took his place. The box, secured on a long rope, was hauled up for the next picture, and so it went on, endlessly for as long as there were people eager to re-enact the tourist idea of the Boston Tea Party.

They passed the turning that the leaflet hinted might be risky to explore, but Carl ignored it. 'If your feet are killing you as mine are, let's stop for the best ice cream you'll get outside of Italy,' he said, and they went into the Italian quarter down narrow lanes and found an ice-cream parlour.

'It's better than the pudding they offer-ed me for lunch,' she agreed when she had eaten half of her gelati and nuts. 'This is delicious. Even Mrs Morgan would ap-prove.'

'She sends her love,' Carl said.

'When?' Sarah stopped eating, her spoon poised half an inch from her upper lip and a blob of ice cream on her nose.

'Last night. I timed the call to catch her in her nightie at seven a.m. over there, and she was very pleased.'

'But why? Did you leave your toothbrush there or are you sucking up to her to make sure you are welcome again?'

'Of course; all that, but I had to know if my friend Myfanwy was OK.'

'I think...' She caught her breath and found difficulty in speaking. 'You bothered to take that trouble for one awful bundle of canine sexual mismanagement because your mother bred wonderful borzois and Great Danes?'

'You rang, too,' he accused her.

'That's different. Mrs Morgan is my responsibility.' She smiled and her eyes showed how much she cared but Carl couldn't tell if the caring was for him or for Mrs Morgan.

'So we both know that Myfanwy is back in Leigh Woods with a stitched incison that she tries to lick, a flat belly and a certain loss of libido.'

'It happens after operations,' Sarah said. 'Women lose their desire for men.'

'I disagree. It may be postponed but never lost,' he said.

The blob of ice cream on Sarah's nose

melted and dripped. Carl leaned over and licked it away.

'Do you *mind?*'

'Not at all. It was pistachio and my favourite,' he said calmly. 'And I could never marry a woman with a runny nose.'

She wiped her nose with the paper napkin and pushed the dish away. 'What now, wise guy? The witches of Salem?'

'Too far for this trip but one day we might take in that, and the Fall in New England, and whale watching off Cape Cod,' he said.

'No oil wells in Cape Cod or Martha's Vineyard,' she said lightly.

'And Dr S. Brackley isn't allowed to take time off to be really self-indulgent,' he said, mocking her.

'This is sheer indulgence,' she retorted.

'I thought it was just an escape from the blue-rinsed and militants.'

'No, I've enjoyed every hard step on these awful paving stones, and I adored the ice cream.'

'Thanks, ma'am,' he said dryly.

'I couldn't have done this without you, Carl,' she conceded and he laughed.

'That's better. Hang on to that. I'm good with dogs and plump housekeepers and I lead a mean road workout. I might send in my tax deductable account later, but for now, I'm content,' he said and held her hand in his, in a friendly way.

He looked at his watch. 'I have to get back to the hotel,' he said.

'Are you lecturing tonight?'

'No, not tonight.' He seemed reluctant to say more.

'You have a date?' she asked as if it was a good idea, but she hated the thought of him dating another woman. 'Don't keep her waiting.'

He gave her a long cool look and she looked away. 'I have to get my arm dressed. A friend of a friend is here in surgery at the local hospital and he will do it. Wanna come along and have him look at you, too?'

'No need,' she said crisply. 'I use cream only now and most of it is healed.'

'I'll walk you home,' he said. 'Pick me up at the hospital at eight tonight and we'll have some food.'

'A taxi now would be nice,' she said, flexing the ankle that had suffered slightly over the cobbled street. Carl gave a whistle that would have put a London hotel door-man to shame, and minutes later, Sarah edged her way through the lobby of her hotel to avoid being seen by any culture vulture and reached her room safely. The evening paper lay by her door.

'Oh, no!' She studied the picture and the caption. 'Beauty and Brains,' the blurb went and said a lot of fairly erroneous things, flattering her, and hinting at a liason with a handsome Arab prince. The byline showed it was written by a girl who usually wrote about fashion models and film stars, and the picture was made up of two separate photographs, skilfully linked to look as if she was with Hussain.

So I have to be glamorous and give the Great American Public a vicarious thrill, Sarah thought sourly. The reporter hasn't the ability to take on a serious subject. But as she showered, she thought that she was being unjust and had to admit that here, in modern America, it was still a man's world and women were expected to be glamorous if they were in the public eye and leave the heavy stuff to the men.

She almost wished she'd talked to the militant women. They had a point. Cloistered in university campuses, it was easy to be liberated, and within her own profession it was so, but out in the so-called real world of ordinary people, had things changed all that much?

Maybe I should wear a caftan and a hairband to justify the piece about my dowsing, she thought with wry humour as she changed to meet Carl. Where do they dig up these articles? Resolutely business-like, she put on a plain black shirt and matching skirt and added a long chenille sweater of dark blue that hung loose and did nothing for her figure. She saw her reflection and grinned.

All I need is my old straw hat and he'd really, really fancy me.

'Kinda homely, but right for this evening,' he said when she met Carl at the hospital.

'Where are you taking me?'

'Don't look so scared. I'll look after you.'

'Should I think I need to be looked after?'

'Only if you yell for the wrong team,' he said.

'Team?'

'Don't be dumb,' he said as if she was all of five. 'I'm taking you to see the Red Sox.'

'What?'

He laughed and eyed her with incredulity. 'You don't know what the Red Sox are? Lady, you have not mixed with the right people. How can anyone not know about them. They are the champions and I've bartered my soul for tickets tonight, just to make sure that you have the best night of your life.'

'I can think of better ways to spend a night,' she said without thinking.

'So can I, but I thought you'd never ask!'

'I'm not! You can forget that.'

'Pity.' He grinned, seeing her rising colour. 'You're real pretty when you blush, Mary Lou,' he drawled.

'Don't we eat?'

'Greedy. You've been at the flesh pots all day.'

'I ate some seafood and a little chicken

and that wonderful ice cream but that's all.
I never eat much breakfast when I have a
lecture to give and I need my calories.'

He sighed. 'OK, it's going to be a fine
night and the river is high. We can grab a
burger and a can of Coke and see the moon
rise.'

'A burger? Why didn't I say I'd marry
David?' she said.

'Lady, you need education,' he replied. 'I'll
buy you a burger that surpasses all those
you've ever eaten.'

'That wouldn't be difficult. I've only had
one in my whole life and that was in Glas-
gow. It gave me heartburn.'

'A haggis burger?' They giggled and he
hailed a taxi. 'It's a burger or nothing, as
you don't like any sport I suggest,' he said
severely. 'And you can say thank you to the
nice gentleman.'

They went down by the river and walked
along the bank and over a bridge. The lights
of Cambridge winked at the brighter lights
of Boston and the night air was warm. Sarah
distrusted the effect it was having on her.
'At least if we'd gone to the stadium we'd
have been sitting down,' she grumbled.

'Not far now,' Carl said and walked on.

She followed. 'Is this it?' The stall was
painted white and looked very clean and the
smell of very fresh ground beef cooking over
a grill was irresistible. A boy on a skateboard

286

swanned past them and came back to buy popcorn.

'Hi there!' called Carl. 'Want to take in the game?' He held out the tickets.

'You crazy, mister?'

'No, she is,' Carl said soulfully. 'Can you believe it? She doesn't want to go to see the Red Sox?'

The boy, who was all of twelve, eyed her scornfully. 'Women!' he said and went off at speed, clutching the tickets as if he had won a fortune.

Sarah watched the girl behind the grill toss the burgers in between soft rolls and Carl added relish to his. Sarah cautiously examined what was on offer and decided that tomato ketchup might be safer than some of the hot spices.

'Very wise. Some of them would take the top of your head off and you'd never know it was beef in there.'

'This is good,' she said in surprise.

'What did you expect? I'd never take a lady anywhere that wasn't five star.'

She kicked a discarded can that lay under the high round table by which they were standing. 'I'd never have guessed. I suppose this is all part of the ambiance?'

'OK, back to the hotel for coffee and brandy,' he said.

'No rush,' she said and smiled. 'Let's give them time to be out of the lounge and bars.

I don't want to be recognised and I don't feel like dowsing tonight, even for an avid audience who are now sure that I am sleeping with Hussain.' She sighed. 'Such is fame. I work my fingers to the bone in my real job, but they have discovered me overnight as what one person called me – a kind of guru in the Middle East with great influence over the Sheikh, and now I'm a woman with a dark romantic secret, or so they hope.'

'You'll make the front page of *Vogue* yet,' he said laconically and found a cab.

A group of people stood by the bar as if rooted there until morning. Sarah drew back. 'The man with the ponytail is a reporter,' she said. They went into the smaller lounge and were alone. Carl ordered coffee and drambuie.

The bellboy brought a selection of petits fours and savoury blinis topped with cream and smoked salmon. Sarah raised her eyebrows. 'Did you order this?'

'I thought it might fill a gap,' Carl said.

'Great. How did you know I was still hungry?'

'I knew because I am hungry and we have so much of our basic needs in common,' he said, grinning. 'We like the same things and both have good appetites. Remember how we ate all the cookies and drank all the coffee when we were watching the turtles?

Dwight was livid.'

Sarah giggled. 'Mrs Morgan must miss us now. She was thrilled to see all her good food vanish when we were there. She loves cooking for a crowd.'

'We weren't a crowd.'

'We ate like one,' she said.

Carl eased his arm into a comfortable position. 'More coffee, please,' he said when he saw Sarah watching him.

'Dressing sticking?' she asked.

'Not really. Just stiff,' he replied.

She poured the coffee and decided that the pink and grey cups were not what she would have chosen. 'Is that strong enough? It's difficult to see the colour of the coffee in this china.'

She handed the cup across to him. 'How bad was the burn?' she asked reluctantly.

'Healing fast and no third-degree patches,' he replied. She knew he was regarding her with intense concentration, as if to read her mind. 'I may have to wear long-sleeved shirts for a while to hide my embarrass-ment,' he went on, 'but that's a common hang-up, like having to wear a leotard in the water and high-necked dresses.'

'A leotard would look odd on you,' she said and bit into a gooey petit four that tasted of synthetic vanilla.

Carl saw the reporter pass by the entrance to the lounge and was glad that Sarah was

289

seated in the shadow of a fake palm tree.

'I think that you should get down to Texas as soon as possible,' he said, seriously.

'I leave in three days' time. Isn't that soon enough? Do they want the schedule brought forward?'

'No, but I think you'd be safer there.'

'Safer?'

'No physical danger,' he assured her quickly. 'The media have cottoned on to the fact that you are a bit unusual. That dowsing business was reported by a stringer who is in cahoots with the Sheikh and the press have gotten their bloodhounds on to it. You saw the picture of you and Hussain?' She nodded. 'They'll not stop there. Some little eager beaver will be even now be riffling through the files for any mention of you and they'll find the account of the London bombing and Mark's death.'

'Who on earth will want to read about that again?'

'You must have noticed the increase of interest among the public today? It makes a story when linked up to what they think gives with you and Hussain. Possibly an escape to the peace of the harem to forget, sort of thing. A will-she-won't-she cliff-hanger.'

'Oh, no!'

'You know it could happen. Even the fact that you dressed so modestly in the sheikhdom will be used to guess when you are to take the Muslim faith.'

'What do I do, Carl?'

'Skip the media interview tomorrow and fly down with me to the ranch and stay there until you visit the rigs and keep to your schedule.'

'I can't just go.'

'Sure you can. Go to bed now and leave it to me. I'll get the tickets and check you out from the hotel. No hassle as you don't have to pay anything. I'll leave a note of apology for the lady with the tight butt and say you have a sick friend to visit.'

'She'll know you're lying.'

'Who cares?'

'How shall I know that you are ready?'

'I'll ring through. Let it ring three times but don't answer any calls, and when it's me, it will stop. Ten minutes after that, be at the entrance with your baggage. I'll have a cab waiting.'

'Do I have breakfast?'

'At the airport.'

'I'll be ready. I'll pack tonight.'

# Fourteen

A long black limousine waited by the narrow strip and Sarah stepped out of the shuttle plane on to a parched area of grass by the airport tower. Hot, dry air eddied round the buildings and caught at her throat. A chauffeur wearing jeans and a denim shirt took her bags and she followed Carl out to the car.

'Didn't know you'd got lucky, boss!' The man's wide grin split his dark face.

'Cool it, Morton. Any wisecracks will be unwelcome as she's smarter than me and doesn't even like me!'

'Pity. She's cute.'

Sarah laughed. 'Are they all like him?' she asked. 'Maybe I'll decide to like Texas.'

'You'd better,' Carl said. 'I want you to fall in love here.'

'I fell in love with the desert,' she replied. 'Look where that got me!'

They drove for about twenty miles and passed a derelict oil rig, then on for more miles and saw active pylons on the horizon. 'That's where you go for your first meetings,' he said. 'We're a bit further on and we've landscaped so that we don't have derricks and towers dominating us.' The car purred smoothly and ate up even more miles.

Carl pointed to the east. 'The ranch is over there and we should see it in about fifteen minutes beyond the trees.'

'You really feel at home here,' she said, watching his eager expression. The hard lines by his mouth softened and he looked young and boyish.

'That, too.' he said.

'What else? You said that, too.'

'You being here,' he said simply, as if that was obvious.

'I'm flattered,' she murmured.

'So you should be. It isn't every woman I'd bring out here.'

'But as a colleague, I'm OK?'

'Try telling that to my old man,' he said cryptically. 'He'll take one look at you and decide you're no roustabout.'

'You mean, I don't have to share in the bunk house?'

'Not unless you want a riot on your hands,' he said coolly. 'You'll wash your face and look pretty. My father likes to meet intelligent and pretty women.'

'Can't I wear my straw hat?' she teased.

'I shall personally burn it on the barbecue,' he said.

The ranch house was cool with deep

porches and long windows covered with fly screens that kept away the dust but not the air.

The glint of a huge pool, fringed by green shrubs and bright flowers, invited her, but Sarah resolutely turned away, knowing that it was not for her, and joined Carl in the house to meet his father. She held back until they had greeted each other with fervour, then Carl took her hand and led her forward as if performing a ceremony.

'I've brought Sarah to meet you, Father,' he said.

Paul Ward laughed and kissed her cheek. 'Where's the formidable Dr S. Brackley we were expecting?'

'She's here too,' Sarah said. 'It's wonderful to be here, Mr Ward and I can't thank you enough for putting up with me at such short notice,' she began.

'Carl said you'd be coming to stay,' he said as if it was settled weeks ago. He grinned. 'I think you'll be safe if you call me Paul,' he added. 'Hester, take Miss Sarah's things and show her where she will sleep,' he ordered. 'I have to see a groom but bring her along to the stables in half an hour, Carl, and we'll show her some of the stock.'

'What a lovely room!' Sarah looked about her at the pale walls and luxurious drapes. The bed, covered with a patchwork quilt that picked up the colours of the hangings, was right out of the Deep South and the polished wooden floor was covered with scattered rag hook-rugs.

She admired them and Hester smiled shyly. 'My mother and my granny made them for Missus Paul.' Her huge brown eyes were solemn. 'She was a good woman and Mister Paul still misses her,' she said.

Sarah nodded. She knew so few details of Carl's background, and yet as soon as she arrived at the ranch, she had been made to feel as if she was expected to know about them or would know, soon.

She changed into jeans and a soft blue shirt and hesitated when she saw her battered old hat waiting to be picked up. A tap on the door made her say, 'Come in,' and Hester handed her a wide-brimmed bush hat.

'Did Mr Carl send this?' The girl nodded.

'Fair exchange. Take this to him with my compliments,' Sarah said and Hester departed giggling when she saw the awful fraying straw that had been such a friend in the past.

'You made the supreme sacrifice?' Carl eyed the replacement with approval. 'Come on, Paul has a new foal and some rather fine Arabs to show us.'

'No dogs?'

'Two that are out there with him, but after my mother died, he gave away all the pedigree Danes as he couldn't bear to see them around as she was not here.'

'The horses are different?'

'He had horses long before he married,' Carl said. 'It's his life now.'

'I hope you ride?' Paul asked as if it was inevitable for anyone visiting him to do so.

'I can stay on a horse,' Sarah said cautiously, eyeing the lively mare that Paul was stroking and wondering if they might have something a bit more pot-bellied and calm.

'You'll find it easy over here,' Carl said reassuringly. 'With Western saddles and high pommels it's armchair riding.'

'Oh, yes?' Sarah needed convincing. 'But they are beautiful,' she told Paul and ran her hand along the soft flank of a palomino that searched her pockets for titbits.

They wandered through the paddocks and Paul told her something of the stock and the pedigrees of the valuable beasts. Carl wondered when the Sheikh was expected to arrive and Paul asked him if he'd meet him at the airport the next day. 'He'll bring two servants who will use the smaller guest house and the Sheikh will live in the house,' Paul said. He glanced at Sarah. 'The gossip columns are having a ball over you and Hussain but I take it that there is nothing in that?' he asked bluntly.

She looked at him with direct and assured eyes. 'Nothing,' she said. 'Hussain asked me to marry him and the Sheikh wanted a tame scientist at his beck and call but I refused.' Suddenly, she looked fraught. 'In any case, I think that Hussain has gone off the idea,' she said, remembering the look of horror on his face when he saw her mutilated back.

'So you won't be embarrassed to meet the Sheikh again?'

'No, I'm fond of him and now he knows the score, he seems to have accepted the situation. He wrote to me and I may go back next year to work for two months but I've given no promises.'

'Even if Hussain is there?' Carl asked.

'Hussain will never be a problem to me again,' Sarah said.

'You sound confident,' Carl said as Paul moved away to give orders about the foal. 'What happened? I haven't heard that you murdered him?'

Sarah looked into the distance and sighed. This was a different world, although in its way it too had desert vistas, but here was a gentler peace and relaxation and she knew she wasn't threatened.

'Hussain wanted me and tried to rape me,' she said quietly. She heard the hiss of indrawn breath but Carl's face was without expression. 'He said he'd make me pregnant so that David would not want me and I would have to marry him.' She raised tragic eyes to Carl, wondering how much he would understand. 'He stopped before any harm was done because he saw how ugly my body is. His dream of possessing a woman with exquisite skin was destroyed.'

'I know you may have scars,' Carl said impatiently. 'Don't we all?' He touched the sleeve covering his own burn.

'I have a disfigured back that looks like something from a horror movie,' she said.

'So, what?'

'It means that I can't marry or have any deep relationship,' she explained, as if he must understand. 'I freeze as soon as a man touches me.'

'I had noticed,' he said dryly. 'How come a horse can make you limp with adoration and I can't get close enough for a hug?'

'I can't explain it, Carl, and if I had begun to feel normal the expression in Hussain's eyes told me all I didn't want to know.'

'He is a skin fetishist,' Carl said, grimly. 'I am not. I think I see something deeper and I like what lies lurking there under that tragedy queen attitude.' His voice took on a harsh tone. 'Are you going to waste your life in self pity?'

'It's not a false attitude,' she retorted, her eyes filling with tears.

'Well you won't be asked to strip off here,' he said, dismissively. 'Come on, Paul is waving to us to see the foal. You can drool over her and make me green with envy,' he said, and laughed.

The two springer spaniels were weaving busily among the bales of hay, as if sniffing for drugs as Sarah had seen other springers do at Heathrow, and they ignored her in their efforts to find something exciting. 'Not as elegant as Danes or borzois,' Sarah said, 'but I expect they're more suitable for Paul, and less demanding.'

A waggon drove up to take them back to the house and dinner on the broad patio. 'You can have your third burger, or lots of steak and chicken,' Carl promised her. 'Stay in jeans and we'll be informal until the Sheikh arrives, and then we'll put on our best clothes. Paul is good at entertaining and we have a few really good friends who I want you to meet tomorrow, but tonight, just eat and drink and let your hair down. It's just family.' He grinned. 'You won't even be asked to go dowsing. We have our own artesian wells.'

Alan Humbert, the ranch manager and his wife, Addie, came over from their bungalow to eat with them, and a couple of student relatives bumming around the States for a year before graduation consumed steak and roasted potatoes as if they had to stoke up for a long and arduous journey.

Sarah smiled. That could be true. They told her that they were leaving for Mexico in the morning and then to South America and Paraguay. Wonderful to be so free and careless of what life could offer, she thought, and tried to visualise Mark as he was when they were at university together, but his face refused to form in her mind and he was becoming a blurred vision of the past, weakening in the haze of blue smoke as more sage sent its bitter scent from the barbecue and the hickory chips died down to a dim red glow under the bars supporting the food. The only face that now dominated her thoughts was Carl's, and she didn't need to think about him as he was there, close by her side all evening.

'Grab a can of beer and come for a walk,' Carl said. He zipped off the ring and handed her the foaming can. 'Tomorrow, we drink like civilised people and eat from good china, but tonight, I just love all this.'

'You are a very lucky man,' Sarah said slowly. 'I had wondered what you were like at home and now I know. This place...' She gazed into the near distance across the white corral fencing and the tall bushes and heard the night-time whinney of horses. The dogs followed them, still weaving and sniffing as if they could never be tired and Carl's hand was warm when he held hers so gently that she could hardly feel the pressure. 'You have everything,' she whispered and was suddenly lonely.

'Not everything.' His hand cupped her

cheek and turned her face towards him. His kiss was light, then more questing but with a controlled passion that showed the depth of his wanting.

Instinctively, she responded, her body drifting close as he turned to his embrace, but she felt her tears begin to flow and when he touched her cheek with a gentle finger, he traced her agony.

'Damn Hussain,' he said in a low voice. 'You were coming back to life and I believed that you had put the past behind you, but he has set you back again.'

'He only showed what I already knew,' she said.

'Rubbish! He's a madman, and has nothing to do with ordinary people like us. He's the kind of man who would look at a wonderful emerald for an hour and reject it because the colour was too pale or too dark or he imagined there was a flaw. He searches for the perfect jewel, the perfect woman and the perfect result in his work in the oil fields and will never be a happy man. I know him and he was like that even when roughing it with us students in England.' He gave a short laugh. 'He hated you as much as he desired you.'

'That's impossible!'

'You, a woman, showed him that there were things you could do better.'

'Like what?' she said scathingly.

301

'You can dowse for water, the most precious commodity in the desert, and he had to fail, in front of his servants and his father.'

'But that isn't important! A lot of people have the gift in an unexpected way and many of them are not even literate. It's the same as people dealing in the paranormal and mediumship. We are instruments of some force that can't be explained scientifically, so he should have no feelings of failure. It's luck.'

'I couldn't dowse. I've tried,' Carl said.

'Did it make you want to rape the nearest dowser who put you to shame?' she asked, laughing weakly.

'Hell, no! He was a grubby wino who never touched water in the normal way but could find drains and water courses as if they leaped up to his rods.'

They walked by the main stables and the guard emerged to check who they were. 'The Sheikh will have no need for his own security corps,' Sarah said.

'Sure, and the press can be kept away from here. Even telephoto lenses are not a lot of good with all these bushes and if they came within a mile, we'd know.' He glanced at her in the dim moonlight. 'I had a few faxes from a friend. The media were baying after you and Hussain but it's cooling now as he is out on a rig with Dave and you are here, with us, and they are not really sure where

302

that could be.'

'With Dave?' Sarah felt more concerned about the fact that Hussain was on the same rig as David than she was about the press trying to make footage out of her and the Prince.

'It's OK,' Carl said in a mild tone. 'With you out of the way, they can work together, and by now, Hussain will have forgotten his passion for you. He can switch his emotions off and on like a light bulb, all brightness and heat one minute and deep oblivion the next. He will remember you only as a woman he rejected and therefore will have no need to waste precious time over you.'

'Is that possible?'

'He dismissed all traces of his wife from his emotions and memory. She had a settlement, largely due to the Sheikh, and that was the end. Zilch!'

Sarah shivered. 'He is a monster.'

'When you meet him again, if you go back to the oasis, you can feel safe. He will treat you with distant respect due to your professional status, still pay lip service to your beauty, but you'll never be sexually harrassed by him again.'

'And you like this man?'

'In his terms, we are brothers,' he said simply. 'He is a brilliant man and a good companion and I like him.'

'Takes all sorts,' she said in a tired voice.

'I said I like him, Sarah, but until you marry me, I'll never forgive him for treating you as he did.'

'Then you'll never forgive him,' she said flatly.

They met the manager and Addie who were going back to their bungalow. They refused to join them for a last night cap. 'Busy day tomorrow,' Carl said. 'The Sheikh will expect a good mount and a few horses to inspect as Paul thinks he might want to buy.'

'I'm glad to have you here to deal with him, Carl. I never feel right with people like him and you know all the wrinkles,' Alan said easily.

'You'll bring Addie to dinner tomorrow?'

'Sure he will. My only chance to wear a pretty dress,' Addie said firmly. 'G'night, Sarah.'

'If you get up early, we'll have time for a ride before I leave to pick up the Sheikh,' Carl promised.

'A nice quiet horse?' Sarah asked.

'The slowest one we have,' he offered.

The barbecue had been cleared away and the dogs looked for the few bits and pieces that had been left for them. 'Coffee?' suggested Paul, but Sarah was tired and said goodnight, aware that the two men might have private matters to discuss.

Her bed was soft and the moon hidden

behind the thick drapes, she could still smell the wood smoke and she drifted off to sleep aware that she felt blissfully at home.

The smell of fresh coffee made her stir and the swish of curtains being pulled back from the daylit windows brought her back to full consciousness. 'What's the time?' she asked, and yawned.

'Ten o'clock,' Hester said and Sarah sat up in bed.

'How did I sleep so long?'

'Mr Carl said to leave you to rest and he'd be off to fetch the Sheikh, so I'll run your bath and after you've had coffee, you can get up slowly.'

'I am ashamed,' Sarah said, smiling. 'But you shouldn't have made me so comfortable.'

'Everyone who comes here is tired,' Hester said. 'They go away much better and Mr Paul likes to have me spoil the ladies a little.'

At least I didn't have to show my incompetence on a horse, she reflected as she wallowed in the deep, scented bath. She brushed her hair vigorously and left it loose, then pulled on a pair of pale blue linen trousers and a shirt of fine Sea Island cotton that had flecks of yellow among the grey and white stripes. The wide brimmed hat was great against the sun and she wandered down to the stables and found Alan who was overseeing the grooms curry-combing a line of beautiful horses.

'Those five are for export,' he said when she admired them. 'Paul hopes the Sheikh will have them as he knows his stable and the fact that he treats his horses right. If they are here when he arrives, it will give him something to consider without comment or embarrassment before we talk business.'

'I can imagine,' she said. 'You won't offer him interminable glasses of mint tea as a build up, but the idea is the same.'

She peeped into the compound where the foal was in the shade with her mother and admired the cleanliness of the tack rooms. 'Why the gun?' she asked Alan when he stopped to share coffee with her. 'Not expecting trouble when the Sheikh arrives, are you?'

He touched the leather holster on his hip. 'Routine,' he said. 'We get a few snakes out here and they frighten the horses.'

'They'd frighten me!'

'Not to worry,' he said laconically. 'We sorted a nest out in the scrub, a week back, and I've seen none since.'

On the horizon, a cloud of dust preceded the two limousines that brought the Sheikh, driven by Carl, and the two servants brought by Morton. Paul joined her to see them arrive.

'Makes me feel a slob,' Paul said quietly,

but with humour. 'So I play up the Texas thing and wear this gear.' He tipped the six-gallon hat forward and stuck his thumbs into the armholes of his thin calf waistcoat. His embossed leather chaps and custom-made boots were polished and supple and the holster was edged with silver.

'I think you look wonderful,' Sarah said. 'You'd be a riot in a Western soap.'

'Thank you, *ma'am!* Carl had better scoop you up fast or I'll be in there.'

Carl drove up to the stables where his father was waiting and opened the door of the car. The Sheikh stepped out, looking cool and fresh and the men greeted each other warmly. Sarah smiled and the Sheikh took both her hands in his and kissed her brow. 'It's good to see you again, my daughter,' he said.

His gaze swept the line of horses and his eyes gleamed with pleasure but he said nothing. Paul led him over to a stall where a big stallion thrust his head over the half door. 'This might suit you, Your Highness,' he said. 'Tomorrow, we shall ride.'

Paul drove the Sheikh to the house and Sarah walked back with Carl. 'He has no idea what Hussain tried to do,' Carl said bluntly.

Sarah shrugged. 'Just as well,' she said.

'Loyalty makes it impossible for him to say a lot about his own son but I found a pile of newspapers in the airport lounge that splashed Hussain over the front pages, with several different pretty women, and I think that the Sheikh believes that you refused his son because of his love of women in general.' He laughed. 'You, my poor neglected darling, had not so much as a paragraph, so you can take off the dark glasses when you return to England. Your fifteen minutes of fame is over.'

'Thank God for that,' she said with feeling.

'Something wrong, other than having me with you?'

'Not really.' She frowned. 'I can't get Dave out of my mind. I dreamed about him last night as if he was in danger.'

'Relax. Now that Hussain has no claim on you, he will be impervious to the fact that Dave wants you. He is convinced that no man can equal him in anything, and so can almost pity you now if you marry Dave, as nothing could compare with life as his princess.'

'You think there is no danger for Dave?'

'While Hussain was hot for you, I hated the idea of Dave being on the offshore rig with him, diving,' he admitted. 'Strangely enough, Dwight had the same idea and warned Dave to be careful.'

'I felt it too,' she said. 'I tried to convince Hussain that there was nothing between us

308

but the Sheikh wasn't a lot of help there as his spies saw us kissing goodnight. Two and two made a hundred!'

'Nothing can happen now. You have left the oasis, Hussain has had a pleasant fling in London to bolster his ego and the Sheikh is resigned to the fact that you will never be his daughter, so all you have to do now is to marry me.'

'You know why I can't.'

'It's not because you don't love me,' he said, firmly.

'Mind your own business,' she said waspishly, but knew that she was blushing.

'I have to get back or the Sheikh will be insulted,' Carl said. 'He'll want you there, too, just as you are. You look quite delectable now that you've given up wearing that donkey's breakfast.'

'Flattery will get you nowhere,' she said and smiled rather sadly.

The day went quickly and Sarah watched the men and the horses, aware of the charisma of all of them. She was persuaded to go for a sedate ride with Addie, both on mature bays, used mainly for riding when the men checked and repaired fences. The western saddle was comfortable and gave her a sense of security and she began to enjoy the sensation of being on a horse again.

'I could get to like Texas,' she told Addie.

'Maybe when I give my lectures I shall change my mind, but this ranch is sheer heaven.'

'Pity you have to go over there,' Addie said. 'Carl will be lost without you.'

'He has things to do,' Sarah said. 'I'll be back before he knows I'm gone. I give one lecture then come back here for two nights before I give another and use their laboratory for illustrations of various methods of analysis.'

'Rather you than me. What happens when you get married?'

'I'm not,' Sarah said and surprised her mount by urging her to greater speed.

'Carl can be very determined,' Addie said and laughed. 'Run for it if you find him breathing down your neck, or he'll catch up with you.'

'Just as well I have work to do,' Sarah said the next day. 'I could become a lotus eater if I stayed here.'

' "Ah, my beloved, fill the cup that clears today of past regrets and future fears. *Tomorrow!* Why, tomorrow I may be myself with yesterday's seven thousand years." ' Carl's smile was forced.

Sarah shivered. 'You are right. Life is short and some of us, like Mark, don't make it to the end.'

'So, fill the cup,' Carl said and gave the

Arab obeisance of hand to heart and palm up towards her.

'Find Morton and ask him to bring the basket of fresh oranges,' Paul requested. 'I have the juicer working and the Sheikh is thirsty.'

'I have to go, Paul. Thank you for the loan of the car. I have no idea when I shall be back but it should be some time after lunch tomorrow.'

'Take care, now. Have a nice day.' Since the Sheikh arrived Paul had been progressively more American.

'Is he staying much longer?' Sarah whispered.

'Christ alone knows! I shall be the last to know,' Paul replied. He wants four of the horses and has arranged by fax for transport and I think he wants to go with them, so he may have gone before you return.'

'Not a very long holiday,' she remarked.

Paul grinned. 'If I had a son as crazy as Hussain, I'd want to check him out from time to time. The grapevine reaches even here and told him that Hussain is being rash and diving too much and for far too long each time.'

'He thinks he's immortal,' Carl said soberly. 'Bloody fool.'

Sarah picked up her briefcase and tried to turn her thoughts to work as she drove out to the rig. Gradually she was able to concentrate and the lecture went well. Lunch in a long wooden hut was simple, with bacon and chicken and beans and fresh fruit and the staff were attentive but full of respect for her work. Her room in the modern prefabricated bungalow was adequate, the water warm in the shower and the efficiency all about her very impressive.

The next day flew by and she was almost sorry to return to the ranch as there was so much to discuss and so many innovations that could be introduced even to this laboratory. Memories of the wonderful equipment in the oasis kept intruding, and she wished she could combine that with the skills she found in Texas.

'Goodbye, Gus,' she said to the rig superintendent.

'You'll be back in three days' time?' he asked anxiously.

'Try to keep me away,' she said warmly. Then, 'Why? What's wrong?'

'There's been a bit of trouble,' he said as if he was at a loss how to describe it to her.

She leaned out of the car window. 'Trouble?'

'The Sheikh left in a hurry last night. There's been an accident at home and he was anxious.'

'Anyone hurt?' Sarah's hands on the wheel were clammy.

'Carl didn't say. We spoke briefly on the

phone and he said not to worry you.' He shrugged as the dust under her wheels spurted and the tyres squealed.

Sarah couldn't recall that ride afterwards. She knew that there had been a tragedy and she wanted to be sick, but she came safely to the ranch and Carl ran out to meet her.

'It's David, isn't it?' she asked as soon as she left the car.

Carl put an arm round her shoulders and kissed her cheek. 'He'll live,' he said simply. 'He's out of decompression and will be fine in a week.'

Her eyes searched his. 'Then why has the Sheikh left? He wasn't exactly fond of Dave.'

Carl made her sit on a cane settle in the shade of the porch. 'Hussain dived too deep and the back rush of the eddies round the struts sucked him too close to the rig. Dave was there but higher in the water when he saw that Hussain's cylinders were caught and he dived down to free them but the tubes were torn and Hussain was getting nothing from the cylinders.'

Sarah shuddered, wide-eyed. 'And then?' she asked in a faint voice.

'Dave got him free and brought him up too fast for his own good and if Hussain had been OK it would have given him the bends, too. Dave tried to save his life and nearly succeeded, at the risk of his own, but it was

313

too late to save Hussain. He died on the way to hospital.'

Sarah buried her face in the comforting shirt and Carl stroked her hair. 'Such a waste,' she whispered. 'Poor Sheikh Abdul.'

'One beautiful and talented and pig-headed animal,' Carl said harshly, to hide his own grief.

'What do we do? Is there anything we can do?'

'Like send Dave some grapes?' He smiled sadly. 'Paul has sent the usual formal, banal messages of condolence to the Sheikh and will make sure the horses get there safely, which might be of practical help to take his mind away from the death, but they will bow to fate and the will of Allah and we can have no part in that. That door comes down firmly on outsiders like us.'

Sarah wiped her eyes. 'I'll go and freshen up,' she said quietly.

'We need to ride,' he said. 'Don't be long away. I need you and you need me now, Sarah.'

She nodded and after she had flung herself on the bed in a storm of sorrow, she washed her face and and put on dark glasses to hide the drying tears. Outwardly composed, she joined Carl again and they walked silently out to the stables.

'You may need this,' Alan said and gave Carl a hand gun. 'Think we got them all but

314

there might be a stray rattler.'

Sarah climbed on to a small Arab mare and Carl rode by her side on the stallion that had been ridden by the Sheikh. The arid earth beneath the feet of the horses sounded almost metallic and the sun was hot. They rode for a mile and Sarah stopped under a tree. 'Give him a good burst of speed,' she suggested. 'You need it. I'll wait here.'

Carl looked like a flying Pegasus as the stallion thundered over the hard ground, and Sarah knew that she had held him back from losing his tension.

From being a speck on the horizon, he came closer and closer again, seeming to grow larger as the distance between them decreased, and then Sarah heard it!

At first she thought it was a dry leaf in the breeze, then her mare began to weave rest-lessly and to back away from the rattlesnake, into the sun.

Carl was a hundred yards away when he saw the mare rear and move sideways. He spurred his own mount and drew out the gun, hoping that Sarah could hold on. The mare tossed her head and Sarah could smell the hot manure that poured out in fright. She clung to the pommel but slackened the reins.

'Hang on,' Carl shouted, but saw Sarah slip sideways and the mare, sensing that her weight would soon be gone, reared again and tossed Sarah off on to a pile of stones.

She heard the shot and lapsed into unconsciousness. Carl called Alan on his mobile phone and within minutes a small ambulance arrived and Sarah was lifted on to the stretcher.

'Careful!' Carl said as Sarah was carried into her room. 'I'll need the First Aid box. She's bleeding but she'll be OK. Put her on her side in recovery position.'

Dimly, Sarah heard voices and felt her shirt being taken gently away from the blood that welled from the torn scar where the last plastic surgery had been done. Firm fingers swabbed the area and she lay on her stomach as she had done so often in hospital, her mutilated back exposed.

'Does she need hospital?' asked Paul.

'No,' Carl said decisively. 'I can cope here. I've got all my Brownie points for First Aid and she is breathing well. I doubt if her stubborn thick skull has been hurt.'

Sarah opened her eyes. She was hurt and this moron was insulting her!

'About time too,' Carl said without sympathy. 'That was a dumb thing to do. No, don't get up. I haven't finished.' She winced as the antiseptic hit the scar. 'Soon be better, but I'll drive you out to the rig next time if you can't look after yourself.'

She felt his fingers tracing the worst of the

316

healed injuries. 'Great job they did,' he said. I'm going to have the most interesting wife in Texas. You'll be great at shutting up bores who want to tell you long stories of their brave deeds. I shall show them your back.'

'You won't!'

'No, I won't,' he agreed. 'I shall keep you all to myself like a good Arab.' He gathered her carefully into his arms and kissed her. Her breasts were warm and soft and beautiful against his chest and she sighed. 'That feels good.'

'What kept you away for so long, you silly thing?' he said.